Fire and Glory: THE MILLENNIAL STORY

Part I

Fire and Glory:

THE MILLENNIAL STORY
Part I

A NOVEL

Sequel to
"Lightning and The Storm"
"A Love Beyond Time"

MARSHA NEWMAN

WELLSPRING PUBLISHING * Salt Lake City, UT

ISBN # 0—9608658—5—3

Printed in the United States of America

Wellspring Publishing & Distributing
P.O. Box 1113
Sandy, UT 84091

June 1989

"For each of us there is a journey,
a long road —
a time of trouble and pain,
a moment of sunshine and joy.
No one else knows the path,
for no one else has traveled there before.
We walk alone;
courage is our only companion.
We may travel in darkness,
or we may travel in light —
it is our choice.
But meeting Christ
is the final destination of the soul!"

DEDICATION

I wish to dedicate this, the final book of the trilogy, to my understanding husband, Gene Newman. He has been my best support and has maintained patience and encouragement throughout the time the book has taken me away from him and our family.

ACKNOWLEDGEMENTS

My sincere appreciation goes to Kris Amussen and Barbara Miller for their editing suggestions and the many hours of discussion and encouragement. Special thanks go to Lt. Gary Clayton of the Utah County Sheriff's Office for extensive military and nuclear information. I also wish to express gratitude to Floyd Holdman, Lorin and Judy Pugh, David Nelson, and Merlene Fieldman for background information on various portions of the book. I am deeply indebted to W. Cleon Skousen for his insights on prophecy and certain political aspects of the book.

AUTHOR'S NOTE

In writing The Millennial Story, I experienced one of the most meaningful conversions of my life. The study of the prophecies of the last days, combined with research into the political and military international situations of today, brought the realization that we are, indeed, living in the last days. I didn't realize until the second editing how powerfully this book testifies of Jesus Christ as the creator and redeemer of this earth. It is my own testimony that He is the God of all people: Hindus, Buddhists, Moslems, Jews, Christians, and — whether they accept it or not — even the atheists. Every man and woman will eventually come to know Christ as their brother and Savior of the world. Acquiring that personal knowledge is the sweetest experience of all.

The Millennial Story is just a novel. It is not meant to be prophecy by the author as to how the last days will unfold. I have done an immense amount of research on all aspects of the book — military, financial, nuclear, and prophetic — and I have been as accurate as possible where they are concerned. However, this is merely one fictional — but, I believe, plausible — scenario created to include my characters. It is my hope that no one who reads this book will panic, sell his home, or apostacize because of the things I have written. Rather, I do hope to motivate my readers to study the prophecies and be as well informed, prepared, and watchful as possible.

There is a great deal of material available for those who desire to learn more about nuclear survival, emergency preparation, and the U.S. military capability today. You may contact Lt. Gary Clayton, Utah County Sheriff's Office, Emergency Services Division, Provo, UT, 84603,. Phone 1-801-370-885.

Now, I give you the most difficult, most cherished, of my three works — Fire and Glory: THE MILLENNIAL STORY.

"But if from thence thou shalt seek the Lord thy God, thou shalt find him, if thou seek him with all thy heart and with all thy soul."
(Deuteronomy 4:29.)

Chapter One

Paulo sat back on his heels, inches above the frozen ground. Click. Click. Move a fraction to the right. Shoot again. Three more frames. Move. Click. Steady. He lowered his camera, stuck it inside his down jacket, and thrust numbed hands into his pockets. From eighteen thousand feet, tucked into a crevice of Kala Pattar, he was somewhat protected from the quick-freeze wind that swept ferociously from the face of Mount Everest. From this small hillside, Everest was directly in front of him. Kala Pattar was indisputably the best place from which to photograph the mountain. One roll of film was already spent on the Mother Goddess of Earth, or "Chum-a-lunga," as the native Sherpas called her. Rotating on his heels, he looked out across the foothills of the Himalayas, over which he had made his way on foot for the past eighteen days.

The day was dying a brilliant, blood-red death in the west, its glory cast in splendor upon the layered mountains of Nepal. Liquid gold ripened into salmon and rose, and Paulo pulled his camera out again, adjusted the lens and froze into concentrated professionalism. Click. Click. Wait sixty seconds. Shoot again. Then he turned back to his heart's quest. Everest hung over him like an Amazon queen, immortally regal, blushing pink as a maiden. Click. He shot several pictures in fascination. His

1

fingers were numb, his body stiff, knees aching, but the mountain held him captive. He studied it, searching for words to describe the essence. It was the frozen thrust of a great primeval beast, cast eternally in the throes of death. It was God's sentinel at heaven's gate, and one could step from its icy pinnacles into the vales of paradise. These were the pictures Paulo sought.

Below him some fifty feet, a faithful Sherpa guide sat huddled in another crevice shielded from the ranting wind. He had walked from Lukla to base camp beside Paulo. He would not leave until his guest was safely back at camp. This man was different than most trekkers. The watchful Sherpa privately thought that the trip was not just an adventure for the American. It was a holy pilgrimage. The man's reverence for the earth was similar to the Sherpa's own. This was unusual. Even now, the Westerner sat oriental fashion, enduring the wind and the cold, seeking a spiritual union with Chum-a-lunga. The little Sherpa nodded. He understood.

Paulo sat back against a rock, his arms wrapped around his knees and gave himself up to reflections. The ebbing golds and pinks, the encroaching indigo of night, these were his life — colors, shades, light. His whole life was painted in such terms. He was an artist with a camera, faithfully reporting the world, the masterpieces of God. And he saw his own life as a series of photographs — scenes, people, faces, feelings, frozen in time. But asked to choose one representative picture of his life, Paulo would have selected his galaxy shot. It was a mystical picture of the star-clustered night sky, with the faint, misty suggestion of a child's face floating through the stars. It was his face. It was his son's face, the child he had never had. It was God amongst the stars.

Paulo touched his own face. It was almost numb. He rubbed it to bring circulation back. Then he turned once more to the lady of his heart. Across the alabaster shoulder of Mt. Everest, the moon came rising, even as he watched. A tiny sliver, a rim of light, then a slice of radiant globe, and then — full-bodied and sailing across a darkening sea, the moon floated free of the grasp of Mother Goddess.

Paulo sat motionless as though stunned by the moonlight, pinned beneath the staggering weight of the mountain which rose triumphantly some twenty thousand feet above him. As he sat staring up into the immutable, pristine magnificence of Mt. Everest, Paulo's life force ebbed away until his breathing was shallow, his senses suspended, and time and space existed no more. Here the summer winds never disturbed the eternal snows. Shattering the inky sky with moonstruck whiteness, the peak now accepted his admiration regally, as just tribute. Like a bride she stood, forever dressed in the splendid, white covering that captured both the morning sun and pale moonlight, grasped it in her shimmering folds and flung it back to the astounded world.

This is what he had come for. Here, at the top of the world, Paulo D'Agosta was a pilgrim. Here he would touch souls with Deity. His need had become so intense that he was willing to leave his body at the base of the magnificent mountain if the loneliness of his spirit could be relieved. Paulo Giuseppe D'Agosta was a man of God, but he didn't know it. And in his separation from God, he was homeless, but did not understand his sense of isolation. He no longer believed in the traditional Catholic God of his youth. He had rejected the idea of a mysterious being who was not a being but an essence — one God, but three in one — and now he searched for some universal, great soul that would satisfy his own. Never having understood his Catholic God, Paulo had lost his religious faith, but not the sense of solemn reverence for Deity.

A deep need to comprehend his own nature and God's had led him here to the top of the world. At twenty-nine he had known the answers, but at forty-nine he was dissatisfied and sometimes felt the touch of fear when he tried to look into the years ahead. In his profession of photography, Paulo's camera often captured the questioning, haunting expressions of people, or the grandeur of the earth as he examined it through a camera lens. He turned his camera to the skies and became known for his panoramic shots of sunrise, sunset, worlds beyond his galaxy. What lay out there? "The poet camera," the critics called his photographic pieces. But the man behind the pictures was never satisfied. For Paulo, the earth lived and breathed. Sometimes it called to him, and he could never surfeit that restless call.

3

Whispers of ancient wisdom lost, of universal secrets hidden, teased him with a promise of answers. Who am I? Why am I? What am I to God? Does he care? Does he know? Am I crazy, or is the world? Philosophers coolly explored the maze of questions and came back from mental expeditions empty. So Paulo had turned from the hope of philosophical enlightenment to a tender, artist-like worship of Deity through his creations.

Gold trailed the high clouds as the sky sank into darkness. Golden wisps fanned out from atop mountains in the distance, like waving hair moving in the breeze. How many years ago had it been that he had seen a woman with just such golden wisps of hair and a face like a sunset sky? He had been nineteen, a novice photographer, struggling with a decision about the Catholic priesthood. That vision had changed his life. He was immediately wed in the spirit and abdicated all thoughts of a career as a priest. So young! He had been so young — nineteen, perhaps twenty, and he had thrown away his youth pursuing a vision, a dream of love.

Tonight the sting of love lost was sharper than usual. Her face came again to the fading glow in the west. Paulo shuddered with sudden pain, not so much for the woman who haunted him as for the terrible loss of young love and the loneliness he still endured.

"Curse you," he whispered without vehemence. "If we had never met, I would have eventually stopped believing in my vision. I would have loved someone real. But you, you stole my chance to love anyone else. Curse you, Shielah. I've never found another woman that matched my vision. You are the only one." Paulo drew a deep breath and set his jaw. "I hope you're happy, my love. I never have been."

The face in the sky was fading fast now, the golden wisps disappeared. "Go on. Hurry up," he urged, willing his torment gone. But even as the clouds darkened with the advance of night, he left the Himalayas and lived again the warm, indolent summer evening in Honolulu when he had seen Shielah Sorensen for the first time. She was the fulfillment of his vision. Paulo gave himself up to the warm sensations that flooded through him. Other arms had held him since then. Other women had loved him. But no one had touched him so. What was it? Her innocence, her

4

beguiling youth, her sensitive spirit — those had charmed him.

"Shielah," he whispered, "go away. I thought I had given you up for good. Are you still there? How can you still be there? I need an exorcist. My devil has golden hair and beautiful eyes, and she stole the love from my soul."

Then he laughed. For a girl, a mere girl, he allowed himself to be tormented. Sunset brings fantasies, and he was indulging the child in him, dreaming of youth — an old man's pastime.

The earth was rocky and frigid beneath him, and his bones rebelled after a time. The moon floated serenely above the massive peak, throwing both Everest and Lotse into bright relief against the dark sky. The wind whistled and slapped at his nylon snowsuit so that Paulo couldn't hear the bursts of laughter of the trekkers. The bitter cold began to take its toll. Moving reluctantly, he brought his camera up to his eye, encapsulated the mountain in the viewfinder, held his breath, and gently pressed the button. Several more shots, some with colored filters, one with a starburst glinting from the peak, and finally Paulo stood up. He had been there two hours. The temperature had sunk to ten degrees, and even in his down jacket and layered thermal clothes, he was chilled to the bone.

In the meager spot of his flashlight, Paulo picked his way back to camp. The native guide joined him silently, with just a smile of greeting. The Sherpanis and porters were finishing the clean-up after dinner. A lantern on the table gave a yellow light and took the chill from the main tent. It was too cold for much socializing at Everest base camp. This was the culmination of the trek but not necessarily the most comfortable part of the journey.

Paulo had spent six days in Katmandu, sight-seeing and taking photos, before joining his scheduled trekking party. Even to the experienced traveler, Katmandu was a kaleidoscope of the exotic — bronzed statues of caricature beasts with huge eyes and bared teeth, Buddhist temples with curving roofs stacked layer upon layer, emaciated beggars sleeping in the streets, marriage processions and death processions, and American cars moving precariously amongst bicycle rickshaws and bazaar goods. Paulo had visited and photographed many of the beauties of the world as a popular photographer for *National Geographic* magazine. And while he had not come on assignment, he was too much of a professional not to make use of a once-in-a-lifetime experience.

Here was a melting pot of Hindu and Buddhist philosophy and worship. Here, also, India met China, and the faces of the people reflected ancestry of many different groups: Indian, Tibetan, Sherpa, Limbu, and Newar. The ancient stories were still retold at festival times, and the storyteller drew crowds of hundreds in the town square. Those stories told of original valley people of Nepal, but the centuries had erased the knowledge of how they came to be there or where they came from. Over thousands of years, migrations of different peoples had turned the Katmandu valley into an exotic, colorful, many-faceted land — a photographer's dream.

Paulo photographed a Tamang woman with hair, lips and nose adorned with gem-studded brass jewelry. She spat in his direction, disdaining the invasion of her privacy. He wandered down the narrow, dirt alleys where yellow-clay brick buildings crowded shoulder to shoulder. He photographed the children in their baggy clothes, with their brown eyes bright and mouths trying to hide smiles.

Katmandu would have held him with its charms if he had not already determined to make the trek to Everest. Two years prior, he had visited New Delhi on assignment with the U.S. Embassy and spent an evening with an Englishman who was just returning from Everest. The man's account of his trip captured Paulo's imagination, and he set about immediately to arrange a similar trek for himself. Contacting the Mountain Travel Company in Katmandu, he was told it would be two years before they could take him. The delay was attributable to the Nepalese government. The travel company explained that government officials limit the numbers of travelers allowed per year in order to preserve Nepal's natural resources. It took one year to obtain a permit.

The last week of April, Paulo took an eight-seater airplane from Katmandu to Lukla, the starting point of the trek. It was a flight he would never forget. Lift-off from Katmandu was breathtaking. The mountains rose, range upon higher range, to form the white-tipped sides of a gigantic bowl, with Katmandu cradled at the bottom. The pilot circled once so his passengers could have the full effect, then headed northeast to the tiny airstrip at Lukla.

Lukla was cut out of a mountain and perched precipitously some four thousand feet above the Dudh Kosi river gorge. The sheer mountain rose another six thousand feet on the opposite side of the strip. The length of the single airstrip was no more that one hundred and fifty yards, and as they neared the mountain range, Paulo felt the small airplane begin to twist and bump with the conflicting drafts of air. The white peaks seemed within an arm's reach. Unconcerned, the pilot was chattering with the American nurse, whom he had seated as his co-pilot, until the moment before he set the aircraft down. The plane landed sloping upward, and taxied quickly to a stop. Before the craft was completely stationary, a native man ran out to block the wheels.

In his best tourist English, a smiling Sherpa in a baseball hat with "Snowbird, Utah" printed across the front opened the airplane door and said, "Welcome to Lukla." The native knew exactly why they had come and led the group immediately away from the airstrip, down a winding trail to tiny tents in the village, where the head guide or "Sirdar" awaited them.

Mountain Travel Company had put together an international group for this trek. In Katmandu, Paulo had been met by a young man, perhaps twenty-five years old. Greg Morris was tall and lean, his face already leathery from exposure, and he was very American. He was the product of the hippie wave that had swept over Nepal in the Sixties. His mother was American, his father unknown. He spoke both English and perfect Nepalese. Now he introduced Paulo and Lisa Brown, the American nurse, to the company they would come to know rather intimately in the next twenty-three days.

There was a Frenchman and his twelve-year-old son. There was a Russian couple dressed in the best, most fashionable European clothing. Last of all, Paulo shook hands with a young man, slender, broad-shouldered, black eyes like a hawk, a white triangle of cloth fastened about his head with a red-and-white band — Omar, an Arab.

Louis, the Frenchman, smiled as they shook hands. Maurice, the boy, pumped his hand vigorously and compared cameras. Gustav and Katrine, the Russian couple, smiled politely. Gustav was not as tall as Paulo,

7

but broader, his biceps hard and his short legs muscular. The couple seemed two people carved from one mold, so alike were they in their frank, direct looks and matching clothing. But Omar Abdul Mohammed ibn Azziz Sayd glanced at Paulo's outstretched hand, then into his eyes, and only slowly did he extend his own hand. Paulo maintained his smile and held the Arab's gaze. Then, all at once, the wall cracked and a slight smile widened to a genuine grin on the Saudi's face. They clasped hands a moment longer than necessary, each testing the other's lasting power.

"It will take ten days to reach Everest" Morris began. "We will leave tomorrow morning at seven a.m. You only have to worry about one thing, and that is yourself. The Sherpanis will cook for you, clean up after you, put up and take down your tents. You have only to walk and watch yourself for signs of altitude sickness. You are at nine thousand five hundred feet here in Lukla, and you will climb to about eighteen thousand feet. If you feel nauseated or unusually sleepy, if you have headaches or trouble breathing, let me or your Sherpa guide know immediately. Even if you live near mountains, or do a lot of climbing or skiing, you may still develop altitude sickness. It is very common, and you must be treated quickly, as it can be fatal."

"Please, monsieur, what is the treatment?" the French boy asked.

"You go back."

The Russian woman frowned. "After so much money we pay?"

"Yes ma'am. Altitude sickness can definitely kill you. Better to see the sights of Katmandu and Baaktapur."

The morning air was chilly at seven o'clock. The climb began immediately across the curve of the foothills. The group was small, only eight including Morris. White peaks towered above them. The Sherpanis and porters had long since gone on ahead, hiking at mountain-goat speed. Paulo later found that there were seven Sherpas who walked by the side of the guests, five Sherpanis, tiny women who carried more than their own body weight on their backs, and three porters of definitely lower mentality.

"So, you are not with the American woman?" the Saudi observed after an hour of walking. Lisa walked beside Morris, asking questions about the foliage and the Sherpa people.

"No. I travel alone."

"And that is the way you wish it?" Omar tested delicately.

Paulo glanced at him. "Not always. Where are you from?"

"Do you mean where do I live? I live everywhere. I have a home in Riyadh. That is where my family lives."

"Where did you learn your English? It is perfect."

"I graduated from Oxford. Of course, it took me eight years." The Arab laughed. "But I received a thorough education in more than language and philosophy. I made an exhaustive study of the pubs of London, the restaurants, the women, and the stock market."

Paulo nodded his appreciation. "I see. And what will you do with this valuable information?"

Omar shrugged. "I will eat well, love well, and keep my country out of the hands of international money thieves."

Paulo looked at him quizzically. Omar answered the look. "My father is king. He does not trust the British or American banks."

"Then why do you invest so heavily in us?"

"My people were foolish. We are novices at world finance. Forty years ago when oil became the world's food, we were counseled by certain European bankers to raise our prices and invest our money with them. We did, and now they have squandered it on stupid investments with countries that cannot and will not repay it. They are bankrupting our assets. Now we are trying to protect ourselves with land. Land is constant. Land, we know."

"Many Americans resent Arab investment," Paulo spoke frankly.

"Ah, yes. Many other people also resent Americans." Omar was just as frank. "And many Americans do not care whose money it is when they put it into their own pockets."

"What is your total investment in America — land, stocks, bonds?"

Omar smiled, chewed on the question, and then

9

answered, "Many millions. You would not wish to know."

"What makes you think that our economy will not fail?"

"Anything is possible, but you are the best hope we have — if you are smart enough to elude the Soviets." Omar looked ahead to the Soviet couple walking some fifty yards ahead. "If you are not, no investment anywhere will be safe."

"I didn't think Arabs were mountain people," Paulo deliberately changed the subject. He was not interested in a political discussion. This was his rest, his time away from the world.

"They aren't. I am not. I do not ski, although I possess fine equipment and spend delightful hours in the ski lodges of Europe. I am also not a camper or hiker. How do you think I will do?" the Arab grinned at Paulo.

"Great. I'm sure of it."

"I see you know me already. I decided it was time to challenge myself. The ocean, I do not like. I would never make a skin diver. Space, I have conquered. I fly my own Lear jet. So what is left of any consequence? Everest! The government would not issue me a permit to climb. I am inexperienced. But, they tell me I can climb to base camp at Everest, and this is enough for me. Eighteen thousand feet is enough. Twenty-nine thousand feet is insane."

Paulo found the Saudi interesting company. Omar was astute, honest, appreciative of his surroundings, self-confident, and occasionally obnoxious in all those qualities. It was young Maurice whose companionship never wore on Paulo.

Maurice Boyer was a perfect gentleman even at twelve years old. This his father openly attributed to his mother. Louis was a gambler — on a very large scale. He owned three casinos on the French Riviera, and he was never home. He provided his wife with a villa, two children, servants, and a Lambourgini, while he lived, ate, and slept — usually — at the casino. This trip was to satisfy Maurice's pleadings to spend some time together. Louis was not sure he was glad that he had come. But Maurice was certain.

The trail was seldom steep. The pine trees, the fir, the rhododendron, the fields with their yellow wildflowers and mani stones (or prayer flags) were all remarkable to him. No less than twenty times a day, the boy exclaimed *"Tiens!*

Look at these mountains. They are beautiful, yes?" And he discovered Paulo's magic with a camera.

"I too have the good eye for a picture. What was your shutter speed for that picture of the yaks on the trail? What is the best camera for micro work, *mon ami?* Do you develop your own film?"

The boy had endless questions, but Paulo enjoyed teaching him what he knew. The days went quickly — too quickly. The pattern of the day emerged. Breakfast by six-thirty, on the trail by eight, walk until twelve, rest and eat for an hour, then walk on until four. They always stopped for the day around four o'clock, and the Sherpas would set up camp. The natives were up before them, preparing breakfast. The porters and Sherpanis stayed behind to strike camp and pack up. Then, inevitably, the string of porters carrying gear hurried past them on the trail and had the next meal set up when they arrived at camp. There was no hurry for the trekkers. The slow ascent allowed their bodies time to acclimate to the high altitude. They walked casually, sometimes through valleys dropped like green jewels in the lap of the mountains, sometimes along the mountainside, criss-crossing and climbing.

The weather was temperate, the days about seventy degrees, clear, sunny. Paulo was surprised to learn from Morris that Nepal was actually the same latitude as Florida. During the day, he walked along in a tee-shirt, his sweat shirt tied about his waist. About three o'clock, the sweat shirt was pulled on, and by five o'clock the down jacket came out as the temperature dipped to twenty degrees and lower.

"Ah, potatoes tonight!" Omar clapped his hands in mock surprise. Potatoes were their standard fare for lunch as well as dinner. Buffalo meat was cooked in a variety of ways, but mostly stewed. There were a few vegetables supplied by villagers along the way. The lettuce they boiled. Paulo could barely choke down the meat. It was gamey and wild. But the bread the Sherpas made was delicious, quite like New York style French bread.

Maurice warmed his hands over the little charcoal burner set in the middle of the dinner table. "Tomorrow we will be at the Namche Bazaar," he informed them with aplomb. "Monsieur Greg told me this. He says there will be many strange things to buy and good things to eat and other boys my age. Do you think they may speak to me, Papa?"

"If you speak Sherpa," his father answered practically.

Maurice's face fell. "Oh, I am forgetting that. Oh, *trés bien,*" he brightened. "I can still make friends. Candy is good for making friends."

"Monsieur Omar, do you like to be a prince?" The boy was very serious. He had been greatly intrigued by the Arab.

"Absolutely! There is nothing like it in the world! Everyone should try it. Would you like to?" Omar's eyes twinkled as he regarded the serious young man.

"Oh, yes!" Maurice glanced quickly at his father, then back to the Arab. "I should like this very much. Can you do it? Can you give me this title?"

"Certainly. You shall make a marvelous prince. Won't he, Paulo?"

"Well, he makes a pretty fine boy. I would think he'd be a good prince."

"However, there is one thing," Omar said soberly. "You must learn to ride a camel. You must be able to cut off a man's head with a sword, if necessary, and you must pray five times a day. Do you pray five times a day, Maurice?"

"No," the boy replied with regret. "I do not pray at all."

"Ah, this is difficult then. To be a Saudi prince, you must pray five times a day to Allah. He will be displeased otherwise and will not give you the strength of the lion when you need it. Also, you must marry a girl you have never seen. Would you like that?"

Maurice was looking very doubtful now. "I. . . I do not know. Why can you never see her? Is she not pretty?"

"Saudi women are very beautiful. They have pretty brown eyes, like you, and long, black hair. They are our jewels, and we keep them sacred, not for every man's eyes. Only for the husband." He shrugged. "Your sister, she can see the girl and tell you if she is pretty or not. If she is not. . . Oh well, you can marry another, and another, and another. If you are an Arab prince, you may have four wives. But no more." Omar shook his finger at Maurice's wide eyes. "You must not be greedy."

Now Maurice looked at his father, who was trying to keep from smiling. "Papa, I do not think Mama would like me to have so many wives, do you?"

"I'm quite sure she would not," Louis agreed. "She won't let me."

Maurice turned back to Omar. "I would like to be a prince, but I do not think I could cut off a man's head or ride a camel or pray five times a day. And I am very sure Mama would be quite angry with me if I had four wives."

Omar shook his head. "Ah, well, this is too bad. You would make a lovely prince. However, you would have to be a Moslem, and you are not."

"No," the boy said solemnly. "I am a Catholic. What are you, Monsieur Paulo? Are you a Catholic?"

"I was born a Catholic. My mother is."

"Then so are you."

"Not necessarily. I am just a seeker."

"What is a seeker?"

"One who questions, one who searches."

"Do you believe in God?" the boy asked.

"Yes, I think I do. But I don't understand him."

"Neither do I," Maurice nodded his agreement.

Omar listened to this exchange with curiosity. "You should be a Moslem. Then you would understand him. Allah is the one true God. He is great. He is infinite. He is strict but merciful. He is the Creator, the only God, the beginning and the end. And we must worship him. It is very simple — he is God, and we worship."

"Is he my god too?" Paulo asked quietly.

"Yes," Omar confirmed.

"And the Jews?"

There was silence. After a moment Omar said, "Yes, even theirs."

"Then why do you kill them? And why do they kill you? Does Allah approve of this?" Paulo was not reluctant to challenge the inconsistencies of the Arab.

Omar's eyes narrowed, and his voice was cold now. "Allah protects his people. He knows that men will be unjust. That is why an Arab must not be afraid to use a sword."

"You haven't answered my question." Paulo persisted quietly.

"Your question is foolish! Killing is sometimes necessary. If a bear attacks you, you will kill him, no?"

"No." Greg Morris answered the question as he swung his leg over the bench and joined the group at the table.

13

"Not if you are a Hindu or Buddhist. Taking a life of any kind is forbidden, except at sacrifice time. Then life is taken. Goats, chickens, fowl — they are all slaughtered as sacrifices to the gods. But not in anger. They are killed with compassion and in order to relieve their souls of the bodies that imprison them. Then their spirits are free to take another, hopefully higher, form of life."

The tension was dispelled by his matter-of-fact presentation of the Eastern philosophy. Paulo was interested. "Do you mean, if a bear attacked you, you would actually not kill him? Are you a Hindu?"

"If I could possibly avoid killing the animal, I would. Yes, I am a Hindu — Buddhist — whatever. The two religions are so closely intertwined here, it is hard to remember where one leaves off and the other begins. If I had to kill him, it would be with great respect, and I would ask his forgiveness."

They all stared at him. Lisa had come in with him and sat down at the end of the table, dinner plate in hand. Her expression was filled with admiration and amazement. Omar registered disbelief. Maurice was fascinated.

Greg continued, "You see, life is precious. All life is precious. And all life has one eventual goal: to reach perfection — perfection of mind, perfection of soul, perfection of goodness, of compassion. When that perfection has been achieved — only after many centuries of reincarnations and effort — that life force may finally be reunited with the universal source of life and goodness. God, in other words. He is the source. He is our beginning and our end. To be joined with him forever is to be complete, to be home, to rest from endless striving. This is the basis of Eastern belief. This is why our people seek enlightenment, not accomplishment, as the Western world does."

Innocently, Maurice spoke up. He was fascinated by the adult conversation, so unlike anything he had heard in Catholic school. Turning to Gustav and Katrine he asked, "How do you believe about God?"

Decisively, Gustav answered him. "We do not believe in God."

The boy was taken aback. "Then what do you believe in? What do you say your prayers to?"

"We do not say prayers. We work for what we want.

God is a figment of the common man's imagination. Our people are taught to be independent and self-reliant and not to lean on wishful thinking about some super-being who will give them what they want."

Maurice looked away from them. He looked at Paulo as though hoping for an answer. Paulo did not respond. Then the boy sat down close to his father, a frightened look on his young face.

"I think you're right," Greg agreed with the Russian. "Sometimes God is a figment of people's imaginations. We see him as we want to. Hindus and Buddhists alike have many gods. Some are delightful, some are fierce and terrible. But the Nepalese are not so different from you." He looked at Gustav. "Or you." And he looked at Paulo and Omar. "Their gods are the visual representation of legends and, often, the many aspects of man and nature. You have your gods and you also give them form. You worship strength. Omar worships his sword, the Soviets their armies, the Americans their marines. You worship prosperity. And you represent it with banks and tall buildings and jewels on your fingers — instead of the Hindu's beautiful young goddesses with flowing hair and green eyes. You also worship destruction, though you were all repulsed with the blood sacrifices of the animals. But the Arabs seem to wait anxiously for the day they can declare holy Jihad on the Jews and slaughter them. Americans and Soviets alike build their missile silos to assure their mutual destruction. Are these not your temples to the God of destruction?"

The group was silent. "The Nepalese culture is a simpler one — clear and innocent. Even their God of destruction is viewed as the means by which new life may start again. That is their whole wish — to live, to live again, to reach perfection, to reach God."

Omar spoke thoughtfully now. "That is also our goal. An Arab lives with all the passion of his soul, and we expect, as the Christians do, to live again after death with God, in paradise." Then he turned to the Soviets. "Katrine, what do you wish for? What is your goal if it is not God?"

"I wish to be a good comrade," she answered. "Nothing else. A good friend to my countrymen, a good citizen of my state, a good wife to my husband — a good comrade — that is all. You cannot wish for anything after life. Death

15

is the end. That is the definition of death — 'the end of life.'"

Maurice spoke with a tiny voice. "Mama said that Jesus Christ came back to life from death. She says we will too, if we are very good."

Katrine shrugged. "People believe what they want to. It is as simple as that. Greg prefers the simple life. Omar prefers the passionate life. We prefer our disciplined life. There is great satisfaction in a disciplined, orderly life. Paulo, what do you prefer?"

Paulo had become very uncomfortable. The discussion had led to probing questions for which he had no answers. He had hoped to find the answers here. "I prefer to keep my mind open to all answers that may be right. Not to believe in a supreme being is, I think, unreasonable in the face of so much grandeur. All this which we admire each day as we walk — this is so much superior to missiles and tall buildings. The mere fact of our existence and the magnificence of the world in which we live is the burden of proof for God's existence. The burden of proof against him is nothing more than words. Somehow, words are not as convincing as the mountains."

That night Paulo lay awake for a long time. Where were the answers for him? Omar had his faith, Greg was quite satisfied with his. Even little Maurice would speak up for his belief in Christ. Paulo felt cheated and very lonely.

At the Namche Bazaar, they replenished their food supplies. Omar bought an ornate silver dagger, with a handle studded with gems. Maurice and Louis bought one slightly smaller. Maurice bought bags of candy and then gave it away to a crowd of barefoot boys. Paulo was anxious to go on. They had had glimpses of Everest and Lhotse on the way to Namche. Now he was becoming impatient to reach the great mountain. What he expected to happen, he didn't know. Was he insane, thinking to find God on the mountain as Moses had? He was irritated with himself, but still he couldn't wait to get back on the trail.

Three more days and they approached the Thyangboche Monastery. The building itself was not spectacular, just a two-tiered, red-brick monastery with a a few clay homes clustered about it. However, the town was built on a large plateau above the Imja Glacier. Encircling the tiny village, a small stone wall meandered, breaking up the landscape and defining the perimeters of the town. The trail was steep now, and no one spoke as they concentrated on putting one foot in front of the other, hoping for the crest of the hill, not even noticing the mountains that had been their constant companions for days.

At last they emerged from the trees and mounted the crest of the hill. Paulo stopped. The monastery and town were dwarfed into mere nothingness by the monstrous mountain behind. Ama Dablam rose up like a colossus twenty-two thousand feet high. It overhung the monastery and imposed its presence on all the senses. There were gasps of delight through the trekking party, though they had, by now, become used to magnificent surroundings. Paulo's was not the only camera clicking. Maurice crept up beside him.

"*Voilà!* This is the 'payoff,' as American gangsters say. I did not know it would be like this. Did you, *mon ami?*"

"No," Paulo shook his head. "I had no idea."

"Can Everest be more beautiful than this?" the boy asked reverently.

"It will have its own beauty, as we all do. Have you got all your pictures?"

"*Oui,* I think so. Can we come back here in the evening when the sky is pink?"

"Sure. We should get some good shots then. Those clouds will turn pink, and probably the mountain, too."

Ama Dablam remained Paulo's favorite mountain. It had a haunting look. The pinnacle rose like a huge knob above the mass of the mountain. In the moonlight, it seemed a gigantic ghost rising up into the heavens. He never tired of looking at it or photographing it. While the others sat around the table after dinner and talked or read by flashlight, Paulo endured the frigid night air to exhaust his special-effect lenses and filters.

Base camp was now only three days away. They took the ascent slowly. They walked a ravine, and then the canyon widened into a narrow meadow with a shallow lake. A few mangy yaks grazed, and a native attempted to drive two of the beasts burdened with his possessions. The obstreperous animals were balking every few feet. Ama Dablam rose above the meadow so imperiously one could see nothing else.

"How will you use your photographs?" Gustav asked Paulo as they strolled along the meadow trail.

"Oh, I may not use them at all. I'll print two or three of my favorites, and the rest I'll put into my library until a magazine or a government project requests something on Nepal. Often, commercial businesses use such pictures in advertising. But, I don't worry about the use. I photograph simply because I love to do it."

"That is a fine luxury. I have observed your love of the land. For you, it seems a religious experience."

Paulo laughed at the irony. "I have no religion, Gustav."

"That is just as well, I think. Religion is for the intellectually weak."

"Have you considered that you might be wrong? It seems to me the religious life is very demanding. It requires great self-discipline — something you admire so much — patience, tolerance, service, sacrifice. None of those qualities are natural to most of us. It is work. Therefore, to be highly religious is not easily accomplished by the weak."

"Highly religious men are rare. Most men who call themselves religious are frauds. They claim to believe in high principles, but most will kill another person and justify it as a religious commandment."

"Gustav, you are religious."

The Soviet laughed. "There you are mistaken."

"I don't think so. Your country, 'the Motherland,' is your religion, and you would also kill for her and claim it as a commandment."

Gustav frowned. "This is not a religion. This is patriotism, and it is so in every country. Without such patriotism a country would not be strong. Your own country has lost much in this area. For all the benefits of capitalism, there are also losses. America's prosperity has smothered her patriotism."

"Not all," Paulo refuted. "If you believe that, you will be surprised one day. The American people are sleepy patriots, but they awaken quickly. Their freedom is important to them."

Gustav nodded in agreement. "Surely. It is important as long as it gives them comfort and prosperous lives. But your freedom is proving its own downfall. It allows loafers and leeches, drugs and pornography and violence. It even allows stronger foreign economies to buy up half your land and businesses. It allows gangsters and murderers to go free. It allows . . ."

"It allows the Communist party to work for our overthrow. I know. You're right. Our freedom walks a precarious tightrope, and a small percentage of people abuse it, but the vast majority enjoy a fuller, happier life than anywhere else in the world. Gustav, what is your profession?"

"I am a military man. That is why I cannot understand your preoccupation with religion."

"It is the time in my life. Don't you ever question your purpose, your values, your destiny?"

"I am satisfied."

"Be careful. It's good to be satisfied. It is not good to be smug, to stop questioning. A military man? Army, air force, navy? What rank?"

"I am in the army, a colonel."

Paulo gestured to the meadow and the mountains cutting a jagged edge from the blue sky. "This we share now. Because it isn't my land or yours, we share it happily. If it were America, you would feel yourself an outsider looking on. I would feel the same in your country. But here we are, sharing this equally and cheerfully. If we could only see that all the earth is the same. It belongs to God alone, not to you or to me, to France or to India."

"Paulo, you are an idealist."

"But you like me. Why would a military man like an idealist?"

Gustav put his hand on Paulo's shoulder briefly. "Because you are honest. Such a quality is rare. I hope you find what you are seeking. Also, I would like to think we could be friends."

"So would I. If our countries ever get over their paranoia about each other, perhaps many friendships would be possible. How is your new prime minister inclined to view America?"

"Vladimoscov is a pragmatist. He sees the problems of our society. He also see the problems of the West. America is both strong and weak, and Vladimoscov has no use for that which is weak. He will do whatever he must to solve the problems of the Soviet Union. Already he has solved one of the largest, the money problem. The Politburo will vote next month on joining the European World Wide Monetary System. They will most certainly vote in favor. Europeans and Americans have looked on the Soviet Union too long with suspicion. Now we will be united economically. This should help put many fears to rest. We shall be interdependent."

Paulo answered cautiously, "Interdependency of equals is good as long as independence is preserved."

Gustav smiled wryly and shook his head. "Old prejudices take a long time to die."

"Some lessons you don't want to relearn."

"Believe me, we want only peaceful solutions to our problems. As a military man, I can assure you that I do not see force as the answer. Peaceful interdependence is the only way."

Paulo nodded his agreement. Gustav was probably sincere, but how would Vladimoscov use the World Wide Monetary System to solve his problems? What if it didn't?

*"And he causeth all, both small and great, rich
and poor, free and bond, to receive a mark in
their right hand, or in their foreheads: and that
no man might buy or sell, save he that had the
mark, or the name of the beast, or the number
of his names."*
(Revelation 13:16-17.)

———————————— Chapter Two

Base camp was primitive and unimpressive; just a small warming cabin and a Coca-Cola machine marked the spot. Everest was the only focus. It was what Paulo had wanted — solitude and grandeur.

He pushed back the tent flap and threw himself onto his cot. Despite the long, lingering sunset and the photographs he had taken, Paulo was disappointed. What had he expected? A burning bush? A voice from Sinai? Must he actually get down on his knees, or stretch himself upon the ground as Augustine had done? That was ridiculous. If God had any respect for humanity, he would never require such a thing. How was it done? How did one tap into the infinite?

Omar stuck his head into Paulo's tent. The trip had forged bonds stronger than a casual friendship between the two men. Paulo D'Agosta was an unusual man, quiet but not shy, congenial but not exuberant, thoughtful but not withdrawn. They were fifteen years apart in age, but the Arab had begun to think of them as brothers. Omar had watched Paulo's sunset vigil and sensed the purpose. The man searched for the impossible. D'Agosta had never married. Here was the problem. A wife and children would settle all the searching. A man sees himself eternally young in the faces of his children. In them he sees life

21

stretching on beyond his own, and that comforts him. In a wife he finds love. That is all Paulo really seeks, Omar reasoned silently — love. He thinks it is God, but it is love. To be a part of love and beauty, he must have a wife.

"Did you find your answers?" Omar asked.

"How do you know my questions?" Paulo asked wearily.

"I don't. But you are obviously a man seeking answers. You did not find them, then?"

Paulo lay down on his cot. "No. Maybe there aren't any."

"I don't believe that. Everything fits. Allah did not make an imperfect world. If you can conceive of a question, Allah's mind can conceive the answer."

"Well, if it can, he sure isn't telling me."

"What are you searching for, my friend?"

Paulo turned his head slowly and gazed at the Arab. Omar's face was in deep shadows, but his white head gear and hawk-like nose stood out in the dim light. His intense eyes were merely black hollows. "Do you know who you are? What you are to God? What your place is in the scheme of an eternal universe? Have you asked these questions and know the answers?"

Omar didn't answer. He had never thought to ask such questions. He knew instinctively who he was. He was a royal prince of Saudi Arabia, chosen in the sight of Allah and his fellow men. His place was to worship Allah and serve his country and then . . . to take a few wives and enjoy the sweetness of life. It was very simple.

Omar sighed. "These questions do not bother me. I have my place already assigned. But it seems to me you would find such questions not nearly so obsessive if you had a good woman to enjoy."

Paulo turned away. "I've had women. They only satisfy for a few moments before sleep. The hunger I have is not for a woman. It is for my own identity."

Omar stood up. "If anyone deserves to find it, you do. I think, however, in your intense concern you may be missing an obvious answer. You are just as magnificent a creation of God's as this mountain you worship." He stepped out of the tent. "Good night, my brother. Sleep well."

They stayed at the base camp of Everest for three days. He didn't receive any momentous answers to his questions, but gradually, his heart and mind found greater peace. He began to laugh more, to talk more with the others, to enter into their word games as they tossed French, Russian, Arabic phrases about trying to guess the meanings. Maurice asked the Sherpas about the Yeti, and the group sat enthralled for hours listening to the many tales of Nepal's famous Abominable Snowman.

Taking a different route back to Lukla, they hiked across the Gokyo valley to Gokyo Ri. The valley was filled with rugged canyons, the Dudh Kosi river, and three exquisite turquoise lakes. Above the lake rose the peak, Gokyo Ri, which the group climbed upon some urging from Greg. The view was worth it. From the summit, they could see the panorama of many Himalayan peaks. That day had been somewhat cloudy, and now the peaks were lapped by wave after wave of oceanic clouds, only the very highest crags showing above the cotton-like tufts.

Although Greg had told them they would be walking along the Khumbu glacier, none of the small group realized that they were on it until they were halfway across. The glacier was embedded with small rocks and dirt so that it looked like most of the other terrain they had been walking. Tramping along across the side of the mountain, they approached a thousand foot crevasse. The trail ran along the edge, not more than five feet away from the sheer fall down.

"When will we get to the glacier?" Lisa asked Morris.

"You're on it now."

"This? This is just the side of the mountain, isn't it?"

"This is the glacier of Khumbu. It's three hundred feet thick, at least."

Lisa turned and called to Paulo and Omar trudging behind. "This is the glacier. We're on the glacier now."

"It still looks like dirt. Are you sure?" Omar called back.

"Just scratch through the dirt and pebbles." Greg answered. "It's pure ice below for three hundred feet or so. Let's wait and let everyone catch up, and we'll talk about it then."

Greg sat down on a large rock. Paulo bent to adjust his boot. Omar and Lisa moved off the trail and knelt to dig through the stones as Greg had suggested. A gust of wind snatched Lisa's hat as she hollered, "Hey, it took my hat!"

She started for it and Greg shouted. "No! Lisa . . ."

But Omar had reacted first. He said gallantly, "I'll get it," and took a broad step to reach for the hat. But he lost his footing, sat down, and began to slide. Still intent on getting the pink and purple hat of the young nurse, Omar did not have the perspective of his position relative to the sheer dropoff of the glacier. Paulo did. Greg did. Greg quickly looped the end of the rope he carried around the boulder he had been sitting on. Paulo had already started for Omar when Greg hollered out to him.

"Not without a rope! Grab my hand first!"

Omar had still not grasped the danger of the situation and was laughing like a child on a slippery slide as he helplessly slid nearer the edge.

Paulo called out to him. "Here! Omar look up here and grab my hand."

"Why? It's okay. I can get back up." He stood up to prove it and tried to get a toehold to climb back up the two feet he had slid. But the ice was impenetrable, and he slid another few inches. When he stood up, he could see over the edge. He glanced back over his shoulder and down to a jagged ice bottom a thousand feet below. The Arab's face went white. His eyes were like saucers, and he looked back up to Paulo in panic.

One hand in Greg's, Paulo was reaching for him, leaning as far as he could to grab something of the Saudi's clothing. He grabbed the arm of Omar's well-padded jacket first. That stopped the skidding.

"Give me your hand and be careful. Don't move quickly. Don't lose your footing. Take it easy. Nice and easy. I've got you." Paulo called out directions to the frightened man. Omar was almost frozen to the spot. He stood precipitously, staring down at the icefall below him, not able to move. Paulo had a firm grip on his hand. But, if the Arab should loose his footing and lurch, Paulo knew he would not be able to hold him. Lisa stood on the trail, her hand over her mouth to keep from screaming.

Gustav and Katrine had come upon the scene. The Soviet immediately saw the situation and responded. More length was needed. He inserted himself between Greg and Paulo, grasping Greg's free hand. Pulling up Paulo's jacket, he grasped his belt. Now they had lengthened the chain by a yard and freed both Paulo's hands. Carefully testing the snow, Paulo inched closer to Omar. His other hand now free while Gustav held him by the belt, Paulo reached for Omar's shoulder, turned him from his dangerous, unnerving perspective, and began to talk him back.

"Okay now. Easy does it. Come on, come on. One big step up here. This is level. You can get a toehold. You won't slip. I've got you. That's it. One more. One more step. Almost there. Okay, my friend, we're home free. Let's get back on the trail."

He had brought Omar slowly, carefully back, and when at last they stepped back onto the welcome gravel and dirt of the trail, the relief was overwhelming. Lisa sat down in the middle of the trail, uncovered her mouth, and sobbed in relief.

"It's all my fault. My stupid hat! He almost died over my stupid hat!" The hat was nowhere to be seen, swallowed forever by the glacier.

Gustav and Greg slapped each other on the back. Morris was visibly shaken, though he tried to hide it in the busy work of putting away the rope. Omar and Paulo stood in a long embrace, both arms around each other, thumping the other's back and trying to catch their breath. Too choked up to talk at first, Omar stepped back after several minutes and looked at Paulo.

"You are my friend, my true friend. You have saved my life. I owe you everything, everything, anything. Anything I have is yours, my friend."

Paulo smiled shakily, "I have what I want — you, safe and sound. That'll teach you to go chasing hats."

"I am serious. Anything you want, I will give you. Just name it."

But Paulo shook his head. "Your friendship is enough. Now will you please stay on the trail?"

Omar tried to laugh and failed. His breath came out in an explosion. "Hah! this puny, stinking, pig-lover of a trail is too close to the damned edge! Who made this lousy trail?" he bellowed.

Greg hollered back, "Someone who didn't like Arabs."

"Aha! So it is! No doubt a member of the Jewish cabinet has been here and cut out this trail so that I would fall over."

"No doubt," Paulo smiled wryly.

Maurice and his father had joined the group and sat on the ground watching as each person gave way to the tension. Maurice kept looking from Omar and Paulo to the edge of the glacier, his eyes round.

Before they left, Omar turned his face to the east and bowed down to Allah. The rest of the day, they walked in silence. That night they camped in a narrow meadow between the glacier and Lobuje Peak.

After that, the return trip seemed to take on a more earnest aspect. The trek back to Lukla was often broken up with a few switchbacks that took them briefly uphill; however, on the whole, going back was easier and more swift than the long slow climb.

"You must come with me to Riyadh," Omar began to press Paulo as they drew closer to Lukla. "You will stay with me in the royal palace."

"I'd like that. I've never been in a royal palace. And I'd like to see your country, especially those oil fields that make you so rich. But, unfortunately, duty calls. I've been away from the company for almost a month now, and I have to go home and try to look as though I am working for my keep."

"Do you own this Vista Color?"

"No, it owns me. I'm just a photographer at heart who got pushed up into the job nobody wants — vice president under Isaac Zimmerman."

"He owns it — this, this Jew?"

"No, even he doesn't own it. He is the president and chairman of the board. The American stockholders own it. But I do have a healthy investment in it. So does he."

"Are you part of the D'Agosta clothing designers in New York?" Omar asked after a moment of silence.

Paulo glanced sideways at his companion. "Yes. I'm the renegade. It was started by my father. My older brother, Roberto, runs the business. We try to stay out of each other's way."

"Ah, you do not get along well?"

"Correct."

"Why is this? You do not approve of him?"

"How do you make so many correct guesses?"

Omar shrugged, "I just watch your eyes. They speak before you do. If you do not approve of your brother, he must not be a good man."

"He is . . . an opportunist."

"Aha!" Omar jumped on Paulo's hesitation. "You think he is a thief."

"I didn't say that."

"No, but that is what you meant. See, you frown when you speak of your brother. It must make you very sad."

"It does. I am most concerned for Mama. She is afraid to know how far he goes, just as I am."

Omar was quiet for a few minutes. The day was sultry, and he brushed perspiration from his forehead. As the trail wound between the pink rhododendron bushes and the fir trees, he dampened his white, cotton head gear with canteen water. Then he spoke carefully. "I have heard some things."

Paulo stopped. He took Omar's arm and pulled him to a stop. "You have heard . . . what? Across the world you have heard of the D'Agosta name? What have you heard?"

Omar looked at him levelly. "That certain secrets can be obtained through D'Agosta. Or, more correctly, that he is a part of a chain that trades drugs for American secrets."

Paulo was paralyzed. "No. No! I don't believe it! That can't be true. I know he dabbles in the Mafia. I know he is into some things that are not legal, but not . . . I can't believe that!"

Omar inclined his head, acknowledging. "It is a hard thing. I also have an uncle who, some say, poisoned his brother. It is hard. Our family is our pride."

"Where have you heard this?" Paulo insisted. Now he too wiped his face.

"I have Shiite friends. Not close friends, you understand. They are too . . . too crazy for me. But these Shiites claim they get information from America — military information, which tells them when ships are moving, arms are arriving. This is how they can strike so effectively. This information comes through their chain. Drugs for secrets, for weapons."

Paulo swore and turned away. The others passed them on the trail. The chatter was now of home and friends. He opened his canteen and splashed water on his face. It took Paulo many minutes to recover his composure. Each time he tried to speak, only swear words came out. How could he do it? If Mama ever knew, it would kill her. "I'll kill

27

him," he finally exploded. "I swear I'll kill him."

Omar's face darkened. "Do not swear, my friend. Allah will hold you accountable for that which you swear."

Paulo stared at him with a bleak expression. "How could he do it? It's not as though he needs the money. I've got to stop it. I've been partly to blame. I haven't wanted to know. I should have been more active in the business. I should have watched him. Mama asked me to, but I didn't want to be bothered." He sat down on a stump and looked up obliquely. "You are telling me that my brother, my own brother, is betraying his country. Working with terrorists, selling military secrets." A deep groan escaped him. "What can I do?"

Omar put his hand on Paulo's shoulder. "Come, my friend. Nothing has changed. Only, a moment ago you were not aware. Now you are. The situation has not worsened in the past few minutes. You will simply take up your responsibility now. You will oppose him at each turn. You will try to take the D'Agosta link out of the chain. But do not be deceived. You will not break the chain. Nothing will. As long as some people can be bought, other people will purchase. If enough Americans are willing to be bought, your country will one day be slaves."

Paulo found it hard to breathe. Omar might speak philosophically about it all, but it was his country, his brother, his name at stake. Paulo didn't have much. He had no wife, no children, but he had his name, his father's name, and it meant something to him. It was a name he had always been proud of, and now, for the first time, he was ashamed. Slowly something clicked. "That is why you didn't shake my hand at first, isn't it? Remember? You held back. I thought it was just because I was an American. But it was the D'Agosta name, wasn't it?"

The Arab answered truthfully. "It was both. I am not a fool. There may be many D'Agostas."

Paulo stood up. He sighed deeply and began walking again. "Well, that settles it. I will be going straight home. Some other time I'll come to the royal palace."

The take-off from Lukla was even more hair-raising than the landing. The plane was packed with the seven of them and their backpacks. The plane rested on a downhill slope. All Paulo could see was one hundred and fifty

28

yards of runway and then the edge of the cliff. The props started, and the engine growled, then whined. Their Sherpa guide gave one last friendly wave as he unblocked the wheels, and the airplane rolled. The pilot gunned the engine. The sudden momentum pressed them against the back of the seats. From the window, Paulo saw the earth fly by, felt the wheels leave the ground. And then the strip of dirt was gone, the craft was airborne slightly; a downdraft from the canyon hit them, and the airplane dropped almost six hundred feet before the pilot pulled it out and up.

Omar took this experience better than Paulo did. He merely sat back in his seat, his eyes closed, "Allah" upon his lips. Paulo's face drained of all color, and his eyes were glued to the boiling river at the bottom of the gorge. When it was over and the airplane was soaring smoothly, Omar spoke.

"Ah. So, that was the final excitement! Well, it was worth it. We didn't see any tigers. We didn't see the Yeti. But, I must have something grand to tell my brothers and sisters about my trek."

Paulo glanced at him in disgust, his stomach still in his mouth. "This is your idea of something 'grand?' You're sick."

Omar laughed. "I was just about to mention that word to you. Do you need this airbag?"

"No!"

"Hah! So, you are sensitive about your weaknesses! I am not surprised. Quiet men often are. Not me. I am weak. I am strong. So what!" After a few minutes of silence, he asked, "If I should come to New York sometime, where should I stay? What place would you recommend?"

"My place. Best accommodations in town."

That was exactly what the Saudi had hoped to hear, but he demurred. "I travel with too much ceremony. There are bodyguards, cousins, a room of baggage. We could never fit in your place. But I am glad to know that you would want me."

Paulo was amused. "Were you testing my friendship?"

"I suppose. People are not the same on a vacation as they are at home. I might be an embarrassment to you."

Paulo laughed. "Yes, I guess you might. Who will believe me when I tell them the Saudi Royal Prince is my

29

friend. They'll think I am lying."

"Not if they know the Saudis. There are nearly a hundred of us. We are a very prolific family, many wives, many sons, many cousins, all of them hoping to be king someday."

"Do you hope to be king?"

"Not until I am very old. I enjoy my freedom too much. The king must be very responsible." He sighed. "However, one must prepare. Paulo, I am thinking I too will go to New York. Would I be in your way, if I went with you?"

This time with Omar had been among the most enjoyable weeks Paulo had ever spent. The thought of extending that companionship warmed him immediately. "Yes, most definitely. I wouldn't get a thing done with you around — and I'd love it! Have you seen New York?"

"I have been there several times."

"But you haven't seen it the way a native son can show it to you. The tourists' New York is cold and gaudy. My New York is warm and unforgettable. And you must meet Mama."

New York City had just been scrubbed clean by a two-day rainstorm. The afternoon Paulo and Omar flew in, the sky was clear and fresh. The Boeing 747 circled the Statue of Liberty, and the buzz of conversation in the aircraft quieted while they all strained to see the Lady with the torch. Paulo had been gone a month, and, all at once, it seemed like years. The Lady was even more impressive from the air than from the ground. Paulo's eyes felt the sting of pride. From the back of the airplane, a child's voice exploded, "I see her! Mommy, I see her! The Statue of Liberty, just like in my school program. We sang 'My Country 'tis of thee, sweet land of liberty, of thee I sing.' Isn't she beautiful?"

Paulo hadn't realized how glad he would be to see New York. He wasn't prepared for the depth of emotion that came over him. The expansion of gratitude and love in his heart choked out his ability to speak. It was several minutes before he turned away from the window and back to his companion.

The Saudi smiled. He had not missed a thing. "Ah yes, she is beautiful, your Lady." He patted his friend's knee lightly. "I, too, feel just that way about my homeland. My deserts are beautiful to me, as well as the faces of my people."

When they stepped from the airport wind tunnel into the terminal, Paulo and Omar were engulfed in a mass of white-robed Arabs. Omar had called from Katmandu to inform his father that he was going on to New York City. Waiting for him was his entourage of bodyguards, servants, advisors, and close friends. Paulo's inclination in a crowd was to back out of it, but Omar would not let him. He kept an arm around his shoulder and presented him to each man.

"This is my friend, my brother, Paulo D'Agosta. To him belongs my life. No, this is true! Let me tell you. I was sliding down the glacier. I was inches away from the edge. One thousand feet to the bottom! Yes, it is true. Tell them, Paulo, one thousand feet. I stand up. I look over. Aaiee, I see the bottom! I cannot move! If I move this way, I slip. If I move that way, I slip. This brother of mine, he risks his own life. Reaches out for me. 'Give me your hand,' he says. I cannot hear him. I am frightened. Allah, I am frightened! He grabs my coat, then my hand, then my shoulder as well, and he pulls me back up the slope onto the trail. My friend, Paulo, is a very important man to me, a very brave man. Now he is your friend too."

They took him into their midst and into their arms in enthusiastic embraces, one after another. Paulo and Omar moved slowly toward customs. With only one suitcase each, they had little to declare and went quickly through what was usually a long process. Waiting for them outside the main terminal were three black limousines. Paulo and Omar and two bodyguards took the lead limo.

"I have a social obligation, Omar. My calendar tells me that tonight is the annual charity benefit for the Metropolitan Art Museum. I am on the board of directors and am expected to be there, if at all possible. It might be interesting for you too. Lots of the big money of New York will be there."

The prince was interested. "Who?"

"The mayor, the governor, the Rockefellers, the Fords, the Rabinskis, the —"

"I'll go. So, you are on the board of directors with the big shots. There is a lot about yourself you haven't told me. You are too modest."

Paulo laughed. "One of us has to be. No, not modesty. I just keep things in perspective. I'm not there for my importance or my money. I represent Vista Color. And, I have a certain amount of knowledge."

Omar grinned at him. "I'll bet you do. Where is the party? At the museum?"

"No. We tried that once and they almost wrecked the place, spilling cocktails, bumping into the art. It's at the International Concordia. We can go together."

"If you don't mind, I think I'll take a nice long soak and rubdown at the hotel. Maybe also a short nap. The jet lag has found me. I can meet you there. What time?"

Paulo looked at his watch. Five-fifteen already. "Let's make it eight-thirty. The boring dinner speeches will be over, and we can get down to the serious business of partying."

"Good! Eight-thirty is good."

But His Royal Highness did not show up at eight-thirty. Paulo walked through the massive glass doors at eight-thirty sharp. He walked around the lobby for fifteen minutes, waiting for Omar to show. Finally, the hotel concierge escorted him to the banquet area. Floor-to-ceiling, carved doors gilded with gold leaf were opened, and the sound of laughter and music poured down the long hallway. Paulo turned back to the concierge briefly before he entered. "Oh, I have a friend coming. A Saudi. A Mr. Omar Sayd. Will you direct him this way please?"

Paulo paused in the doorway, taking stock, then made the plunge. After the immense silence of the mountains, the noise and clatter hurt his ears. His mind recoiled from it as he forced himself to mingle.

"Oliver, nice to see you again. I agree, once a year is not enough. Mrs. Goff, it's a pleasure. Have you found any good Persian pieces of art this year? You should go to Nepal. Katmandu would fascinate you. No, I wasn't looking for art, I went purely for pleasure. Trekked into Everest. Have you seen Isaac Zimmerman here tonight? The last I heard, he was going to try to be here."

A beefy man about sixty, with a girl much too young for him at his side, interrupted the conversation. "D'Agosta! Didn't know you were back. Zimmerman said you'd deserted him and run off to the Himalayas. I told

32

him he'd better not lose you. When the State Department needs somebody really good, we don't want to break in a new man."

"Izzie exaggerates. I just went to Nepal for a couple of weeks. Is he here tonight?"

"Haven't seen him. Somebody else from your firm is though." He turned around, his back to Paulo, and unceremoniously pointed.

A woman was standing beside the curved, sweeping staircase, her arm resting on the banister. She held the stem of a glass lightly with her fingers. She was deeply engrossed in a conversation with a man in a black suit. Paulo couldn't see his face; he could barely see hers. A wave of warmth flushed through him. Rachael Feldman was Zimmerman's niece. She had come into the company eight years before, hired by Izzie and presented to Paulo as his new secretary. She was recently divorced. A young marriage had left her bitter about men when she discovered that her "nice Jewish boy" was an embezzler. Rachael was thirty, with rich, deep-brown hair past her waist, arresting brown eyes that seemed to take half her face, and lips almost too full. When she began working for Paulo, she wouldn't speak to him informally or discuss anything that wasn't work related. She had no use for men. She didn't trust them and she didn't want to get involved. But she was very competent. She took computer study at night school, followed by a succession of classes on photography. She read religiously the two best trade magazines. She soon made herself the most valuable secretary Paulo had ever had. Then she asked for a raise.

Paulo smiled as he remembered. I've never seen that dress, he thought. White looks good on her. He kept staring at her. She turned her head and looked to her left, then to her right. Paulo moved closer, absently greeting a few people, smiling, complimenting, always turning quickly back to the woman by the stair. Still she hadn't seen him, but she kept looking around, losing the thread of her conversation. Then the couple in front of Paulo moved away, and he stood a few feet away, fixed on Rachael and smiling.

Self-consciously, she brushed a strand of hair back and swept the room with her eyes. She was uncomfortable. She wished she hadn't come. But she had come when her uncle Izzie began to wheeze with a cold. She felt that Vista Color should be represented. She felt very much alone and ill at ease in this gathering of influential people. Why wasn't Paulo back? He was scheduled to be home two days ago. Her thoughts stopped with her roving glance. Paulo was standing a few feet away, dressed in a royal-blue dinner jacket that accentuated his dark good looks. He sipped his drink, studying her, barely smiling as though he knew her secret thoughts and found her delightful. Instantly, her heart rate jumped, and his suggestion of a smile widened as he saw her recognize him.

At forty-nine, Paulo was one of the handsomest men she knew. His black hair had turned to silver at the temples, and his skin had drawn taut across the cheekbones and mouth. Eight years before, when she had first sat across from him in his office she refused to look at him. She had been embarrassed by his good looks and her response to them. His dark eyes were fringed with long lashes, which contrasted with his masculinity, projecting a definite sensuality. She had worked for him two years before she had admitted to herself that she was in love with Paulo D'Agosta. For two more years, she had fought it defiantly. For the past four years, she had simply accepted it, hopelessly.

And it was hopeless. She knew it. He was a Catholic; she was a Jew. He was kind, he was tender, he even liked her. But he was not in love with her as she was with him. Jim Polanski said he had loved a girl when he was much younger and she had refused him. He had never allowed himself to become involved with anyone else. Rachael understood that determination. She had felt the same way after Michael. But that was thirteen years ago. Bitterness cannot last that long, especially when you work daily around a man like Paulo.

He moved across the floor to her, ignored the man on her right who was still talking about the racetrack. "The most beautiful girl at the party! I didn't think you'd be here. How did I get so lucky?"

Rachael flushed. "I didn't think you'd be back. Somebody has to represent Vista Color at these social functions. Izzie said I didn't have to come, but he's sick, and I thought you'd want to know who was here, what the

34

scuttlebutt was."

"Hey! I don't think I know your friend," the dapper young man on her right broke in.

"Sorry. I apologize. Joe Salano, this is Paulo D'Agosta. He's my boss. I was just covering bases in case he didn't get back."

"Been gone long?" Salano asked.

"A month."

"That's a long time. Where'd you go?"

"I went to Nepal."

"Where?"

Paulo was irritated by the questions. He wanted to be alone with Rachael. He had missed her and had much to tell her. He looked again at the younger man. Joe Salano, he had heard the name. Then it clicked. He was a friend of Vincent Maretti's. Roberto had once suggested that Joe Salano would be a good match for Paulo's secretary. Salano was lower-level Mafia. Paulo went cold. He turned to Salano, his relaxed manner gone, his eyes unmistakable in his dislike.

"Mr. Salano, my secretary and I have some important business to discuss. Will you excuse us, please?" He had his hand under her elbow, guiding her up the stairs, before he had finished his question. Joe Salano stood below, staring up, puzzled at the instant change. Then he looked around and wandered over in the direction of the liquor bar.

"Rachael, I don't want you involved with my brother's friends. I've told you that."

"I didn't know he was. He's just someone I met at the party."

"He's Maretti's boy. Works somehow for Vincent and Roberto. He's slime. Stay away from him."

Rachael was surprised, and a little miffed, to hear the angry edge in his voice. "Since when do you take an interest in my private life? You've been gone a month. I could have been dead and the company dissolved, and you wouldn't have known it."

He kissed her forehead, disarming her anger. "Jealous, huh? You should be. I found something even more beautiful than you. Ama Dablam and Mt. Everest. I really wish you'd been there. Tell you what — we'll go back. I'll take you, and you can see what kept me. There aren't words, Rachael. There just aren't words."

"Are there pictures? How many rolls did you take? When do I get a screening?"

"In a couple of days. I've got a friend I have to squire around for a while. He's quite a guy. You'll like him."

At that moment, His Royal Highness Prince Omar Abdul Mohammed ibn Azziz Sayd swept into the room, resplendent in white and silver robes with flowing head gear, accompanied by four attendants, all dressed alike. All conversation stopped in the huge banquet room, and eyes turned to the Saudi party. Omar encircled the room with his piercing gaze, then examined the balcony and exclaimed imperiously, "Aha! I found you! Paulo D'Agosta, I am here."

From high above him, Paulo laughed and shook his head. He leaned over the banister slightly and called to his friend, "Wait there. I'll come down."

"Not so," the prince returned. "I shall come up." In a moment, the five white robes crossed the room and fluttered up the staircase. Omar made a great show of embracing Paulo and thumping him on the back. Then Paulo introduced him to Rachael.

She was smiling in amazement. She had never seen Paulo engulfed by another man. "Prince Omar Sayd, may I introduce my best secretary, Miss Rachael Feldman. Of course, she is my only secretary, but still . . . "

Paulo didn't notice the shadow that crossed Omar's face ever so briefly. The Arab smiled and bowed over Rachael's hand. But she saw the shadow. She didn't understand it. She dismissed it as her imagination.

"Ah, Paulo. This is why you did not wait for me in the lobby. You didn't tell me such beautiful secretaries grow in Vista Color. You were, perhaps, going to hide her from me, as we hide our precious jewels. I cannot blame you. I would be jealous of such a prize also. It is my pleasure, Miss Feldman."

Rachael was amused. "This is the friend you mentioned, Paulo?"

"Yes. Omar and I ate a lot of potatoes together this past month. I promised to show him New York, and he has promised to show me the royal palace in Riyadh one day.'

"I hope you like New York. Have you ever been here

36

before?"

"Yes, three times before, but not with such charming company. I usually spend most of my time sitting in bankers' offices or the UN hearings. This time I have only one thing to do; after that, I intend to do nothing more than follow Paulo about. How on earth did my friend, who pretends not to notice pretty women, find you?"

"My uncle is his boss. He forced me on him. I needed a job, and Uncle Izzie hired me and said, 'Like her or not, here she is.'"

"Well, it wasn't quite like that," Paulo objected. "What is it you have to do? Let's get that out of the way first."

Omar looked away from Rachael and back to Paulo. "I have to meet with the Israeli delegation and attempt to persuade them not to put up a manned space station."

"What makes you think Israel is planning a space station?" Rachael asked.

"It is well known to my people. Israel has a space program modeled after NASA. She has two nuclear plants. She is producing her own missiles. Several minor satellites are already up." He remained smiling at Paulo.

"But why?" she persisted.

Omar turned back to her, no longer smiling. "For one purpose, of course — to keep the Arabic world under constant surveillance."

Rachael's eyes were flashing now. "Nonsense! How is it that fifty million Arabs can be so paranoid over a country as small as Israel?"

Omar responded softly. "We are not exploding nuclear bombs, nor establishing satellites. But we shall if we have to. I am here to point out to Israel the disadvantages of escalating the hostility between us. They put up satellites, now we shall have to do the same. I would rather spend our money elsewhere."

Rachael felt her cheeks hot with indignation. "I don't believe it. Uncle Izzie would have mentioned something if it were true."

Omar had stopped smiling now. "Clearly, your uncle does not tell you everything. I am surprised you didn't hear of it yourself. It is no secret. Of course, why should you care? You are an American. Americans care little for the Middle East, or the rest of the world, for that matter. There are so many delightful pastimes in this country that

Palestine and her problems are disagreeable."

Paulo had sensed the mood of the moment change. The air had become charged with challenge and hostility. Rachael would not back down. Her brown eyes were stormy, and she cared nothing for the circle of white-robed Saudis around her.

"Mr. Sayd, we are not all so ignorant as you would like to think. Nor are we unconcerned. I take a great interest in Israel. It is the birthplace of my religion, as Mecca is yours. My people have wanted only one thing — to be able to live in peace without fear. If they are building missiles and satellites, it is only because of the constant threat they are under from your people. They have been attacked time and time again."

"I see. Well, I'm sure they have nothing to fear from the poor Palestinians who live like livestock in the tents without even running water. These are the same Palestinians to whom the land once belonged. Or from Jordan, who has continually appeased them and given up its land to them. Iran and Iraq were too busy for many years slitting each other's throats to threaten Israel. Then there is a peace treaty with Egypt. And you are quite mistaken. The Saudi people have never threatened the Zionists at all. If your people wanted peace, they started about it completely wrong. Moving into a man's land and taking it over as though it was their particular right is not the way to promote peace. If the UN gave Manhattan and the rest of the New York coast to millions of Russian refugees because they needed a home, would Americans stand for it? I doubt it. Jerusalem is no more a rightful home for all the Jews of the world than Rome is for all Catholics."

His voice had built until it carried across the balcony. Groups of people stood listening in rapt attention. Omar looked around, then lowered his voice.

"I apologize, Paulo. I did not mean to bring politics into this evening. Miss Feldman, we should start again. I am happy to meet Paulo's lovely secretary. I hope I have not permanently offended her."

Rachael did not respond to him. She turned instead to Paulo. "It is getting late, and I only came to cover for you. Since you are here yourself, I think I'll go home. I have work tomorrow."

"I'll take you," he immediately responded.

"I can get home. I always have. Thank you anyway, but stay; I'll be fine." She began to move toward the stairway. Paulo walked with her.

Omar was sincerely contrite. "I am to blame. Please do not go. I am inexcusable to treat a lady so. I am certain we could be friends if we gave each other another chance. Miss Feldman, won't you stay?"

She dismissed him coolly, her eyebrows raised. "No. You may be certain, but I'm not." Speaking again to Paulo, she asked, "Will you be in tomorrow?"

"Yes, in the morning."

Paulo walked her to the lobby in silence. While they waited for the cab, she spoke at last, coldly furious. "That is your friend? He is a maniac! Don't let him meet Uncle Izzie. There would be bloodletting."

Paulo sighed. "I know. He's a fanatic about Jews. But I think he really is sorry for what he said."

"He is not! He knew exactly what he was saying, and he wanted his day in court. He used you, Paulo. He used you to get the most influential audience in the city, then he used me to state his case. It was well planned. Be careful of him." As she climbed into the cab, she warned him over her shoulder, "One more thing. The 'crocodile lady' is here tonight. Be careful of her, too. See you tomorrow."

So Elaina was here. He was not surprised. In the past few years since she had married Mafia king Edward Ciardi, she had pretentiously become an art lover and patronized such gatherings religiously. Elaina Maretti Ciardi! At eight years old, Elaina had been a picture-perfect child — large dark eyes, full lips, straight dark brown hair and completely without scruples. Her father, Vincent Maretti, was the kind of man from whom Enrico D'Agosta would not have accepted a check or a favor. When Maretti bought a country home down the hill from the D'Agostas, Carmella and Enrico gently discouraged visiting between families, but Elaina blithely invited herself to be Paulo's constant companion. By twelve years old, she was passionately devoted to the gentle, young poet up the hill. His eyes fascinated her. His lips fascinated her. His easy, graceful walk and movement excited her every instinct. She set her precocious young mind on a match and

39

pursued Paulo with smiles, pouts, hurt fingers that needed kissing, and pious visits to mass.

Paulo had been both attracted and repelled by her. He quickly saw through her childish manipulations, and even though she was eye-catching, he was not captivated. It was the very sensuality she exuded, thinking it would attract him, that scared him away. In the idealism of youth, he was thinking seriously about the Catholic priesthood. As a teenager, Elaina dabbled with many suitors, merely to arouse Paulo's jealousy. It was futile. She became the beauty of the fast New York set. She laughed, played, taunted, and flirted, and she gave herself to the most notorious men in the country. But Paulo D'Agosta refused to notice. She threw herself at his brother, Roberto, in revenge, and when she married Ed Ciardi, twelve years her senior, it was to torment herself for not getting Paulo.

He hadn't thought about Elaina for months. He had been happy when she had married Ciardi ten years before. Ciardi obviously adored her — showered her with his diamonds and D'Agosta furs. Paulo was especially happy that she had given up her determined quest for him. He had never wanted her. Why she wanted him was a mystery. Paulo had always presumed her ardor was like that of a spoiled child who wants what she cannot have. Rachael called her 'the crocodile lady' because of the nature behind the smile.

The evening had gone flat. Paulo wished he could go home as Rachael had. Suddenly, he was monstrously tired. The adjustment from the quiet, simple world of Nepal to this complex world was taking all his energy. Had Omar used him? He didn't want to believe it.

The Saudi prince was not difficult to find. A circle of curiosity seekers had gathered about him as he regaled them with stories of Saudi and of the Nepal adventure. At the inner ring of the circle, face to face with the dazzling prince, was the 'crocodile lady.' Elaina Maretti Ciardi, usually the focal point of a crowd, was now overshadowed by the prince in white robes. She hid her smile behind a cocktail glass. Her figure, fashionably emaciated, was tentatively sheathed in a red satin and sequined gown, cut down at the neckline almost to her waist and slit up from the floor to her thigh. Her neck was wrapped in layer after layer of diamonds. Omar seemed to speak to the entire group as he turned from side to side, but always his eyes were drawn back to her. Like most men, he couldn't help it.

Paulo stood back, not wanting to be a part of the melee. But Omar spotted him, and the crowd began to open up as the Arab began to move determinedly toward his friend. But Omar did not reach him first. As smooth as satin, unnoticed by anyone else, Elaina slipped through the crowd and spoke in Paulo's ear.

"Welcome back. We've missed you."

"Thanks. I'm flattered that you noticed. How's Tony?"

Tony was Elaina's nine-year-old son. He was a beautiful child, guileless and loving. He was raised by a nanny and saw his mother only once a day, before bedtime. Edward Ciardi adored the boy. He worked hard during the week in order to get out to their home in Albany to be with his son on the weekends. Tony and Paulo had been fast friends since the boy was an infant. Tony was the one thing about Elaina that interested Paulo.

"Growing up very fast, and asking when Uncle Paulo will come back from the Himalayas. He is loudly hoping that you will bring back pictures of that Abominable Snowman. Is this your substitute?" She waved her hand at the quickly approaching Arab.

"Now, Elaina, be gracious. He's a stranger. You should be kind. Besides, you seemed quite enthralled just a moment ago."

Omar spoke at his elbow. "You seem to know all the beautiful women. Surely, this isn't another secretary?"

Elaina's voice was like shivers of ice. "Hardly. Paulo and I are old friends, childhood sweethearts really."

Eyebrows shot up. "Sweethearts?" Omar repeated. "Well, this gives me hope for you, Paulo. But your taste seems to be above you, unreachable. This beautiful lady is obviously a queen."

"This beautiful lady is also married, if you hadn't noticed," Paulo said sardonically.

Omar shook his head "Too bad. She seemed to enjoy my little stories. I had hoped . . . "

"They were quite amusing, your Highness." Elaina's

tone was sarcastic. "Are you really a prince? Is that how we should address you, 'Your Highness?' Or is it, 'Your Royal Highness?'" Elaina was playing with him now. She considered him gauche.

Omar did not like being ridiculed. Again his eyebrows lifted. His lips lost their smile and his eyes narrowed. "It depends on who is addressing me. To my friends, I am 'Omar.' To acquaintances, I am 'Your Highness.' To you, I am 'Your Royal Highness Prince Sayd.'"

"Omar, you are going to get me into trouble with all the ladies. Come on, the mayor is standing by the door. It looks like he might be on his way out. I think he was one you wanted to meet."

Elaina stood alone, seething, watching Paulo and the obnoxious Saudi. He's a fool, she thought, a pompous fool. Why does Paulo prefer his company to . . . Too late she glimpsed a dark-suited shoulder as it bumped her arm, splashing her cocktail all down her gown.

The rest of the evening went smoothly. Omar had an open nature and brought a breath of freshness to the society crowd gathered at the art benefit. As long as others were respectful of his position, he had a marvelous time being generous and entertaining. By the end of the night, he had pledged thirty thousand dollars to their benefit and had his picture taken with almost every couple there. Paulo didn't like that much notoriety, but he enjoyed watching the effect his friend had on New York society.

It was unfortunate that the prince met Arthur Rabinski. By the end of the evening, most of the 'art patrons' were resoundingly drunk. Omar was completely sober, as befitting his position, in accordance with his Moslem religion. He did not drink — in public. Sometimes he drank moderately in private. This was not acknowledged, but it happened.

Rabinski, on the other hand, was dead drunk. It was not apparent — he held his liquor well. But it unleashed a certain belligerence. Omar was deeply engrossed in financial conversation with Derrick Ford and Albert Johansen, both with Chase Manhattan Bank.

"You know they'll fail. I know they'll fail. When enough of your investments fail, what will you do? Turn to us and say 'I am sorry, I seem to have lost your fifty billion dollars.' You are playing with a tiger."

"Your Highness, the financial world holds no promises. We do our best. The Third World countries come to us to help them achieve a modicum of prosperity." Johansen shrugged. "They have assets that insure the investment, natural resources pledged to the notes."

Omar stared him down. "What natural resources?"

The banker did not answer. Omar plunged ahead. "All their natural resources? Are they all pledged?" The implications hit him, and his words were measured. "You will own these countries, in effect, when their notes fail. With my money, my father's money, my uncle's money, you will buy up half the world." His voice rose as he marched through the logical process.

No one was paying much attention now to the Saudi prince. But Rabinski heard him. Arthur Rabinski was usually a discreet man. He was second in command at the Federal Reserve. World finance was his love and his expertise. This Arab monkey in his theatrical robes was raking Al and Derrick over the coals. This kind of talk was private, between gentlemen who understood the difficulties and nuances of world finance. He was making allegations that would embarrass them all. Rabinski moved into the circle.

With him came a younger man, not dressed in dinner jacket or tux. His dark suit was modest. He was light-haired and blue-eyed, and his face had a clean look. He was David Cyrus ben Gurion Cohen, at twenty-eight a member of the Israeli cabinet and invited by Rabinski to come to New York City to learn about American finance. Paulo watched the scene apprehensively. He politely excused himself from conversation with two dowagers and started toward Omar.

"You are completely out of order," Rabinski said abruptly as he joined the group. "Mr. Johansen and Mr. Ford represent only a fraction of those responsible for such financial decisions. Those decisions are made by representatives from thirteen nations, including our own. You have no right to embarrass them this way. Besides, I can assure you that your money is safe."

"Who are you to assure me?"

"Arthur Rabinski of the Federal Reserve. And this is not talk for a party."

"You can assure me my money is safe, when you know

43

that banks are collapsing all over your country because they loan out forty-eight times more money than they've got and three nations have already declared bankruptcy? What will you do when the house of cards falls? Simply do away with money altogether?"

"Perhaps. And perhaps that wouldn't be a bad idea. A moneyless society would solve a lot of problems. Credits and debits would be much more tidy, much more efficient. No muggings, no robbery, no bad checks —"

"No manipulating the money supply. Half your job would be over. Ah, but robbery, that would be the worst kind! Robbing every man of control over his life, his wealth, his possessions. If you hold my purse strings, you can starve me to death. I am no more than a slave. You can tell me when I can come and when I can go, when I can eat and when I don't have enough credits to eat. Are you a Communist, Mr. Rabinski?"

Arthur was a slight man. He wore steel-rimmed glasses, and he was balding. He was not as tall as Omar, nor nearly as strong. But he was quick. Rabinski's drink splashed in the Saudi's face, and his right fist connected with Omar's jaw. But he wasn't quick enough to avoid Omar's cousin and bodyguard. In a split second, the room turned into an uproar. Plainclothes policemen hired by the mayor joined the foray. A table was overturned, and a thousand dollars worth of good whiskey was smashed. Gasps turned to shrieks as more men joined the fight. The Arabs were decidedly holding their own, though outnumbered ten to one. Paulo just wanted to get Omar out of there. He heard the prince laugh and saw him swinging happily, apparently enjoying the whole thing immensely. Just as Omar was about to dispense with one brawny young man in a hotel uniform, a foot shot out of the melee and connected with his midriff. His Highness went down.

Paulo tried to thread his way through the chaos and get to Omar to pull him out. He made it, mostly unscathed, to the spot where he thought his friend had fallen. Omar was not there. He turned about and saw Omar's limp body being dragged away from the fight and out a side door. Paulo plunged after him and found the Arab, groggy and holding his midriff, resting none too comfortably against his rescuer — David ben Cohen.

44

The young Jew looked up at Paulo and smiled, shaking his head. "Better that he should live to fight another day. I wouldn't be surprised if he had a broken rib. Can you help me find a way out?"

Paulo and David half carried, half walked, Omar down the side hallway, tried a few doors, and made their way to the lobby. Paulo ran out to summon Omar's limousine.

The Saudi prince looked into the clear blue eyes of the Jew and asked, "Who are you? Why did you help me?"

"Because you needed help. Because you were right. My name is David Cohen, David Cyrus ben Cohen," and he grinned at the surprise on Omar's face.

The prince regarded him seriously for a moment, then exclaimed, "Damn, but you're a good Jew!"

Now David laughed aloud. "Thanks."

Paulo came back in and helped them out the door. Omar groaned loudly as he collapsed onto the back seat.

"If that ever calms down in there, will you tell the prince's friends that he is safe?" Paulo hastily shook hands with the young man and started to turn away. But there was something arresting about David Cohen's face; a solid jawline and strong prominent nose — both balanced by the direct gaze of startling blue eyes. Paulo turned back and looked at him more closely. He felt an immediate sense of trust, and another emotion he wasn't used to — instinctive love — such as he should have for a brother. "You . . . you've been very kind. Thank you. I'm sure he would thank you too if he weren't rolling around in pain. If I can ever . . . well, you know. I'd like to express our gratitude somehow. My friend is not very discreet, but he is honest."

David nodded. "I could see that. Too honest. It is dangerous. I'm glad to help. David ben Cohen is my name," he said, putting out his hand for Paulo to shake.

"D'Agosta, Paulo D'Agosta. I feel as though we've met somewhere? Is that possible?"

"No, I don't think so. But perhaps we will again, though. Good luck."

"And it came to pass that they did have their signs, yea, their secret signs, and their secret words; and this that they might distinguish a brother who had entered into the covenant. And thus they might murder, and plunder, and steal, and commit whoredoms and all manner of wickedness, contrary to the laws of their country and also the laws of their God." (Helaman 6:22-23.)

Chapter Three

Isaac Zimmerman was a short man with gold-rimmed glasses that forever coasted down the narrow bridge of his nose. He frequently wiped both his glasses and his nose. Portly and balding since twenty-five, Isaac looked much like a banty rooster, preening in his gray wool suit.

Paulo spent half a day in Zimmerman's office answering questions when he wanted to be digging into the pile of work Rachael had neatly stacked on his desk. Izzie was only partially interested in Nepal and Everest. He was most interested in Paulo's Saudi friend. He pumped his vice president for all the information he could get. Where was Omar's headquarters? Did all the royal family live in the same city? What defenses had he mentioned? What did they think of the Israeli satellite? What were his holdings in America?

Paulo grew impatient. "I don't know," he said. "I didn't interrogate him. I just made friends with him. He has extensive holdings in the U.S. in farmland. He looks at it as a hedge against losing the money he put into the International Holding Company. He thinks they have intentionally planned to lose it by making loans to bad-risk countries. Once those countries go bankrupt, the bankers will take over all their natural resources, and the Arabs will have lost fifty billion dollars. Of course, he's paranoid. Thinks the Jews of the world are behind it."

Izzie was nervous, tapping the rubber end of a pencil on his desk and twisting a small piece of paper around in a circle. "Arabs have always been paranoid about Jews. It goes back to Isaac and Ishmael. Say, I have a friend you should meet. He is the youngest member of the Jewish Cabinet. His uncle was the first prime minister of Israel, and his father was the best friend of Ralph Schleger. You knew, didn't you, that I am also good friends with Prime Minister Schleger?"

"Yes, so you've told me — several times."

"David ben Cohen is a very promising young man — bright, competent, admirable military background, excellent education from the Institute of Technology in Haifa, very dedicated to Zionism. I think Schleger will use him for important things. He is here in New York learning about finance, on assignment from Ralph. You really ought to meet him."

Paulo fought down his irritation with Izzie's name dropping when he heard David Cohen's name. "I have."

Zimmerman was surprised, then deflated. "You have! When?"

"Last night. You should have gone to the charity benefit for the Met. It turned out to be a very exciting evening. My friend, Omar, was there and dazzled our New York crowd. And your friend, David, was there."

"Well, I dare say he isn't as dazzling as your Saudi prince, but . . ."

Paulo laughed. "Dazzle doesn't impress me. David Cohen is impressive enough just as he is. I agree with you, he's headed for good things. I think he impressed Omar too. He pulled the prince out of a head-breaking bash. I'd like to meet Cohen again. There's something . . . something unusual about him. He's . . . real."

Izzie was pleased. "He is. Yes, he is. Very real, very unusual. Schleger doesn't compliment idly. I can arrange dinner tomorrow."

"Good. Tomorrow night would be good. After that, I'm taking Omar up to meet Mama."

New York City wasn't quite as wonderful as Paulo's fond memories. He had promised Omar to show him a native son's New York and found himself a little disconcerted by what they saw. Omar always traveled in style. The black limousine rolled slowly through streets that had once been Paulo's childhood playground. Here he had learned to catch a football, kick a soccer ball, and ride a bicycle. Now, the houses his mother's friends had kept spotlessly clean were hardly more than a rubble of bricks. Many of the windows were broken. Holes through the brick let daylight onto the apartment floors within. Porches were no longer used for sitting and playing cards at night, or for drinking coffee and talking during the day. It was too dangerous. Restaurants that once boasted authentic Italian pasta now dispensed crack, heroin, opium. Violence erupted regularly on the street corners. Black, Spanish, Italian and Oriental teenagers hung out around the corners, often roving the streets arm-in-arm, sweeping everything before them. Cars that cautiously slowed to avoid them were taken over and sometimes rocked and rolled over on their sides. The geranium-filled window boxes Paulo remembered from his childhood were gone. No flowers or trees graced this neighborhood. It was not the neighborhood Paulo had loved. They didn't stay long.

Broadway was so jammed with crowds of people, the limos inched along like snails. The New York women were not beautiful. They were fashionable but hard, oblivious to their own femininity. They strode along, tight-lipped, narrow-eyed, smoking cigarettes, slim cigars, and marijuana. Their skirts were either tight and very short or mid-calf and wrinkled. There were dozens of women on every corner with sheer, see-through blouses, wearing little or nothing beneath. Sex was their trademark, product, and reward.

Central Park was out of the question. It was completely controlled by gangs, and unwary strangers who occasionally wandered there usually did not return. Coney Island also was not on the sightseers' list. It was still an amusement park, but dominated by youth, it had become a center for drugs and Satan worship. On the island one could get any kind of drugs imaginable just as commonly as candy or beer. Blood sacrifices of animals had become a nightly ritual. The newspapers had stopped carrying reports of the youths who were killed by the devil worshippers. Even the policemen had been pulled out of Coney. Several shows of force had resulted in ten men killed, riots in which property damage ran into the millions, and fires that took life indiscriminately amongst teenagers and officials. For a while, patrolmen went in pairs, then, after three pairs had simply vanished, the New York City police unofficially gave Coney Island to the brave or foolish. Only the Mafia was able to keep peace on the Island, and they ruled it as they pleased, with fear. Here, Roberto D'Agosta's and Edward Ciardi's boys received and processed all the illegal drugs they smuggled into the country. Every kind of sex was available, and young, diseased, or drug-ravaged bodies were found dead on the Island every day. Of course, D'Agosta and Ciardi never soiled themselves with direct, eyewitness knowledge of how their men ran the place. As long as the money was good and consistent, they would rather not know everything.

Paulo and Omar finished up their sightseeing early. "Tomorrow I'll take you into upstate New York to meet Mama. You won't be disappointed there, I promise."

"I am not disappointed now. I have spent the day as I wished, with my very good friend, Paulo. Only you are disappointed, I think. I have been often enough to New York to know what it is like. You have obviously been too much the traveler to notice changes at home. Don't feel bad, my friend. Nothing remains the same. Scientists say we are always either evolving or deteriorating."

The day would have been a real disaster for Paulo if he had not agreed to meet Zimmerman and David Cohen for dinner. When he mentioned it to Omar, the Arab immediately invited himself.

"I have wondered about this Jew. This cannot be a coincidence. I do not believe in coincidences. Allah directs all, and he directed me to this David Cohen."

Paulo shook his head, "I don't know, Omar. You are not exactly a favorite of the Jews you have met. I don't want to get into politics or —"

Omar brushed away his concern with a wave of his hand. "Do not concern yourself. I will not be rude to a man who saved my head, as well as my ribs."

"Well, I'm sure you'll be polite to Cohen. Zimmerman you might have more difficulty with. He can be a bit pretentious, a little smug. You'll be impatient with him, I'm sure."

Omar folded his arms calmly across his lap. "I can be the soul of patience."

Paulo laughed. Omar remained aloof, practicing his patience. "Okay, okay," Paulo gave in. "We are meeting for dinner at Jenna's Club, on Seventh Street at 7:30. I'll increase our reservation number." Paulo ducked out of the limousine, and the prince's entourage rolled away, three vehicles long.

Omar came discreetly to the Club, no bodyguards in sight, no flowing white robes, no white headgear. He arrived promptly at 7:30 p.m., wearing a white shirt and gray slacks with a cashmere sweater, casually unbuttoned. He was slender and broad shouldered, an attractive, powerful man. Paulo thought Zimmerman was a trifle disappointed. No doubt he had wished to be impressed. Omar made no effort to impress. He was introduced around the table, and only his slight bow at each introduction marked him as foreign.

Zimmerman nodded and shook hands. Cohen stood and offered his hand, "Your Highness, you seem well recovered. Broken ribs don't slow you down, I see."

"It is nothing. A little bruise. But I couldn't resist the chance to say thank you. Your help was much appreciated. Mr. Zimmerman, thank you for allowing me to join your dinner party. You are the president of Vista Color, is this correct?"

Izzie nodded gravely. "It's my pleasure, Mr . . . uhh, Your Highness. Paulo has told me about your trip together to Everest. Quite an adventure. And you are just visiting in New York?"

"Exactly. Today we did a little sight-seeing. Tomorrow we will go to see Mrs. D'Agosta. I understand she is the special treat."

A waiter came to take their orders. Over french onion soup, conversation resumed.

"Mr. D'Agosta, I am well acquainted with your work," David Cohen said. "And I admire it. There is a certain quality about your photography. It strikes me as curious. The faces you photograph seem to be questioning. Whether young or old, there is a quality in their eyes of questioning. Why do you think that is?"

"I'm not sure what you refer to. Perhaps there is a

51

certain questioning in all of us. Those who don't question at all seem very smug."

"Confidence seems smug to those who don't have it." Izzie managed to sound very satisfied.

"I think one may have a great deal of self-confidence and still question," Paulo countered.

"It depends on what you may be questioning." Omar looked at his friend, knowing Paulo as neither of the others did.

"I agree," said David. "Questioning is most often good. We must examine events, philosophies, intentions, and especially our own motives. But I sense a different question behind your pictures. Your children often look lost, or very sad. Your old people are usually not peaceful, having found life's answers. They look as though they might ask 'What is this all about?' Is this your own question, perhaps? Have you not found your own answers?"

"Maybe it is not given for some people to find answers. Are you quite comfortable with all your answers? Omar is certain that the heavens revolve around Allah and the earth around Saudi Arabia. It would be nice to have things so neatly arranged."

David nodded agreement. "Almost everyone sees the universe as revolving about oneself. It is a rare man who sees all people as equals before Deity and his own relative importance in being one in three billion. Then, to be able to turn around and with confidence say, 'Yes, but I, myself, am important to Him.' This is a very great trick." David went on eating and talking, zeroing in on the very area of Paulo's greatest difficulty.

Paulo watched the younger man. He seemed to look beyond the smile and into the heart. His blue eyes were guileless and yet wise. Paulo looked from Omar to David. With his black hair and sharp eyes, Omar might have seemed more Semitic than David, whose light, sandy hair and straight nose reflected a European ancestry. He was, in fact, a German Jew. His parents had been playmates as children just before the second World War broke out in Germany, and his grandmother had walked out of Mannheim, Germany, into Switzerland, shepherding her own two children and four other playmates. They waved good-bye to their parents and never saw them again.

"Is this what your religion teaches you?" Paulo asked. "Or have you simply come to it by yourself? If your analysis of my art is correct, I would not photograph you, David. There are no questions in your eyes."

The young man's face opened into a wide smile, his eyes crinkling. "No, there are not many. A few. A few. My greatest question right now concerns not just myself but the lives of many others." He resumed eating. "I am questioning the World Wide Monetary System that is becoming so popular now in financial circles. Mr. Rabinski, whose nose is still recovering, thanks to Your Highness," and he nodded to Omar, "seems to think it is the wave of the future, the magic wand that will make all poverty disappear, and crime as well. Why did you call him a communist?" His eyes were clearly fixed on Omar.

"I didn't. I simply asked if he were a communist. I think that is a fair question. Either he has not grasped the implications of the system, or he supports economic control. Economic control is as effective as military control. It is even more effective, actually, because you can fight an army — even missiles you can fight — but when you cannot even obtain a loaf of bread unless a computer says you may, then you are a slave."

Cohen continued to probe. "That is how you see it then, as a control device?"

Omar shrugged as if it were of no importance. But Paulo knew how deeply he felt. "Of course. Here, let me illustrate. You have given over to me all your shekels. Paulo has given me his millions of dollars." He glanced at his friend and flashed him a smile. "And Mr. Zimmerman here has turned over to me all the assets of his company. All of you no longer have currency. You only have credits and debits in my computer system. Isn't this convenient? No longer do we have to bother with exchange rates for foreign currency. It is simple. All monetary transactions go through a central bank."

Izzie broke in. "Exactly! International business would be immensely facilitated. Fluctuations in value would be obsolete. Saudi Arabia either has so many credits or it doesn't. Israel either has so many credits, or it doesn't. There would be no concealment of assets possible, no bad checks. It would be wonderfully simple, and we could get on with the important things in life — business."

The Arab sat back studying Izzie Zimmerman. Paulo had been right. He was a smug little man, and either a fool or dangerously shrewd. "All for the sake of business, pure and simple! Ah, yes, it seems like a fine idea. But let us continue the example. Now, I am the banker. But one day my computer system has a mechanical failure. Paulo's funds are mistakenly transferred to another account. Paulo needs to pay his rent. But he cannot do it. His landlord must wait until the account can be settled. Uh-oh, there is no mistake. His credits have been seized by the government for back taxes he didn't even know he owed. Can he protest? It won't help. His credits are gone. I have given them away. He has no purchasing power.

"That is not much different from today." Paulo ventured, sardonically.

"Not much, but the significant difference is that you will not be able to buy or sell anything unless you belong to the system. It will not be a voluntary matter. Now you can use cash, if you like. You may have a secret fund, if you choose. You may have objects of value that you can sell whenever you want in order to raise money. Under the World Wide Monetary System that will not be so. There will be no secret funds, no cash under your mattress, and if you wish to sell an art object, you must do it by debits and credits, with the government able to control your account as it chooses by computer."

They ate in silence for a few minutes, mulling over Omar's charges. Paulo asked, "How do you know this, Omar?"

The Arab smiled humorlessly. "It was explained to us by the large bankers, Mr. Fellerman of the Chase Manhattan Bank, Mr. Wilson of the Lloyds of London, Mr. Guettenborg of Switzerland. Of course, it was explained very positively. It will all be very convenient for governments in ruling their people. The Soviets have embraced it wholeheartedly. Vladimoscov is leading the push for world adoption of the system. It will give government ultimate control over protestors, renegades, dissenters, even its own officials. A king will be a king indeed."

Cohen stared at Omar in fascination. Then he recounted Jewish history for them. "In Babylon of old they did this. They began by calling in all the gold and silver

54

and issuing clay scarabs. The gold and silver in their treasury the kings used for their own pleasures and traded it away. The scarabs were no longer redeemable by gold and silver, but now, by brass and copper. After a long time, the brass and copper were also used, traded and depleted; then the scarabs were worth nothing. So, the king ascribed a fixed price to the scarabs, though they were redeemable by nothing of value. We have done this also. America accomplished it under Mr. Roosevelt, then Mr. Johnson. Your paper money only has worth as measured against my economy, the German economy, the Japanese, and so on. And the bankers set the price. The worldwide central computer would be one more step beyond paper. I see what you are telling us, Your Highness."

"Do you? Then what? Will you tell your prime minister? The rest of the Israeli Cabinet? Will they say it is the ravings of a crazy Arab?"

Zimmerman spoke. "I think this is a classic case of paranoia in the extreme. Money is a system of business exchange. It does not matter if it is gold or silver or paper. A nation's economy is as strong as its resources and the resourcefulness of its people. Business is a measure of that. Who cares if our money is backed by gold? It will be as strong as our business, technology, production, creativity is strong."

Omar turned to him and pinned him with a look. "And will you say that when you are no longer the first world power? When your international bankers say that Germany or Japan or China or Saudi Arabia is more productive? And the assets you thought were worth three hundred million dollars are only worth fifty million, not because of anything you have done or not done, but because they have said so. What about the man who runs the deli down the street? He is not worried about fifty million versus three hundred million. He must simply pay his rent and clothe his children, and under the WWMS his credits are cut to one sixth their original value. There will be no stable, objective value at all. No one has any security, no matter how productive, creative, or capable he is. I cannot imagine any greater control. And they are proposing it world-wide. Who will be audacious enough to propose to control this monster system?"

No one spoke. Omar looked around the group. Quietly, he spoke. "Mr. Fellerman, Mr. Wilson, Mr. Guettenborg, and Mr. Ralph Schleger. These men I know. There are others — of different nationalities — nine other bankers. Most of these are not government officials answerable to their people by election or impeachment. These are independent businessmen who have a thirst for power. And there is one other, Mr. Vladimoscov. Perhaps he is ambitious enough to control the system."

Zimmerman was uncomfortable and squirmed in his seat. David looked not at Omar but beyond him. And Paulo sat without eating, his dinner spoiled, his stomach vaguely sick.

Izzie spoke. "You make too much of it."

David spoke decisively. "This is wrong. It is evil."

"Can we fight it?" Paulo asked. "How? How can we?"

Omar resumed his dinner with relish, his points having been driven home. "The only way to fight it is to refuse their number. Each business, each person will be issued a number, much like your Social Security number. It will be coded by country. You must have this number in order to buy even a hotdog at the corner deli or to sell a roll of film. You must not accept the number. The European Common Market already has its central banking system. It is primed and ready to extend the system, join forces with the American Federal Reserve and the Soviet central bank, and project the system to other countries. America could stop it if she wanted to. She is strong enough; her economy influences the world. If she falls, the rest of us will have no choice. The interlocking of international trade would demand it. You must refuse it. You must!"

Carmella D'Agosta was in bed at two o'clock in the afternoon, and much against her will. At seventy-nine years of age, she was not yet old enough to be tended by her daughter-in-law like some senile old vegetable. But last night her blood pressure had shot up, she had become dizzy, and her heart had begun to beat very fast. Ruth D'Agosta had shooed Roberto away and put Mama to bed. The medication should have worked faster, but Carmella was in such a state over something Roberto had said that Ruth could scarcely get her calm enough to stabilize.

56

It was after ten o'clock the following day before her heart rate was normal enough that and she could sit up in bed without getting dizzy.

"Where is my dress? You know, that pretty silk one you gave me at Christmas? My Paulo comes today, and I will not be here in bed in my nightgown. Paulo, he never sees me in a nightgown. Ruth, here! Help me to get up."

"Now Mama, you shouldn't get up. You've been sick. The doctor said if I can't keep you down and quiet while your blood pressure stabilizes, he will have to send you to the hospital. Do you want Paulo to come to see you in the hospital?" Ruth played now to the old woman's vanity. "After all, you know those hospital gowns aren't nearly as nice as your pretty ones." Ruth smiled encouragingly.

But Carmella was not being humored. "Those doctors, hah! All they do is threaten. Hospital, hah! Not for me. When I die, I go to the hospital. Before that, I sleep in my own bed. Now be a good girl, Ruth. Help me into my silk dress."

"Nope, not this time. Here, I'll help you sit up, and we'll see if you get dizzy. I'll just sit here with you. There, are you comfortable? Do you want to lie back down? Okay, we'll just sit together for a while. Then I'll get you some juice if you want it."

By noon, Carmella seemed quite stable and was able to get up to go to the bathroom. She ate sparingly of the lunch Ruth brought, but her hands had stopped shaking, and she sat up determinedly in bed. So, when Paulo entered his mother's bedroom at two o'clock, Carmella was in her silk dress, her hair in a neat bun, sitting up in bed with pillows behind her.

"Mama! You are becoming a high-society lady and sleeping past noon, I see," Paulo leaned over to kiss his adoring Mama. Mother and son had always had a special affection for each other. The older he grew, the more he looked like his mother. Paulo had inherited her warm, limpid brown eyes with sweeping eyelashes. He had also inherited her stubborn though spiritual nature. As a child, he often had spiritual experiences that forewarned him of certain events. He was a serious student of the Catholic Catechism and often asked questions — which she generally could not answer. Carmella loved her religion with all her heart, though the fine points of doctrine were beyond her. The Holy Mother Mary was her chief confidante and consolation since her beloved husband, Enrico, had died. Carmella had encouraged Paulo as a youth to go into the seminary and become a priest. It is an honorable thing for a family to have a priest. But Paulo had his own dreams, and he found his own religious experience with his camera. This she did not understand, had never understood. How could one worship God just by taking pictures? One worshipped on the knees. The knees should hurt, for God to know you loved him.

She reached up to touch her son's cheek. But Paulo, this darling one, he was still a boy, a boy who was still searching for that which she had long ago found — faith in God. Such a good boy. He should have gone into the priesthood. He would have been a good Father.

"Hah, I am not sleeping! I wait for my boy. And who says I cannot rest while I wait? Besides, Ruth does not let me out of this bed, or I would come downstairs to meet you. That Ruth, she is a stubborn girl."

Paulo laughed and sat on the edge of the bed beside her, holding her hand in his. "So, Ruth says you've been seeing lights dancing off the ceiling. Have you been forgetting your medicine? It should keep you well, as long as you take it just as the doctor ordered. Do we need to have Mark come and give you your medicine every morning?" Mark, eleven years old, was Ruth's youngest son.

"Just let him try!" Carmella scoffed. "I am taking my medicine fine. Every morning, every night, just like Doctor Huang ordered. Now stop fussing over me. Tell me, I want to know all about your trip. You said you would bring me pictures of the Mountain Everest. So, where are these pictures? Did you have a good vacation? Were there any pretty girls?"

Paulo grinned and shook his head, then kissed her soft, wrinkled cheek. "None as pretty as you. That's my problem. I've just never found a girl as good as the one that married my father. But I did have a wonderful vacation, and the mountain Everest is every bit as grand as I thought it would be. If only you could have gone, Mama. That would have made it perfect — to be able to share it all with you. If you're feeling stronger tonight, I'll show you my slides of the trip and tell you all about it.

We are talking about mountains, Mama, real mountains. Standing at base camp we were about eighteen thousand feet, and the mountain went on up to twenty-nine thousand feet. It is not to be imagined. I tried to capture just a little of the perspective in my slides. I can't wait to show you. And I have brought you a present!"

"A present, is it? No need, there is no need, Paulo. You are present enough." But she was pleased, nevertheless.

"This is a very special present. You will never guess. And it is not useful. You can't do anything at all with it except enjoy it."

"Ho, this is curious. When do you give me this strange present?"

"When you come downstairs. I don't think you would want it in your bedroom." Now he was deliberately teasing her.

"Oh, you naughty!" She mimicked him, "'I don't think you would want it in your bedroom.' This is to tease me. I know you, naughty boy. So, I must go downstairs! Let's go now!"

"No. Ruth gave me strict instructions. No excitement, and no moving until after your nap. Tonight, if you're a good girl, we'll bring you downstairs for dinner with Ruth and Roberto and the children and me."

A frown passed briefly over Carmella's face. "Is Roberto still here?"

"Of course he's still here. He was going back to New York today, but not until you're better."

"He should go back. I am fine. We just fight when he is here, anyway. Maybe I should just die and leave him alone." The old woman began to wipe at her eyes with the edge of the sheet.

Paulo's jaw hardened with anger, and the tenderness left his eyes. "Mama, you stop that. There is no reason to talk about death. And what are you two fighting about this time? The children? The business?"

She shook her head no. "What then?" Paulo demanded.

"He wanted me to sign some papers. I cannot understand these papers. Such writing is not English, is not Italian, is some foreign language I do nota understand. I don'ta sign papers if I don't understand them. Papa, he tell me this a long time ago. 'Do not sign your name,' he said. So, I tell Roberto we wait for you. You can read this lawyer English and explain it so I understand."

"Didn't he tell you what it said?"

She looked down at the bedspread and smoothed an imaginary wrinkle. After a moment she answered with a sigh. "Yes. He said I am to sell this house to him and he will rent it to me. My own house that Papa bought me! I ask him if he cannot wait till I am dead to take my house. Oh, Paulo, I am afraid I do not trust Roberto, my own son." And she began to cry.

Paulo put his arms around his mother and patted her back. "Shh, it's all right. It's all right. Really it is. Roberto loves you. He wouldn't hurt you. He has been so worried about you. Now, you dry your eyes and don't think bad thoughts. Come on now, be a good girl. I want to see a smile. Just a little one. Do you love me?"

That, he knew, would bring a smile, and it did. "See, silly, you were worried and sick over nothing. Roberto is just following our lawyer's advice. But Mama, if you are concerned, we won't do it. It's as simple as that. I know this house represents security to you. And if you don't want to sell it to the corporation, we won't. We'll do what you want to, and that's final." He smiled reassuringly at her and patted her hands.

"Now, do you feel better? Good. That's good. Just a misunderstanding, Mama, that's all. You take a nap, now. Later we'll have dinner, and I'll show you that present."

Paulo was relieved. With what he now knew about his brother's drug-ring involvement, he knew his discomfort with Roberto was well-founded. Still, he didn't believe Roberto would do anything to hurt Mama. He was, in most ways, a faithful son. He and Carmella had occasionally fought over the business. She owned the controlling stock in the company and had, in the past, prevented him from issuing more stock and selling it to his friends. She had also insisted on retaining her voting privilege on the board of directors in absentia. Even though Roberto ran D'Agosta Furs, Inc., it was still the business that Enrico and Carmella D'Agosta had started in the 1930s. Carmella held on to ultimate control long past the time she actually contributed to running the business. It was not her son she distrusted so much as his friends. Why this was so she couldn't say. Certainly they were kind to her, even jovial and very friendly, but it was in the eyes. Papa used to say that — it was all in the eyes. Their eyes were not honest.

Omar was waiting downstairs. He and Ruth and Roberto were relaxing in the den.

Roberto asked as Paulo came in, "How is she?"

"She's in her best silk dress. Does that tell you something? Ruth, did you help her?"

"No. I told her to stay in bed."

"Well, you know Mama. She is in bed, all right, but she has on that navy-blue dress you gave her last year. And she wants to come down to see slides. I told her if she would take a nap and felt strong enough for dinner with us, I'd show her the slides of my trip. We'll see."

Omar spoke regretfully, "I have come at a bad time for you. I am sorry."

"No," Paulo answered quickly. "Not at all. I also promised Mama a present. You're it. She'll be delighted to meet you. She'll talk about it for years. I also threatened to have Mark come over and give her the medicine every day if she doesn't follow the doctor's orders."

Ruth laughed. "I'll bet she liked that. She will hardly let me give it to her. She'll be independent to the end."

"I'm sure. Roberto, I explained to her again about the house. But I don't think you should push it if she doesn't feel comfortable with it. This house represents security to her."

"Yes, but the family will lose it through probate when she dies if we don't do something now. "Roberto frowned. He was taller than Paulo. His once slim frame had gone to paunch, and his face was too full. His eyes constantly calculated odds.

"That's probably true," Paulo nodded. "But our wants are not as important as hers. I'd love to keep the old place too. It has years of good memories. But Mama is worth more than the loss."

"She's as stubborn as a mule," Roberto said morosely, twisting his vodka glass in his hand.

"Why don't you give me the papers? If she gets stronger while I'm here, I'll go over them with her again and maybe we'll put her fears to rest."

Roberto was hesitant. "I don't know. I'm afraid it'll set her off again."

"I'll be careful."

Still cautious, Roberto said, "I'll dig them up. They are somewhere in the stack of my other papers to work on." It would be a long time before Paulo saw the papers.

That evening, Carmella descended the stairs slowly, with Paulo on one arm and Roberto on the other. Her dress was scarcely wrinkled. She had slept without even turning over. The nap had been peaceful for the first time in two days, and her eyes were bright again. Paulo noted how much thinner his mother had become. The years had taken their toll since her invalid daughter, Maria, had died of leukemia.

Omar was waiting in the dining room, dressed in full regalia. He was backed by two royal cousins, also in white robes. When she entered the room, Omar bowed deeply from the waist and said in a resonant, deep voice. "My dear Mrs. D'Agosta, the king of Saudi Arabia sends you greetings. The queen of Saudi Arabia sends her very best wishes for your recovery. And the prince of Saudi Arabia gives you this small token of esteem." The prince moved forward and knelt on one knee before Carmella, holding out his small token — a velvet box containing an ornate necklace of Saudi diamonds and one deep red ruby. The other two cousins remained bowing until Omar arose.

Paulo was all smiles. Ruth stood with her hands clasped at her breast, delight written on her face. Roberto watched it all curiously, and the D'Agosta children, Mark, Elise, and Ricky could scarcely refrain from rushing in and interrupting the scene. Carmella stared at Omar, then his cousins, and then back to the splendor of the prince's costume. The box was opened, the necklace held out for her approval. Then her stupefaction changed into sweet, gracious acceptance. Her eyes twinkled, and she accepted his offering.

"Your Highness, I accept the greetings from the king and queen of Saudi Arabia, and I accept your beautiful gift with one condition, that you should put it around my neck and seal it with a kiss on both cheeks, like we do in my country." Then she turned to Paulo and giggled. "I have not been kissed by such a handsome man since Papa died."

Omar stood, clasped the necklace, and bent ceremoniously to kiss Mama on the cheek. She whispered in his ear, "Are you the present my Paulo tolda me about?"

He smiled and kissed her other cheek. "Yes. He bought me with his life, and now he has given me to you."

"This I must hear." said Carmella.

The evening was spent with Omar and Paulo alternately narrating the trip to Nepal, the incident of the glacier, and the harrowing take-off from Lukla. But Carmella's strength was waning by the end of dinner. So the slides and the account of New York City were saved for the following day. It was a mild, calm evening in late May. The rolling Catskill mountains were green from the spring rains. Paulo suggested a walk outside to Omar and Roberto. The D'Agosta home was set on the gently sloping side of the hill. From the patio and sprawling lawn one could see into three different states, and the gentle Appalachian mountains rose, mound after mound, in the distance. So unlike the rugged Himalayas, Paulo thought, as he stood in the moonlight studying the shadows.

He spoke rather absently to Roberto. "We met an interesting man this week, didn't we Omar? Have you ever heard of David Cohen?"

"No." Roberto shook his head. "Should I have? Who is he?"

"A member of the Israeli cabinet. He's quite young to be in such a position. Zimmerman says his uncle was David Ben-Gurion. Anyway, he's Schleger's pet. I can understand why. Seems very sharp, very bright." He turned to Omar, teasing him a little. "Even my Arab friend here liked him."

"Why shouldn't I? He saved me from even more broken ribs. He is a Jew I could like. Most Zionist Jews are very militaristic. They are determined to take over all the land that was theirs before the Dispersion. It is impossible. This land has belonged to others for more than two hundred centuries. This Cohen seems different. Him I can talk to. He is not pushy. He is reasonable."   "What do you want to talk to him about?" Roberto probed.

"Border clashes, permanent peace, Israel's space program. Their advances in space brings many sleepless nights to my father and the other Arab leaders. Russia constantly courts us, pointing to Israel's advances, persuading us to buy Soviet missiles, to build silos, to test satellites. It is never ending, and it is cowardly. If we fight, we should fight like men, face to face. If he kills me fairly,

63

he is the better man. If I kill him fairly, I am. This kind of war is honorable. Missiles, bombs — hah! They are the coward's way."

Roberto spoke decisively. "They are the winner's way. In all respect, your Highness, face-to-face war is over. To win or not to win is the question, and space is the winning edge."

Omar sighed. "Ah yes, this is what the Russian envoy tells my father. But the world already has two superpowers shaking their bombs at each other. Why should we get into that as well. If Israel will recall her satellites, stop building the space station - which some say will carry nuclear bombs - we will negotiate a permanent peace. A permanent peace! Yes, even to sacrifice the lands they have taken away from us. We do not want this nuclear escalation."

"Do you speak for all Arabs or only yourself?" Roberto asked.

"For all the leaders."

"But there are many renegades amongst you. Maybe, it's these the Israelis fear."

"The terrorists can do some things, but they cannot carry on a nuclear program."

"I wonder," said Roberto.

Paulo asked softly, "What do you mean?"

"Oh, you hear things. Some say the terrorists have nuclear secrets. After all, they are easily obtainable by almost anyone."   "From whom?" Paulo pressed. "The arms runners?"

"They're published in this country. Very easy to get. The terrorists seem to have their own ideas. I don't think they would fall into line even if the Arab leaders commanded."

"I didn't know you were so knowledgeable on the subject," Paulo said.

Roberto shrugged. "I listen. Sometimes I get information from friends in Europe." His vanity began to take over. "In fact, I have access to information that even you do not, your Highness. I know, for instance, that there are some who would like to see your father dead."

Omar was nonchalant. "This information is old. This is well-known for years. There are also those who would like to see me dead. That is why my friends are always with me."

"And did you also know that an attempt will be made on King Sudani this week?"

Roberto's face was in the shadows when they both turned to him in surprise. He stood quite still, focusing on something far away, not looking at either Paulo or Omar.

"How do you know this?" Paulo asked sharply.

"I told you, I have friends in Europe. They have friends."

"When?" Omar asked. "How?"

Now Roberto smiled. He had their attention. "I don't know everything. I just know it will be sometime this week. Shiite terrorists, and it will be made to look like an Israeli attack."

Omar stared at him for one moment more, then turned and strode off. Roberto called "Shalom to you" as the Arab hurried off. Paulo heard the patio door open and close quickly.

"Why do you think the Shiites will attack one of their own Arab leaders?"

Roberto laughed. "Very simple. They hate the Jews more than they love the king of Jordan. If they are successful, the rest of the Moslem world will declare jihad and wipe the Jews from the earth."

"What makes you think they can do it? They haven't been able to in the past."

"They never had the backing or the support they have now, and the whole Arab world has not been mobilized before."

"What backing? What support? Whose?"

Now Roberto began to pull back. He started across the lawn. "There are many. I know of only a few, and I can't jeopardize my sources by blabbing. Let's just say I know."

"I'm sure you do," Paulo answered, stopping his brother with a hand on the shoulder. "I have a few sources also, and my sources say the D'Agosta name is well-entrenched in passing secrets to the terrorists."

Roberto's hooded eyes didn't waver under the angry gaze of his brother. "I mind my own business. Sometimes I deliver a letter from one friend to another. What they write is their business."

"You're a liar," Paulo attacked. "You know damned well

what you're doing, and what information is in those letters. You and Maretti and Ciardi and probably all the other big-time hoods in New York are hauling in big bucks from drugs traded for military secrets. What in hell do you think you're doing, Roberto? This is not neighborhood shakedowns anymore. You jerks are jeopardizing the peace of the whole world. Don't be crazy, for heaven's sake."

Roberto smiled and shook his head. "You're out of your league, brother. Go on taking your pictures. Leave the business to me. You never wanted to be bothered with the business. That camera is your only love. So don't start lecturing me now."

"Stop patronizing me! I'm too old to be your little brother. I don't fit those shoes anymore. Your name is my name, and it came down clean from our father. He deserves better than this. Mama deserves better than this. When are you going to grow up and stop playing bully? It's gone too far. I want the D'Agosta name taken out of the chain."

"Why? What do you care?"

"What do I care? I care that my name is respected, that I don't get a suspicious look or a sneaky wink when I'm introduced. I care that my family runs a clean business, an honest one."

Roberto was derisive. "Come on, Paulo. Where have you been? The mob runs New York. It runs the garment industry. Every piece of clothing from your shorts to your wool sweater has had duty paid on it to the mob. I wouldn't stay in a business a week if I tried to pull out. If you don't know that by now, you're blind on purpose. I have bought your right to your pastime with my commitments. D'Agosta money has been tied into the mob for years. This house has been paid for with that money. You think it's tainted? Well, hear this: you couldn't afford this house or your lifestyle without our subsidy. Besides, you don't simply pull out of the brotherhood. It's not that easy." He rubbed his forehead, weary now.

"I have spent years carving out my place in the Mob, keeping our business prosperous because of them, keeping it from Mama. She's as idealistic as you. After thirty years, they are my brothers now." He looked at Paulo. "Not you. You never have been. You should have been a priest. I'd have liked you better. But you couldn't commit even to that. You haven't ever committed to anything. That's your problem. It's not the D'Agosta name. You still don't know what you are or who you are."

Paulo was silent, stunned by the cavalier confession. Roberto softened. "It isn't too late. Go be a priest. That's the best place for you."

Like a shot in the dark, Paulo's fist connected with Roberto's cheekbone. The older brother was taken by surprise, knocked off balance. Before he could recover, Paulo connected again, in the midriff, and a knee came up, clipping Roberto's chin. Roberto was broader and heavier than Paulo, but he was out of shape. He swung wildly, a token attempt to defend himself. Paulo was not put off. In the dark, he swore at his brother, and when Roberto was down, kneeling on the grass in agony, Paulo jerked him up and hit him again. "Now, you tell me, damn it, what is your source? How do you know about King Sudani?" Roberto groaned and shook his head. Paulo backhanded him. Roberto's head jerked, and he held up a hand in weak protest.

"Who is it?" Paulo demanded again.

"Mario Villarini in Naples." Roberto gasped out. "He is my connection to Abdul Yassad in Lebanon. Yassad is a Shiite, but he hates Sudani. Thinks he has given Palestine to Schleger. Yassad wants to take over Jordan as well as Lebanon, and Israel most of all."

"This is the man you supply with our nuclear secrets." Paulo stared into his brother's face appalled.

Roberto's eye had already begun to swell. A thin trickle of blood ran from a torn, puffy lip. Still, he had a look of cunning and defiance.

"He gives me what I want. I give him what he wants. He is my brother like you never were. All your talk of God and nature makes me sick!" Roberto spit blood on Paulo's neck. He grunted, "There is no God, you fool," and Paulo's fist caught his ribs again. Finally, when his anger ebbed, he threw Roberto down on the lawn. The older man rolled up into an agonized ball. Paulo stood above him, shoving him with the toe of his shoe.

"You stink! You know that? You'd sell anything, anything, you rotten . . . You'd sell Ruth to a whore house. You'd sell the kids for porno. You're in it right up to your stinking eyebrows. I didn't believe it. I didn't want to believe it. I turned my head. And that makes me almost as bad as you. I never will again, damn you. You get out of that devil's chain and do it now. No more! I say, no more! My family is not a Mafia family! I won't have it. I'll kill you myself first."

"What's the code?" Paulo swore at him. "Tell me or I'll kill you here, tonight. What's the code for the attack?"

Roberto whimpered and whispered, "Shalom to Jordan," and fell unconscious.

Paulo's chest was heaving with the violence of his emotion. His fists stayed clenched as though he would fight the world. He shoved Roberto's moaning body down the hill to the edge of the lawn. Finally, with one last, explosive shove he kicked him into the rose bushes. Then he turned back to the house. Omar had to have the code if he was to convince the Arab world to believe what they had just heard. Breathing heavily, he strode across the lawn and jerked open the door to the den. Omar was holding the receiver.

Paulo's face was a dark storm. "The code is 'Shalom to Jordan,'" he said.

"Thank you, my friend. I am still waiting for the call to go through. If the situation is as bad as I fear, I must leave very soon."

"I'll be back," Paulo said, then left abruptly, pushed through Carmella's rose bushes and emerged on the narrow road. The old mountain road wound across the rounded cheek of the hill, back into the uncleared forest, and three miles later emerged on the other side of the mountain. Paulo's anger had not diminished. He felt as though he would explode. Walking was his release. Besides, he could not go back home. He could not sleep in the same house with his brother. He could not sleep at all. Anger consumed him for several hours.

Combined with his wrath over Roberto was his anger over his own blindness. His brother was right. He had never committed to anything. Why hadn't he given himself to God and become a priest? Perhaps he might have done someone some good. But he had wasted his life, and he was forty-nine years old. What mark had he made? What difference did his life make to anyone, anyone? Life held no purpose for him. God had no plan for him. Even his family was a sham. He belonged nowhere. Carmella was

68

his only family. Except for her, he was adrift with no moorings. All his life, he had fought off the sense of being totally alone in the world. After losing Shielah, he had searched for her replacement. Girls with long wavy blonde hair, girls with deep blue eyes or a certain tilt of the head. Stupid! He knew it was stupid. No one fit. No one belonged to him. And he belonged to no one. At last he began to question his ability to love. Over the years, the pain of rejection and the longing for Shielah had dissipated. His love for her had faded like a delicate rose pressed between the pages of a book to touch softly and remember fondly.

Oh, but the loneliness remained. Tonight he walked mechanically, climbing over debris, pushing his way through the spring undergrowth, afraid to stop, afraid of being engulfed by his feelings of helplessness. He reached the other side of the mountain just before daylight. Exhausted and seated on a large rock, he studied the rising sun without even a wish for his camera. Pictures were far from his mind now. He prayed for a way out. There must be a way out, for us, for me, for the world. This craziness must stop. It'll plunge us all into war. Heaven help us.

Omar met Paulo on the road back home. "King Sudani is dead. I must leave immediately."

"Let us therefore follow after the things which make for peace, and things wherewith one may edify another." (Romans 14:19.)

Chapter Four

Flying into Riyadh, Saudi Arabia, Paulo and Omar flew through Turkish and Iranian airspace. Constant radio communications were kept with those countries over which the aircraft passed. Tensions were higher than usual now. Private planes were at great risk, and even the commercial ones were challenged constantly from the ground. Protection around other Arab leaders was tripled overnight. The Moslem nations were rioting over the shooting of King Sudani, thundering threats against Israel, and gearing up for all-out war. Israel was denying responsibility, and, at the same time, hardening her defenses. That she had superior nuclear advantage over the Arabs did not deter in the least the Moslem zeal for war.

Omar had been successful in reaching his father, King Abdul Sayd, after six hours of transatlantic connections, just before the news broke worldwide of the assassination. It was his warning that kept the Arab leaders from declaring immediate war. Still, his report was sketchy and incomplete. They awaited his arrival to get a full account.

Roberto had not shown himself the next morning. He made no response to Omar's note, sent through Ruth, asking if there was any other information he could supply. Omar's plans had been laid, airline reservations made by the time he met Paulo on the mountain road.

71

"Will you come, Paulo?"

"What possible good can I do? I'm sure your word is sufficient."

"That's true, but we need an emissary to Israel. You are the perfect liaison. I trust you."

"I think I'd be a sore thumb. Our government will be sending negotiators. Let them handle it."

"I'm sure they will come. But, you must know, we do not always trust your negotiators. The wealthy Jews in your government are in sympathy with Israel. They are no friends of ours. I want someone I can trust. And since we know David Cohen, he is the one we will be deal with in Israel. He is close to the prime minister, yet I feel he, also, is trustworthy. Will you come?"

Paulo was still doubtful. "I will if you want me to. I'll do whatever I can. Official negotiations, however, will go through government officials."

Omar smiled wryly. "Yes, that is the way governments work, through official channels. But we are still warriors of the desert. We listen to all the official double talk and we say, 'Bah! Give me a man I can trust.'"

Now Paulo sat beside his friend on the Italian airliner and watched the terrain change thousands of feet below. Omar was unusually silent and wearing his royal robes. He was leaning back in his seat, his eyes closed. Below them Paulo could see the Persian Gulf, and, beyond that, the central plateau of Saudi Arabia, where it's capital, Riyadh, awaited them.

June was not the best time for visitors to Saudi Arabia. When the plane taxied to a stop and the door was thrown open, a blast of dry, hot air shot into the aircraft. Paulo stretched and looked around the plane. Among the passengers were a dozen women. Although most of the trip they had dressed in the Western manner, now, upon landing, they covered their faces with the traditional "shadrah," or black veil. Paulo was to find that he would not see the faces of the upper-class women of Saudi Arabia, even though middle-class women who worked in the factories and went to college did not always abide the custom.

Before Omar disembarked, his bodyguards preceded him, guns drawn, pausing on the first step and scouring the area for danger. Finally, Omar was taken down the stairs quickly, bent and heavily guarded. Paulo followed, also surrounded by guards. All he saw from the time he stepped into the doorway was the flutter of white robes and the ground rushing past his feet. Then the limousine. He was almost shoved inside. The bullet-proof windows were already in place. They rode in silence. Omar's face, always rugged, now had taken on a haggard, set look. Brown circles shadowed his eyes.

The airport was only fifteen miles from the city. Paulo got a cursory view of Saudi Arabia's capital city from the front windshield. The city he glimpsed was filled with high-rise, Western-type buildings, automobiles of all varieties whizzing by, and street after street of light-colored clay homes. The city seemed to shimmer in the heat waves of the Arabian summer.

All too quickly, the limousine paused before the gates of the royal palace. Armed guards unlocked the gates, and they slowly rolled forward, down the bricked driveway bordered by tiled curbs and rich, green shrubbery to the outer courtyard of the palace. The door was opened by a guard who was apparently a good friend of the prince. For the first time in days, Paulo saw Omar smile as he stepped out of the car and clasp his friend in an embrace. Paulo got out and paused a moment to look around before they climbed the steps.

The palace was a gleaming, white jewel, nestled into a verdant, green setting. Grass was not natural to Saudi Arabia; neither was water. Anything green and growing had to be faithfully irrigated. Vast amounts of precious water had been spent here to produce a luscious garden of tropical red and yellow flowers, interspersed with thick-leaved flowering bushes. A mosaic footpath wound through the garden and led to a deep blue pool, overshadowed with a white, arched pavilion. Paulo turned from the peaceful oasis before him and joined Omar on the tiled steps of the palace.

They walked past the official reception room where the king held press conferences and greeted foreign visitors. From a large room connected to his private chambers, they heard voices, agitated, each one striving to rise above the other. They stood in the doorway for two minutes before anyone saw them. The king was in the far left corner of the room, wiping his face and hands with a cool cloth. As the arguing ceased, he turned around and saw his son. Pleasure lit his face, and in a moment he had crossed the room and pressed his favorite son to his breast. Paulo stood aside, respectful of the love that was so evident between them. Now the prince was smiling, his arm around his father. King Sayd was not as tall as his son, but authority was a natural part of him. He was dressed in black robes. Only his headgear was white. He was polite though guarded, and his black eyes seemed to carry their own message — do not be too comfortable and do not cross me. He spoke in English for Paulo's sake.

"You are welcome. My son speaks well of you. This is brave that you should come with him. War may be soon, very soon."

"Let me speak, father. I want them all to hear this the way I heard it."

They stepped down into a large, square room tiled with a green mosaic border. The floor was covered by the largest, thickest Persian rug Paulo had ever seen. It was richly embroidered with reds, purples, golds, and royal blues with birds of paradise everywhere. Cushions of red and purple bedecked the floor inviting repose, but the king was in no mood for resting.

Omar was greeted by each of the thirteen men there. Several of them were relatives; eleven were heads of state of Moslem countries. Emotion was high. Plans for war were being drawn. Only King Sayd had held back.

Paulo sat in one of the few Western chairs in the room while Omar relaxed into his own language, explaining the information they had obtained from Roberto the night of the assassination. Evidently, he didn't convince them. King Sayd had already repeated much of what his son had to say before they arrived. The Arab leaders were bitter. Their minds were already made up. Israel was the ancient enemy. One man's word to the contrary didn't persuade them to the contrary. After much heated discussion, Omar turned in exasperation to Paulo.

"They don't believe what I tell them."

"Will they let me speak?" Paulo asked.

"Certainly. This I didn't expect, that they wouldn't believe me!"

"They don't want to believe you," Paulo assessed. "It is more satisfying to think that they have an excuse for war with Israel. Let me tell them what I know."

Omar interrupted the arguing voices. He introduced Paulo as his friend, one who had risked his own life to save Omar's. He stressed the confidence he had in the truthfulness of his friend, then he gave the floor to Paulo.

The supercharged atmosphere of the room was apparent, even though Paulo didn't speak their language. He looked into their faces. Some were haughty and proud, lean and strong; others were puffy with opulent living. They all watched him suspiciously. He began quietly, deliberately softening the electricity of the debate.

"Omar tells the truth. I am sure you all know him much better than I. He is one of you and has no love for the Jews, as I found out. On the glacier in Nepal he was sure it was a Jew who had cut the trail so close to the edge." He smiled to coax their reluctant smiles. "But Omar is wise in his youth, just as his father is. The night of the assassination, he was with me at my home in New York. We took a walk with my brother. My name is D'Agosta, a name well known in certain Moslem circles. The terrorists among your people know that name because my brother is a member of the American Mafia. He trades military and nuclear secrets for drugs. That night he said his sources had told him of the attempt on King Sudani's life. Shiite terrorists were planning to make it look like an Israeli raid. He also told me that Abdul Yassad hates Sudani for appeasing the Jews and wants to be the leader, perhaps even the king, himself."

Now the room was buzzing. Omar whispered, "You didn't tell me all of that. When did you learn this?"

"After you left and before I beat him unconscious."

King Aradat from Yemen spoke, "How do you know it was true? Such men who sell themselves for profit cannot be trusted."

"He gave me the passcode, 'Shalom to Jordan.' We had a fight, and he was barely conscious. I don't think he could have lied. Perhaps you have your own sources that can be checked. If the password is correct, then the rest of the information will be also."

"Perhaps." Omar's father nodded. "Perhaps. We do have informants, as your brother has. Let us not make more plans for war until we talk to Lebanon."

Suddenly, all the men fell silent. Far away a bell

sounded, followed by a crier, calling "Salat, Salat." It was six o'clock, time for evening prayers. All fifteen men, kings over their own people, stopped their discussion, turned toward the western wall, in the direction of Mecca, and bowed themselves upon the ground. Paulo sat quietly in his chair, watching Omar and his father, King Sayd. The Arab's harsh features had utterly changed. Deep lines relaxed into a devoted expression of exquisite joy. He seemed almost transported, away from a world of trouble into a place of peaceful dreams. Paulo looked around. One or two other men seemed similarly lost in their meditation of Allah. Others merely did their duty, hurrying through the traditional prayers. Paulo smiled. It is always so. There are those who serve with the heart and others with the lips only. King Sayd was still on his knees, lost in fervent prayer, black robes like a dark stain on the opulent Persian rug. A small drop of water slipped from his lashes and trickled down his face. He didn't brush it away. He merely went on praying. The others stayed also on their knees in respect for the man whose palace they occupied. After a few more minutes, the king straightened, opened his eyes, and smiled. His eyes rested first on Paulo. A quizzical look flickered across them, then an expression of empathy. He rose and the others followed. Walking to Paulo, he linked his arm through the American's.

"Come, friend. We will eat now."

They walked the long corridor in twos and threes. Debate had resumed about the information Paulo and Omar had given them. Only the king, Omar, and Paulo didn't talk about the incident.

"You are a Christian?" the King asked.

"Yes, I am. But I respect your devotion."

The king nodded. "Are you also devoted to Jesus Christ?"

Paulo answered honestly. "No. Not as I should be. Not as you are to Allah. It is the religion of my fathers. I search for my own religion, the religion of my heart."

King Sayd looked at him curiously. "And you have not found it yet? I am sorry for you. Religion is a very comforting thing."

"That is true, sometimes. Religion is also a dangerous thing. It kills. Moslems and Jews, Protestants and Catholics, Hindus and Moslems — they all kill each other

76

for religion."

The king shook his head. "No, not for religion. They kill for greed. All men kill for greed. They simply give it the name of religion."

"I think that is true. And it is ironic. I agree that there is one God, Allah, as you call him. And His son Jesus Christ tried to teach all people to love one another, irrespective of race or religion. And yet people hate each other in the name of Allah. It doesn't make sense. If they are merely using religion and the name of God to kill each other, it seems to me that he must be very displeased. How will they live together in paradise if they hate each other here?"

"Ah, my friend, you ask hard questions. This I do not know. This I let Allah worry about."

They turned into another smaller room with cushions on the floor beside low tables. After washing their hands in the bowls of warm water provided by servants, dinner began. King Sayd was a devoted Moslem, so no alcohol was served, although he had become quite fond of non-alcoholic wine. Delicious fruit and cheese, lamb and potatoes, fresh vegetables, and a sweet condiment Paulo had never tasted before was served to him by a boy no more than thirteen years old.

Omar lay nearest to Paulo. "How do you like this method of eating? I think it is more comfortable than sitting upright at a table."

"I think you're right. My only concern is falling asleep and insulting everyone. Jet lag is beginning to get me. What will they do now?"

"Ali Jabri, of Syria, has already started questions down the chain. He has more informants than even the Mafia. They will soon get to the truth of the matter."

"But can he be trusted to report it accurately? Syrians have no great love for the Jews. He might also want to see another war with Israel."

Omar looked across the room to Jabri, prime minister of Syria. He was a chubby man, used to good food and luxurious living. Now with the grease from succulent lamb shining on his chin, he looked much like an overfed jackal.

"We'll see. I do not think he will lie. But he is hungry for Jewish land, that is true. The problem is that all of them think it is time for us to stop Israel's military and space advances. If we wait much longer, they will hold such supreme power over us that we will not be able to defeat them, and they will gobble up more and more Arab land."

"I don't think they will break treaties. If you make a hard and fast, verifiable treaty with them, they will honor it. War at this point could mean the destruction of the globe." Paulo's voice was adamant now.

"I realize that. Why do you think I am talking so hard against it. For myself, I would like to see the Jews pushed back into the sea. They have no more right to that land than my people do, than the Indians do your country. They are the aggressors, but they have America on their side. That forces us into dealing with the Soviets, whom we hate — godless infidels!" He spoke vehemently to Paulo. "The Soviets send delegate after delegate to try to get us to unite with a space program of our own, administered by their technicians. That is what they want — more nuclear sites, located on Arab soil, manned by communists. They are very persistent and very persuasive too. In this room I count six that would agree to the plan. My family, my father, my uncles, we hold out, and the others will not sign such an agreement without us. Bah! The Jews are fools. They think they are only facing us, Arab cousins with a few rifles. They cannot see they are looking the Russian bear in the mouth. His jaws could crush them. And would America risk global war for the Jew? I don't think so. America is too fat and lazy."

The king's hand shot out and grasped his wrist. In his eyes was the warning, do not say too much. No one is to be trusted with everything. Omar calmed as he met his father's gaze.

"Perhaps in the morning we should take a small expedition out onto the desert of diamonds." The king spoke to Paulo. "If all things were normal, we would take you to the racetrack. This is great fun. We race horses, our beautiful horses. And we race camels." He laughed and slapped his knee. "Hah! Such a beast! A camel race is best. But . . . I regret, we must be very careful now. I cannot go to the desert with you. But my sons can, with the greatest of care. Visitors deserve more than the walls of the palace."

Paulo managed to keep his eyes open until an appropriate time after dinner. Then Omar took pity on his friend and excused them from the lengthy discussion that followed. A servant led them through the corridors, up a curving staircase, and to the bedroom wing of the palace. None too soon, Paulo thought. He was utterly exhausted, and his eyes seemed to be playing tricks on him. He seemed to see small flutters behind the columns and wisps of dark hair disappearing at each turn.

He dropped gratefully onto the bed. With great, groaning effort, he forced himself to remove his shirt and trousers. Then he sank into the cool softness of the bed. After a few minutes, when the American was deeply asleep, the door opened, and two pairs of dark eyes peered in at him. After a moment, there was a giggle, a fluttering of eyelashes, muffled whispering, and then Omar's sisters closed the door and hurried down the hallway.

The night did not hold much sleep for Omar. He had come home to the joy of two wives. Both must be visited, petted, admired, and loved. With a small sigh of guilt, Omar thought of Paulo asleep and alone, as he passed his guest's door. He should marry the Jewish secretary. Marriage solves many problems for a man. Then Omar forgot his friend as he opened the door to his second wife's suite. She was barely eighteen years old, betrothed to him since a child and married to him two years ago in vivid splendor and opulence. Omar spent the remainder of the night with her until his watch showed 4:00 a.m. and the desert sky showed faint morning light.

The plateau of Riyadh was long and hard, but not too hard for reddish sand to blow from the tires of the jeep procession. Five jeeps wound through the outskirts of the capital at four-thirty in the morning. The sky was still dimly asleep, and so was Paulo. Omar had awakened him at four o'clock. The Arab was already dressed and promised his friend a unique adventure if he could pull his body out of bed. He had not exaggerated. The world around them was silent and still. Headlights gleamed in the darkness as they jounced along, the paved road giving way to hard clay just outside the city. After a half-hour drive, the jeeps turned off the road and onto a forsaken plain, broken slightly by small dunes.

The Arabs jumped from the jeeps and, waving flashlights, clustered around Omar and Paulo. "Now we shall make you a rich man, in a matter of minutes." Omar grinned broadly. "Remember the beautiful necklace I gave your mother, which you didn't want me to give because it was too expensive? Remember that? Well, this is my secret! Hundreds of beautiful women all over the world wear the prince of Saudi's jewels and think they are rich. And this is where the diamonds come from. We have a desert full of diamonds." He flashed a light round about. "At least, they look like diamonds. Many of your Western jewelers cannot tell the difference. Tourists who come here must always go home with a pocket full of Saudi diamonds to set into jewelry and fool their friends. Shall we go diamond hunting?"

The night air was pleasant. They all fanned out, flashing lights along the ground, exclaiming over sudden gleams and glints that betrayed the desert diamonds. Slowly, the men combed the sandy plain. Paulo and Omar separated around a sand dune. Suddenly his flashlight picked up the telltale glint from the ground, and Paulo heard a swiftly drawn breath and a short laugh. He turned to see where the laughter had come from. A young Arab boy stood two feet behind him. The boy covered his mouth with his hand. His eyes were laughing and his long tunic moved gently with the morning breeze. Paulo almost turned back to pick up the diamond when he caught a glimpse of long black hair escaping from the white headgear the Arabs typically wore. Both hands went quickly to the headgear, pushing and tucking the hair back inside. The boyish face, so smooth and young, was now filled with exasperation. Dark, fringed eyes turned slowly back to Paulo and pleaded silently, don't give me away. Plainly, the boy bodyguard was a girl. Her finger went to her lips in the universal plea for silence. His flashlight beam went to her face, then dropped back to the ground.

"Who are you? What are you doing here?" he asked, wondering if the girl could understand him.

She turned quickly in all directions, then squatted down, her hand in the sand as though searching for stones. "I am Satari, the prince's sister."

Paulo drew a sharp breath. "You are not supposed to be here, and especially not without your veil."

She grinned impishly. She could not have been more than sixteen. "I am bored. The palace is so boring, I do nothing exciting. But men! They do everything! I wish to be born a prince not a princess. Then I travel. I go to exciting places. You are American, yes? In the palace is talk about the American who comes with Omar. I want to go to America. Will you take me?"

Her words had come all in a rush, heavily accented, but understandable. Paulo knelt also, studying the ground and sneaking looks at the fair young face of the princess. He would have laughed but for the seriousness of the situation. The princess had placed herself in danger as well as him. The royal daughters of King Sayd were not to be seen by mere men, much less foreigners. If discovered, she would be severely punished and his credibility greatly reduced.

"You must go back to the jeep. Do not let yourself be seen. Your father would be very angry. I can't take you to America. That is foolish. You are a child. Go now; go back before you are found out."

One full, red lip protruded and dark eyes pleaded with him. "Please."

Sternly, he whispered, "No! Go back!"

She lowered her lashes and rose reluctantly until she was almost standing. Paulo glanced around to see if Omar was nearby and suddenly found the girl kneeling beside him, soft lips pressed against his own. One delicate, petal-like hand touched his face, and she whispered, "An American. I have kissed an American." Then she turned and scampered off around the dune.

Paulo knelt there another moment to regain his inner balance. He chuckled, remembering her impetuous kiss, and breathed a sigh of relief.

Omar called out ahead of him, "Paulo, are you having good luck? I have several stones in my hand for you. Where are you?"

Paulo called out, "Here. I'm over here."

The two men walked up to the top of one of the dunes and watched the spectacle now taking place in the eastern sky. Time had not altered the ancient love-dance of the

81

desert sun with the horizon. At precisely a quarter to six, the sun burst from below the plain and was immediately caught in shimmering air currents. It seemed to undulate a slow, hypnotizing dance as it struggled to be free of the clasp of the desert floor.

Omar smiled as he observed his friend's appreciation. "Do you wish for your camera?" he asked.

"So, you already know me too well. Yes, I wish for my camera. I rarely go anywhere without it."

They sat, lost in thought for several more minutes. Then Paulo asked, "Does your father have daughters as well as sons? You never speak of sisters."

"Yes, naturally there are royal princesses as well as sons. I visited my mother and my sisters last night after you went to bed. My mother is making ready to go to cooler country. The mountains to the west of us are where the more wealthy of my people go in the summer. We have five summer homes there."

"Why five?"

Omar laughed as though at a wonderful joke. "For my father's three wives, of course, and two of my own. And of course there are my sisters and all the servants. If Riyadh is attacked in war, the women will at least be safe."

"It can't come to that, Omar. You must make them listen to reason."

"Last night our story was confirmed. 'Shalom to Jordan' was the password returned. Jabri knows now that we were telling the truth. He has calmed somewhat, but the debate goes on. Now would be the best time to strike. The world still thinks Israel killed Sudani. If we strike now, we can hope to win. Their missiles will only last so long. We have men who will never stop coming. All Islam is aroused. This is the perfect time to rid ourselves of the canker in our gut." Omar stared out across the horizon, oblivious now to the beauty of the pink and gold luminescent sky.

"That is crazy, Omar! Millions of your men would die. Millions of women and children would weep, millions more would starve. War is the last resort — the last unthinkable resort."

Omar sighed. "I know. If it were only us against the Jews, I would not think more than twice. After the heat of insult and indignation, battle would be a welcome relief.

And," he shrugged, "death holds no fear. Allah awaits the brave warrior in paradise. But to blow up the entire world — this is the danger." He shook his head. "We must convince my people, and you must convince these jackals, the Jews, not to press us."

He jumped to his feet and pulled Paulo up. The sun had fully awakened the sluggish sky by now. "Time is racing. Let us go back."

The knowledge that King Sudani of Jordan had been shot by one of their own traitorous renegades calmed the fires of hatred. After a light breakfast of fruit and juices served in his room, Paulo was summoned by a tall Saudi soldier to join the conference in the king's anteroom. Paulo was relieved to see the Moslem leaders seated on the cushions and discussing matters quietly.

King Sayd greeted Paulo as he entered through the archway. "Are you rested? Good. Today you go for us to Israel, yes?"

Paulo was reluctant. "I will if you want me to. I promised Omar to do all I could to help. My family's part in this is shameful to me. But I would much prefer that you deal through my government. There are others much more capable than I at negotiations. I am not political. I am only a photographer, a businessman. Have you spoken with our ambassador?"

The king nodded gravely. "He belches. And he smells of wine. He is useless. My son trusts you and I trust you. He says there is one Jew that we also might trust. This man is a favorite son of Schleger but still a man of honor. We will send Abdul, Omar's cousin, and a royal prince as well. He will have authority to act for us, and you will go to this ben Cohen and tell all that you tell us. Also say for King Sayd, there will be no war if they stop testing their missiles. We want a nuclear ban treaty between us. And we want his name on it besides the prime minister's name. On this condition we will deliver Abdul Yassad and embarrass ourselves. This is a very great compromise to us. Make him understand that. Make him understand what my son says about the Soviets and their missile bases in Saudi. A very great danger. They do not know how great."

83

Paulo and Abdul were to leave at three o'clock for Ankara, Turkey. From there he would fly to Israel on a Greek airplane. No Arab craft was venturing near Israeli airspace. Paulo paced the room, wishing for the first time that he smoked. Or prayed. It was all crazy, and he was a lunatic to get himself into this position. He was no diplomat. His own country wouldn't appreciate his interference. He laid down on the bed trying to catnap, but his mind was a riot.

At noon, the door opened, and a servant advanced, carrying a tray with his lunch on it. Paulo took the tray and looked into laughing eyes. A cloth fell away to reveal the warm olive complexion of the royal princess. A giggle burst from behind a curtain at the window. He turned in amazement to see a smaller version of the princess rush out and over to Satari. The little girl tugged on her sister's dress. She said something in Arabic and handed the older girl Paulo's watch.

The princess giggled, stifling it with her hands. Her little shadow did the same. The princess took Paulo's hand in hers and made as if to clasp the watch about his wrist.

"Your hands very beautiful. Long fingers. Strong hands. My brother says you never marry. You have no woman to dance for you, to make you happy at night." She shook her head, her long hair falling out from under her headgear. "I dance very good." She said something to little Kaleni, and they laughed again. Satari looked sideways at Paulo and lifted one eyebrow. "You like to see me dance?"

"Good heavens, no! I can see you are too experienced for an old man like me."

Her laughter pealed out, and she instantly clasped her hands to her mouth and fled to the corner of the room, kneeling behind a large tapestry hung for display. When no one came to the room, after several minutes, Paulo reached behind the tapestry and drew the princess out and turned her toward the door.

"Go! You will get us all in trouble. I know this is just play for you, but it is not funny. Go on, now."

But she was stubborn. "Please take me to America. The American women do not wear this terrible veil. They walk and do not fear a man to see the face of them. My brother goes to America often, and he tells me of the cities. I wish to go also. I have money of my own. I can take my own care for myself. Please take me," she pleaded. "My mother and sisters and servants, they all go to Dhariya. No one to look for me many days from now. Kaleni will lie for me. Please, Mr. Paulo, take me with you."

She was so earnest and so lovely. She wouldn't last two days in New York, Paulo thought. A pimp would find her, and she'd go to the highest bidder. He shook his head and inched her closer to the door. When she could see he was intractable, she threw herself on him, her eyes overflowing with petulant tears.

"I must go. I die to be free. Free as Omar is free. I will dress like a servant. If a person asks about me, I will say Omar gives me to you." Her cheeks were wet with tears now, and her lips were trembling. She was singularly beautiful. But she was a royal princess.

She sensed him weakening, and threw herself into his arms, kissing him passionately. He responded like any man, his arms encircling her tentatively, then securely, as her softness and fullness entranced him for a few moments. His pulse was beating wildly throughout his body when he finally pulled away.

"You . . . must . . . go! Your Highness, you are beautiful — too beautiful to give yourself away so cheaply. And I am not a fool. I would not live beyond a day if I took you away from here. Besides, I do not travel alone. Your cousin Abdul will go with me." He unwound her arms from his neck and pressed them to her sides. Then he smiled, "You are just a child, a baby, really. A woman would not beg a man. You are too fine to beg. When you learn that, you will not longer be a baby. You go now."

Satari's face was unutterably sad. As she covered her face and started out of the room, the little sister touched Paulo's elbow. He glanced down into eyes as black as night. She smiled shyly as if to say thank you, then waved and ran after the older girl.

85

*"There shall no evil befall thee, neither shall
any plague come nigh thy dwelling. For he shall
give his angels charge over thee, to keep thee in
all thy ways."* (Psalm 91:9-11.)

Chapter Five

Paulo leaned back against the airplane seat, trying in
vain to clear his mind and decide on a speech to give
David ben Cohen. He hoped fervently that Cohen would
receive him alone. He wanted to discuss the
communication from the Arabs with David before facing
questions from other Jewish leaders who might not be so
approachable.

Beside him sat Abdul Jubayl Mohammed ibn Saud
Khali, Omar's first cousin. He was the oldest son of the
king's sister and only six months younger than Omar. The
two cousins were best of friends though opposite in
nature. Omar's quick smile and sublime good humor were
not present in Abdul. He sat with his eyes closed, a deep
furrowed line between his brows. Paulo had asked Omar
what to expect from Abdul, but his friend had only said,
"If Abdul follows you, you need never look behind."

A Greek stewardess spoke in French over the
loudspeaker. Paulo put on a set of headphones for the
interpretation. "Ladies and gentlemen, if you look out the
windows on the left of the aircraft, you will see that we are
directly over the Sea of Galilee. Slightly to the southwest
is the city of Nazareth. If you look closely, you can see
that it is directly west of the mouth of the River Jordan
that flows from Galilee to the Dead Sea. We will be flying

within Israel's borders westward over the plains of Sharon."

At her words, Paulo's stomach seemed to turn over. He looked out his window and saw below him a drop of blue surrounded by a green fringe of farmlands, then rocky, brown desert on the eastern side. He was unprepared for the sensations that hit him. Forgotten feelings welled up, and his heart seemed full, while in his head he heard, "The land where Jesus walked." Not since his youth had he been so overpowered by the old familiar sense of reverence. The surge of emotion was powerful. He was an altar boy again, with the smell of candle wax and the sound of the Catholic mass in his ears. Brilliant pictures of the boy child he had been flashed like bulbs before his eyes. The wafer lovingly placed by Father Rodano on his tongue, the choking tears that testified of God's acceptance — all returned with the one thought, Nazareth, Galilee, Jerusalem ahead.

The mouth of the river Jordan! Could he see it? Yes, he could see the thin, wobbly stream of blue. He searched the terrain, looking for Nazareth. Nazareth, where Mary received the annunciation! Nazareth, where Jesus ate and slept and walked the same hills that still existed today.

There rose in Paulo a hunger, a hunger to put his feet on the same ground where Christ had walked, a thirst to touch the same walls, a tremendous need to kneel and worship and be comforted, to be filled where he had been so empty. This need he had largely buried as he had grown older. He envied Omar the ease with which he fulfilled his religious duties. Paulo had been too often mocked for his priestly devotions and had grown accustomed to suppressing them.

At the same time, another part of him was amazed at the passion of his emotions. After all, he was not a Jew. He wasn't even a very good Christian. This wasn't his homeland. Why should he respond so violently? Swiftly then, he realized for the first time the intense need of the Jews to come back to this land. Their love was not, perhaps, centered on Jesus of Nazareth, but it was the same passion for the hills and valleys of their fathers, Abraham, Elijah, Jeremiah. Their very identity was sifted into the sand and mortared into the walls. The richness of their history was like a magic web that caught at the heart and bound it forever to this dusty soil.

They landed in Tel Aviv. It was the Middle East Miami, built on the sand dunes of the Mediterranean shore. Paulo and Abdul were quickly off the airplane. In the Tel Aviv airport, David ben Cohen stood waiting and hailed him as Paulo exited the door.

The two men shook hands, then impulsively embraced, in the ancient custom of greeting. David glanced over Paulo's shoulder to the inscrutable Abdul behind. "Shalom, welcome," David greeted Paulo.

"I hope so. I hope I'll leave that way, too. David, King Sayd sent his most trusted nephew to represent the Arab position. This is Abdul Jubayl Mohammed ibn Saud Khali."

The two men bowed politely. Paulo continued, "Omar sends his greetings. He says his ribs are better, and he wants you to know that if Abdul had been there, his ribs would not have needed healing."

"So," David said, smiling at Abdul, "he is wishing he had you at his side in New York. He seemed to have an excellent time giving as well as getting broken ribs." He turned to Paulo. "How was your flight? You seem tired."

"I guess I am. At least, I was until I looked out the window and realized that I was directly over the Sea of Galilee and Nazareth, all the places that have been just names until now. I think I am beginning to understand the Jewish passion for their homeland."

David smiled in satisfaction. "Many do not ever understand it. The need to live where our ancestors did is so overwhelming, so undeniable, that we will sacrifice anything to be here. No price is too great."

Paulo nodded, "I understand."

Abdul spoke at last, "We also feel that same passion. This is holy ground to many people."

David accepted his comment and nodded. "Yes, that is so."

"Tell me, my friend," David said as he guided Paulo through customs, "how did you get this job of averting war between two hot-headed cousins?"

"I didn't want it, you may be sure."

David laughed, "No doubt. Meddling in family feuds is dangerous business."

"Omar is responsible, both for getting me into the middle of this and for holding off a war for five days." He stopped walking and looked into the younger man's cheerful countenance. "You know I am here because he trust me. And he trusts you. You are the one Abdul is instructed to deal with."

"That will be difficult. I am not in charge. Schleger is in charge. The Knesset is in charge. I am merely a cabinet member."

"But they will listen to you," Abdul interjected. "And you will know what is true and what is not. That is most important to us — trust and truth."

David nodded his understanding. They walked on through the terminal and into a waiting black sedan. "How is it that the Arab leaders are willing to negotiate? We were astounded. We have expected certain war."

Abdul watched Paulo to see how he would answer. "There is confidential information that has made a difference. I'll tell you all about it on the way to Jerusalem."

David found his way expertly from the airport to the highway that led through the hills to Jerusalem. In Israel, all roads lead to the holy city, and it is always an uphill climb. Anciently, the Jews built their homes and cities on the hills, leaving their valleys free for farming and ensuring a measure of safety against attacking enemies. The bright, modern buildings clustered on the tops of the mountains were evidence that the old custom was still followed. Jerusalem was built on one of the highest mountains; thus the ancient prophets spoke truly in saying, "Let us go up to Jerusalem."

"The prime minister is anxious to meet with both of you. The Knesset is waiting to hear your proposal."

Paulo shook his head. "Before we talk with them, we want your advice on how your government will respond. There is something the rest of the world does not know. King Sudani was not shot by an Israeli. The Shiites assassinated him, hoping to start the war that would eliminate Israel."

Paulo proceeded to tell Cohen all that he had told King Sayd. He tried to represent the Arab feelings as accurately as possible. Cohen was not surprised by any of it. He was aware of the terrorist's plots to foment war. They had already ascertained that the raid had not been by Israeli soldiers. He nodded his understanding as Paulo revealed his brother's part in the affair.

"I, too, have a brother. He is older than I, just as yours is. My brother is a colonel in our army and is well respected by all except me. I know him too well. I know that he kills not out of necessity but because he enjoys it. To me that is evil, the greatest evil, to take the life Jehovah has given. This is pretending to equal power. But the power to take life is only destructive power, and even a child can be destructive. To give life! This is the greatest power, and it takes a higher, creative force to do this."

Abdul spoke from the back seat. "Then why do you agree to the space program of Israel? Do you not understand that you are forcing us to deal with the Soviets? They are pressing us to put nuclear bases on Arab land. Against them you could not hope to win."

"I know this. But Americans and Arabs have never known the history of conquest and enslavement that the Jews have. We can only face the world with strength. Soviets, terrorists — they understand nothing else."

"There is Jerusalem!" Paulo exclaimed.

They rounded a bend and saw the gleaming golden Dome of the Rock proclaiming the Holy City. Paulo put his hand on David's arm. "Stop, please. Can you pull over? I want to just look."

David pulled over onto the narrow shoulder of the road, and the three men sat looking at the city. A kind of magic about the city seemed to change the passing automobiles to Roman centurions on horseback. White limestone buildings gleaming against the spring green hills made it look like an heirloom jewel. Paulo saw the ancient city; David saw the future city. He thought he saw the bright buildings and homes bombed into rubble. He envisioned the destruction of attacking armies with tanks and airplanes. He heard the cries of hunger and pain. He saw an occupying army marching through his beloved streets, murdering as they marched. The vision was too real. It left him heartsick and silent.

David Cohen looked at the American. Paulo D'Agosta was a unique man. He claimed to have no religion, but at this moment he was completely caught up in a devotion that was deep and real. David looked again at his city. The same sense of devotion swept him, and the bonding between the two men was sealed. He wished Paulo had

91

come alone, or with Omar. Abdul was an unknown entity.

"You have much to see, my friends. Jerusalem will not let you go easily. She has as many wiles as a woman, and she is just as complex. Let us take your message to the prime minister and give this heavy burden to him. Then it shall be my great pleasure to walk through Jerusalem with you."

Ralph Schleger was a shrewd man. A politician more than a statesman, he was always careful to see that his own interests did not suffer. In his six years of office, he had become a wealthy man. His power came from his decisive and persuasive nature. He was not a soldier. He hated the business of violence and carefully refused to acknowledge the atrocities that often went on under his very nose. But he was adroit at getting his own way. He was not an impressive figure. He was as tall as Paulo, but his legs were short. Consequently, he seemed always to be in a hurry. Dark, heavy glasses emphasized the roundness of his face, and he frequently looked over them in making a point. A mass of dark, curly hair along with a broad smile made him seem disarmingly innocent.

While Abdul took lunch in his hotel room, David took Paulo directly to Schleger. The prime minister wanted to see him alone.

"Isaac Zimmerman never ceases to tell me about his vice-president. He says you could run the company better than he could. To tell you the truth, I am hoping you will do just that someday. We could use a man of Zimmerman's influence and contacts here in Jerusalem. And your reputation as a photographer is well known. I see you have learned the business of negotiation from your inside contacts in government circles."

Paulo demurred. "Not really. I am apolitical. And I am certainly not a skilled negotiator. I tried to get King Sayd to go through proper channels. To tell you the truth, I'm quite anxious over all this."

"No doubt, no doubt. But we take it all in stride. I'm sure Sayd is sleeping better than you are. Now, tell me, what is it we are negotiating? War? Peace? What price? We look the tiger in the mouth every day. Is the foolish tiger set on war again?"

"It depends."

"Hah! Just as I thought." Schleger was triumphant. "If they had been intending to strike, they would have done so by now. The last twenty-four hours have been the most tense. I knew the possibility was strong that they would strike while you were in the very act of coming to present their demands. They would think us unprepared, and thus they would have the advantage. But we have been on constant alert! What do they want?"

Paulo glanced at David. Cohen was leaning back against a table, his arms folded across his chest, his white shirt open at the neck and accentuating the golden tan of his face. His handsome features were impassive, but Paulo saw a certain expression in his eyes. Was it distaste?"

"Sayd of Saudi, Ali Jabri, and Arikifal all expressed the concern of the Arabs that Israel is throwing them into the arms of the Soviets."

"Nonsense, nonsense."

"Your space program is a great threat to them. Your nuclear missiles are also a constant threat. And the Soviets are on their doorstep volunteering help. They want to put nuclear bases on Arab soil, manned by Russian personnel. That means, of course, that you would not be facing off against merely the Moslem population but against the Soviets as well. I know the Saudi's don't want Soviet help, but you are giving them no alternative."

Schleger was not slow. "So, they want us to get rid of the missiles and the satellites. Hah! I guessed that." Looking over his glasses, he jabbed a finger in the air. "Did they also tell you of their own stockpile of nuclear weapons and aircraft bought from France and Italy, as well as Russia? This whole incident was manufactured to force us to stop our nuclear progress. They are shrewd, all right. But it won't work. We did not kill Sudani. Of course, the world believes we did, despite our statement. Who did?"

Paulo didn't like the quick, peremptory conclusions of the prime minister. "It was a terrorist strike. Apparently, Abdul Yassad engineered it."

"I'm not surprised. He's a butcher. But the Arabs know this. Why then are they demanding anything from us? It is one of their own. Let them punish him and apologize for accusing us."

93

"I'm afraid it's not that easy."

"It never is."

"The Arabs see this as the chance to negotiate for a treaty on nuclear arms. The entire Moslem world is ready to go to war. In fact, their leaders are having a hard time holding back the tide. They feel they could win a war right now."

Schleger was adamant. "They could not win! Our satellites feed us information that makes their every move transparent. Our missiles would knock them out on the first assault. If they attack, we will simply take over and control the entire Middle East. We could, you know."

Paulo was cold now. "Possibly. You know your military capability better than I."

"It's not just military. We have been promised this land by Jehovah! It has been prophesied. The Jews were to be gathered after many years of being scattered among the nations. Well, we are gathered. We are here. The promised land is ours again. The Arabs controlled this land for centuries and did absolutely nothing with it. When the first Jewish settlers came to Palestine, it was a forsaken land." He tapped the windowpane. "Now look at it. We have made it strong and productive. If it weren't for us, it would still be sand, tilled by ragged, uneducated Arab peasants, oppressed by their own wealthy class. We have changed that. We have educated their peasants and given them equal place beside us. We did it all with our own sweat. It has been waiting for us for many centuries, and we will not give it up! No, nor one missile, either!" Schleger's face was flushed.

Paulo spoke carefully now. Fanaticism has many faces. "Possibly you could win the war. But it would not be an easy victory. The Arabs would come at you from every corner of the earth. And, after the missiles were spent, it would come down to guns, knives, and, finally, hand-to-hand combat. They will not give up this time. They see it as their last chance."

Schleger's ebullient mood vanished. To think of missiles exploding and killing the enemy far away was one thing. To consider a personal war of hand-to-hand bloodletting was quite another.

"They want a treaty, is it? What would be the substance, and what would we get from it?" he asked, standing with his feet apart, arms folded.

"No more satellites, no further production of missiles on your part, and no space station. On their part, they will publicly acknowledge that the assassination was done by one of them. They will limit terrorist attacks on Israel; they will turn down the Soviet proposal of a nuclear plant on Saudi soil, and they will not declare war."

"Ridiculous!" Schleger jumped on it. "They give up nothing. We give —"

"Sir! King Sayd said to tell you this acceptance of embarrassment in the eyes of the world is a very great compromise to the Arab leaders. An Arab does not take such embarrassment lightly. And, you must realize, the alternative is certain and immediate war."

Schleger pursed his lips. He turned away and stared out the window. "I will present this to my advisors tomorrow morning. Their terms are not acceptable. Let us see what can be done."

"One more thing. Sayd wants both your name and David's name on the treaty."

"Why? My signature is sufficient."

"I know. It is sufficient for your government. But the Arabs trust David."

An eyebrow shot up, and Schleger cocked his head as he considered Paulo and then his young protégé, ben Cohen. "Oh really? And what power do they think he has? He is not a king."

"He is an honest man," Paulo answered, his gaze never wavering as Schleger frowned.

When the evening bells rang out at twilight, Paulo and David sat on a rock on the Mount of Olives. Abdul elected to stay in the hotel. All Arabs were secluded now. The tension was so high in Jerusalem that a single incident could catapult the nation into war. From the minarets of the Arab mosques, criers called the Moslems to evening prayer. Commerce stopped; horns stopped honking; haggling ceased in the markets. Jackhammers stopped their staccato. Jews, Arabs, and Christians alike turned to evening prayer on the street corners and in their own homes. The sky changed from deep blue, to pink and salmon, to gray, and, finally, to the deepest indigo.

Shadows crept along the Kidron Valley and clung to the ancient walls of Jerusalem. The old city seemed to curl up into the oncoming shadows. Everywhere could be heard voices calling upon God in their various ways. Down the Mount a few blocks, a group of young Christians held a worship service.

David and Paulo sat silently. The city emitted a distinctive odor, the smell of spices and oil and lamb cooking. Sweet, bakery smells wafted about. But mostly it was a pungent, spicy, old-world smell that Paulo would never forget. Lights began to flicker. Modern high-rise apartment and office buildings thrust their heads above the old part of the city. But they had their place too. That was a part of the magnetism of Jerusalem — the old preserved and the new soaring. The Holy City was for everyone, the orthodox Jew with his side ringlets and ancient costume, the bedouin still in his flowing robes, and the young Israeli of today walking the University hallways or carrying a briefcase into tall buildings.

This is the point of it all, Paulo thought. Surely, if there is a God, he welcomes all who come to worship him. The great tragedy would be if the city were in the hands of someone who refused to allow access to all religions. This land must remain free.

At length, he turned to David. "How lucky you are!"

David had leaned back and folded his arms behind his head in a cradle. He smiled up at the twinkling sky. "I know. I don't know why I should be the one chosen to be here at this particular time. I have a sense that there is important work for me to do here. But, even if I should get a job as a construction laborer tomorrow, I would still know how lucky I am to be a part of this."

Paulo gave voice to his thoughts. "If there is a war and the Arabs retake this city, it will be closed to the rest of the world."

"Probably. At least for a time."

"That can't happen. It would be so wrong. So many people love it. There is such a craving of the soul to be here, it is almost like walking through history. Christ sat at evening meal, just as these people are doing tonight. King David hid from Saul on Mount Moriah. Abraham held Isaac by the hand and climbed that hill to obey God's command. David, this city must remain free. I hope I can

96

do something to help."

David was glad to hear Paulo's conviction. "If you believe at all in destiny, or in God's hand in things, I think that is precisely why we hold the city. We will keep it free. No one else is so committed to that. And I will do my small part."

"Schleger didn't like that," Paulo observed.

"No, he didn't. He is the star. And, you must realize that his signature as prime minister should be enough."

"I realize that. I'm sure Sayd does too. I've wondered why he insists on your signature at the risk of insulting Schleger."

David laughed. "I think it doesn't have much to do with my honesty. It has everything to do with power politics, the upper hand. If Schleger accepts that condition, the Arabs will have succeeded in diminishing his power."

"It may jeopardize the whole treaty."

"How firm are they on it?"

"Very firm. They don't trust Schleger. The space station has them convinced they will soon be vulnerable to a first strike from him. They want someone they can trust at bat for them here."

David shook his head. "I never thought of myself as the Arab voice in our government. We have Arabs in the Knesset. Why aren't they sufficient influence?"

"They're not close to Schleger, and Sayd knows he's hard to influence. It will have to be someone he likes and trusts."

David stared off into the darkness, pondering the strange workings of destiny. "Tomorrow morning you must bring your camera," the Jew said, changing the subject. "And come back to this spot. It is the most beautiful picture in the whole world — the sun rising over Jerusalem."

At 4:15 a.m., Paulo walked up the Mount of Olives, carrying his camera case. He sat down again on the same rock where he had rested the evening before. The sky began to take on a faint, golden glow. Paulo worked fast, getting his lenses out, dusting them and fitting them onto his camera. The light was still too dim for good focusing. He played with the telephoto lens for a minute and fished around in the case for special-effects filters. Then he looked up.

97

The Dome of the Rock, with its rounded, golden dome, had caught the first rays of the sun. It fractured them into thousands of radiant beams, illuminating a dim, reluctant sky. The splendor of reflected sunlight made Mount Moriah the focal point of the whole city, and a few meters farther up the hill, Golgotha, the place of the skulls, lay quietly in the morning light. Shadows still clung to the small alleys and rooftops of the city. The deep, sonorous bells of the mosque tolled across the hills their invocation of a bright new day.

The spiritual filling that Paulo experienced then brought him to his knees. His camera lay beside him on the ground. Pictures would have to wait for another day. This was his moment with Deity. Bells were ringing in his ears — not the bells of the city, but an inward, high ringing, so powerful he felt that his head would burst. There was no mistaking the powerful communication of God, as his heart raced and seemed to swell, choking his breath. A burning from inside consumed all other thoughts and perceptions. The brilliance of the Dome became the brilliance of heaven. Paulo could not move. It was this he had desired on his trip to Everest, this communion he had sought as he lay beneath the majesty of the mountain. But God had chosen the place where His son had suffered to speak to Paulo's soul.

Much later, Paulo walked back down the hill, shaken, moved in a way he had never been moved before. He felt blessed, as though a powerful hand had reached from heaven and rested on his head, filling his body with radiance. No longer did he question why he was there. He knew he was destined to come.

At 9:00 a.m., Paulo and Abdul, flanked by David and six crack shots from the Israeli army, were rushed into an armored car and escorted through town to the Knesset. Schleger had carefully set the scene in his office. His two guests sat facing his cabinet and top parliament officers. Schleger gave his own account of Paulo's communication from the Moslem leaders. Paulo gave Schleger his due. He was a good actor. It was little wonder he usually got what he wanted. What was it this time? War? Muscle flexing? He had to know that this was too dangerous a time for posturing.

When Schleger was finished, Paulo stood to speak. He took a moment to look at his audience, then fixing his dark eyes on David, he began his own account of the international event.

"There is a tide in the affairs of men, which, if taken at its flood, leads on to success. I take liberties with Shakespeare's famous words because he could not have known that he spoke to us in our time. We are at the apex of a great flood. The tide is running, and if we ride it properly, it can lead to success of the most extraordinary kind. How many years have you been in conflict with your Semite cousins? How many years have you prayed for peace? This is your chance to realize that dream.

"Prime Minister Schleger has told you of the terrorist strike against King Sudani. That Arabs would strike another Arab makes sense only when one considers their motive. It is not religion. It is not nationalism. King Sayd of Saudi Arabia rightly assessed it — it was done for greed. War is not an expression of religion — not yours, not theirs. Peace is the expression of religion, every religion. War is always the vehicle of greed, and those who foment it are the enemies of every decent person. The Shiite terrorists do not act for the fine Arab leaders I met with earlier this week, nor for the excellent armies of the Arab nations. These terrorists are independent and nonreligious, acting out of their own greed and passion for blood. You can deny them their reward.

"With all respect to Prime Minister Schleger, this treaty as proposed by the Arab leaders is great evidence of their real desire to live in peace with you. In it, they acknowledge to the world the shameful deed of one of their own. They plead with you to reduce your nuclear arsenal and thereby remove the temptation for them to be wooed by Communist powers. The Communists seek a foothold here in the Middle East, one which King Sayd is not eager to give them. This treaty would allay the fears of the Arabs and, seizing on this great tide, lead on to an unprecedented flood of goodwill."

"Prime Minister Schleger is correct. The assassination was not done by one of yours. You have nothing to apologize for, in that respect. But, you have a chance to

99

turn an enemy into a friend. You have a chance to put peace above greed. Now is the time you can save millions of lives with the stroke of a pen. Nuclear warheads and satellites can do that. The moment is yours, the tide belongs to you. Seize this moment with all the goodwill in your hearts, and the world will be blessed because of you. Throw it away, and you may well destroy the precarious balance of peace for the entire world."

The room was silent when he finished, except for determined clapping from David. Slowly, one by one, the others joined him. Abdul stood, turned to Paulo and bowed in respect. Then began the dreaded part — the questions. How did he become the spokesman for the Arabs? Where did he obtain his information on the strike? Why weren't government officials handling the negotiations?

Paulo was careful in his answers. He well knew the international publicity this event had aroused. Roberto was not worth protecting, but Ruth and the children, Mama — they must be shielded not only from the media, but from the retaliation of the terrorists. He explained his friendship with Omar which had led to his nomination as their spokesman; also, he was a solidly neutral party. Information on the terrorist strike came from private sources who had a link to the Shiite leader, Yassad. Would he name his sources? No, he would not. Were the Arab leaders satisfied with the accuracy of his information? Yes, they were. It had been independently confirmed.

"You should have been a diplomat," David said admiringly as they made their way back to the hotel. "You have a way with words."

"I would never have the patience to be a diplomat. I care too much. How will they decide? Do you have a feel for that?"   .

"Not yet. Schleger was correct in pointing out that since we have done nothing wrong, it is unfair that we should be the ones to make the concessions. Our space program is dear to us and, we believe, vital to our security."

Abdul's voice was quiet but pointed. "You may never get a chance to complete it, if war breaks out."

"True, but the plot is revealed now. Surely your people will see that there is no need for war."

"My people see the Jews following in the footsteps of

100

the world powers and threatening nuclear war. That is what your missiles and nuclear plants mean to us. That is what the space station means to us. The race for space is not motivated by peace. If our leaders say it is time to eliminate that threat, the people will follow. Fear stalks them like a panther. D'Agosta is right — only your sign of goodwill can reduce that fear.'

Paulo stayed with Abdul in the hotel until the restlessness became unbearable. Then he donned a baseball hat and sunglasses, slung his camera over his shoulder, and slipped from the King David hotel to explore Jerusalem. In the old city, the streets were merely alleys filled with every variety of people and goods imaginable. Tourists meandered. Small children, shrieking and giggling, streaked by on skates and skateboards. Baskets of fruit and vegetables were stacked along the way. Chickens and butchered sheep hung in clusters in the meat market. Paulo watched a pilgrimage of devout Christians haul a huge cross along the street, stopping ritually at fourteen stations to rehearse the folklore and the scriptures that belonged to each point. It was a pathetic reenactment, yet Paulo was somehow touched. One tiny, scrawny man dragged the heavy beam. He was sweating and breathing in ragged breaths. At last, he could go no further and bowed beneath the thing. Almost uncontrollably, Paulo felt the impulse to help him up, to offer him a drink — something, anything. The he realized that others had taken the cross, and three women now pulled it along.

Between the thick, cream-colored walls that Saladin had built in 1100 A.D., all nationalities of people walked. Paulo passed a small doorway where a goat's head hung. A few steps later, a man leading a donkey came toward him. The donkey was laden with baskets in which he could hear a constant tinkling. Turning a corner, he happened on a small alcove where a gang of young boys clustered, playing video games. The smell of bagels and baklava cooking enticed him into a tiny room. He ordered a breakfast bagel, and the dark, curly-haired young man slapped the bagel dough onto a flat, smooth, metal spatula. This he inserted into a stone oven, blazing hot. In a few minutes, the bagel was cooked. Out it came, piping hot and smelling like heaven. The man split the bagel, cracked an egg onto each half, and slipped the oversized spatula back into the oven for just a minute. Instant breakfast! Paulo went his way eating freshly baked bagel and drinking 7-Up. Turning the bottle all around, he smiled to see an American 7-Up bottle with Hebrew writing.

That was a day Paulo would later remember with fondness. That evening over dinner, he confided to David his afternoon's adventure. Cohen frowned. It was not safe. Cars had been bombed. Tourists were being denied passports to Israel. Until the treaty was signed or rejected, the city was a powder-keg. But Paulo asked so many question about the city and country that David finally agreed to take both Abdul and Paulo for a tour himself.

David was apparently a well-known figure in the country. He was the golden boy of the press. Always courteous, he was a reporter's dream to interview, and he was, therefore, frequently sought out on questions Schleger would not address. He came from an inauspicious background. Born in Haifa, David had only one brother. His father had been killed in a terrorist raid that bombed a bus, killing thirty-five Israelis. His mother lived quietly in Haifa with her sister. Cohen had studied law and finance in the Hebrew University at Jerusalem. But his real love was the ancient scriptures. His grasp of the ancient principles was faultless. As devoted to the Torah as he was, he was nevertheless a practical man. Orthodox Judaism did not appeal to him. Israel today needed people who would wrestle with modern problems while holding on to their religious principles.

David had served in the Israeli army as did all the young people of the country. He was a tough fighter, but he was not ruthless. He had once been stoned by angry Arab youths. He had responded not with his rife but by stopping the hotheaded young boys and talking to them about their grievances.

David drove Paulo and Abdul through the countryside, venturing into Jericho even though the Arabs in that city were particularly hostile. They passed broken hulks of buses, now only bombed-out pieces of steel. Often, they observed Arab families living in the defunct buses. In Jericho, they climbed a mound where excavation was still going on and looked down upon the walls of Jericho that Joshua had rebuilt. Across the street, the clear, sweet spring of Elisha still flowed from the earth.

"What do you think of Jesus of Nazareth?" Paulo finally asked David as they drew near the town.

The young Jew considered the question, then replied, "I think it is too bad that so much wickedness had been done in his name. If his principles had been truly lived by his followers, there might be many Jews today who would accept him as the Christ. Years ago, the name of Jesus would never have been spoken in a Jewish school. Abuse was so awful that hatred was inevitable. But today, many of us consider him to be one of the greatest rabbis. Certainly, his teachings cannot be faulted. But there were many, very many, in his day who claimed also to be the Messiah. Whether he was the true Messiah, I cannot say. This I can say — I have studied his life and his words, and these I revere."

Paulo was subdued. "When I was in my late teens, I studied to be a Catholic priest. I could never equate the beautiful teachings of Jesus with the atrocities that my people committed against yours. I still can't reconcile the hatred of the Irish and the Protestants with the Christianity they both profess. And, like you, I revere him. But I go one step further — and I only just discovered it. I love him also. David, if he is not the Messiah, there is none. And the world has a great need to be delivered."

Late that afternoon, they drove up one mountain and down another from Nazareth to Bethlehem. The tiny village of Jesus' day had sprawled out across the hills and covered the whole brow of the mountain. Bethlehem — House of Bread — was flanked by wheat fields in the valleys 500 feet below.

"I have a special treat for you, my priest," David said to Paulo. "Not far from here is the Shepherd's Field. Since you are so nostalgic, I'm sure you would enjoy a short visit there."

Shepherd's Field was just a few miles to the northeast of Bethlehem. Situated on a small hillside, it was a favorite spot for young Christians to gather and sing Christmas carols, no matter what the season. Tonight there were about twenty young American college students sitting cross-legged on the ground, holding hands and singing "O Little Town of Bethlehem."

The sun had set and the sky was still blushing pink. Shadows were fingering their way across the little town of Bethlehem. As they sat watching the night come on, a bedouin shepherd came walking around the curve of their hill. He was dressed in a long skirt with a tunic over it. He walked with a limp and the help of a shepherd's staff. Behind him followed the sheep, baaing and bleating. He led the sheep along a faint trail a few yards beyond the group and stopped before an old stone well. Letting down the wooden bucket, he dipped water and filled the stone trough with cool liquid for his sheep to drink. Everyone was silent, watching the shepherd. Paulo looked up in the sky and drew a sharp breath. One star seemed brighter than all the rest, and it had risen over Bethlehem.

David smiled and whispered. "It is Venus. At this time of the year it does seem quite large, doesn't it?"

The shepherd's voice called out, and they turned back to watch him. All the sheep had followed after their master except one little lamb. The creature had decided to stay back and have a longer drink. Now, at the sound of his master's voice, he looked up and bleated, drawn by the voice of authority and yet tempted by the cool water. The shepherd called again, and finally the lamb turned from the tough and trotted after his flock.

All the parables of the shepherd and the flock came swiftly back to Paulo. He couldn't resist saying, "So the sheep still know the voice of their shepherd."

David chucked. "They certainly do. Many shepherds can camp together and bed their sheep together. When morning comes, those shepherds have only to call to their flock, and the animals respond to their own shepherd's voice. Jesus used a well-known metaphor when he called himself the Good Shepherd."

Perhaps it was the quiet lulling of the Shepherd's Field that distracted the attention of the three men. They reached David's sedan, still talking of sheep and shepherds, and before they could open their doors, four men sprang up from behind a nearby jeep. In the darkness and the frantic scuffle, nothing could be seen but long, white robes and the flash of knives. David was clubbed with the butt of a pistol, dropped to the ground, and left. Abdul was attacked by two men, pinned by one, and knocked unconscious by the other. Paulo backed up against the car, drew his knees to his chest, and planted a full-force kick in the chest of his assailant. The man staggered backward, cursing, but before Paulo could follow up with a decisive blow, David's attacker used his pistol butt on Paulo's head, and all went black.

. . . Swimming, laughing, in a swelling tide. No, it was a meadow stream. Water splashed and sang while it rolled through a green field strewn with wildflowers. And there was another singing. What was it? Searching, peering through tall grass, Paulo felt the singing grow louder. It was a high, sweet crooning, and it comforted his ferocious headache. Then he saw her. She was sitting in the midst of the flowers, her back to him, rocking back and forth under the golden sun. Light splintered from her hair in golden shafts and almost blinded him. He lifted his arm to shield his eyes from her, and then she turned to face him, and he could not look away.

A rush of happiness warmed him through. It was recognition of someone dearly loved and long lost. But who was she? Once before she had come to him in a dream. One lonely night long ago. When? Too long. He struggled to find a name for her. He remembered the woman and the sense of comfort she had brought him, and then, suddenly, he remembered seeing her as he had seen her thirty years before, standing under a golden light, wearing a long, blue gown and reaching out to him. Now she stood ankle deep in flowers and she again reached out as she began to walk toward him. The breeze was cool. Paulo was unbearably hot, almost on fire. Her hair blew about her, long and coppery, glinting golden red in the bright light. There was no sound except the singing of the stream, but her lips formed his name, and her eyes drew him closer. And in that last moment before waking, he knew her name. "Charlotte," he whispered, "stay with me."

Then he awakened to the harsh voice of the terrorist who knelt beside him to hear his whispered words. The American might reveal something important in his sleep.

105

With a vicious throb of the head, Paulo regained full consciousness, smelled the rank odor of the scarred man, and opened his eyes to find bloodshot, piercing black eyes only inches from his own. Instinctively, Paulo spat.

"Aagh!" Immediately, Paulo's head snapped to the right as the kidnapper backhanded him.

Abdul lay beside Paulo unmoving. Both men were bound hand and foot. On Abdul's left cheek, a bluish-black circle spread from his cheekbone to his chin. Dried blood was a brown mustache above the Arab's lip. Abdul didn't open his eyes, or groan. He didn't move. Except for the warmth of his body shoved up against Paulo, he might have been dead.

"Pig lover!" the terrorist grunted and kicked at Paulo with the toe of his filthy boot. "Now that you are awake, we will talk." He sat cross-legged on the floor, grabbed Paulo's shirt at the neck, and jerked him around until the two men faced each other. His other hand was raised, ready to strike again if Paulo protested.

Paulo tried desperately to hold onto consciousness. His head was splitting, and he kept drifting back toward the bright meadow.

"Answer me!" the scarred man threatened, shaking him to keep him awake.

Paulo vaguely remembered white robes of Arab attackers, but this man wore wrinkled trousers and a jacket. His nose had been broken and now had a hooked appearance. Two small scars disfigured his left eye and nostril. A third, more vivid scar, about three inches long, started below his ear and curved around toward his knotty adam's apple. Long, black ringlets adorned each side of his face.

"How did you know the password? Where are you in the ring? Who is your contact in the Middle East?"

Paulo shook his head minutely at each question. Even if he had wanted to tell, he could not concentrate on the answers for the excruciating pain in his head. His eye rolled back, he slumped, and the scarred man cursed and threw him back against Abdul.

Sometime, hours later, Paulo swam back into consciousness to the sound of boots tromping on a wooden floor and voices arguing loudly. He was careful not to betray himself with any stirring. He could feel

106

Abdul's shoulder still warm against his back. The Arab still had not moved. Paulo wondered how badly Omar's favorite cousin was hurt, and he realized immediately why they had both been taken. It had to be the treaty.

The arguing was in Hebrew and very hot. Three voices slashed at each other. He could understand only a few words, "Knesset," "Sayd," "Yassad," and, once, the name "Schleger." Paulo's eyelids were slitted. In the dim light of the dusty room he could see a tiny window across the room, about five feet from the floor. Three men in combat clothing wrestled over their problem in the corner. "Scarface", as Paulo named him, seemed most angry, and he paced to and fro, berating the two younger men. Once, the shabbiest of the group brandished his knife, shouting and pointing to the prisoners. "Muslim" and "Saudi" were easily distinguishable. Paulo felt Abdul stiffen minutely and understood, for the first time, that the Arab was not unconscious at all.

Scarface hovered over Abdul, shoved him with the toe of his boot, and then bent over, jerking the Arab up by his clothing and slapping him, shouting in Arabic. Abdul opened his eyes slowly and deliberately and stared into the face of his tormentor. Obviously, the kidnapper was questioning Abdul, but the Saudi never spoke a word in answer. Frustration came easily to the terrorist. His knife flashed and flicked the Arab's chin. Abdul did not recoil. It touched his forehead and drew blood. Still the Arab did not flinch. Now the other two men pulled Scarface back, apparently counseling patience. The three men disappeared through the tiny doorway. Paulo could make out a large warehouse cavity beyond the doorway.

"Abdul, are you all right?" Paulo whispered.

"Yes. Are you?"

"I'm okay. Can you understand them? Do you know who they are and why we are here?"

"Not Moslem terrorists this time, although they dressed as Arabs during the kidnapping. These are Jews, and they are against the treaty. Our only crime is to be the bearers of the treaty. He wants to know if I am Sayd's son. He says he will cut off my hand before I can sign the treaty."

"Who's behind this?"

"I believe this man to be Levi Frankel. He was trained by the Israeli army and often protected by them, though that is denied. He is a fanatic Jew who want to see our countries go to war just as much as Yassad's terrorists. Our informants call him the Serpent, for the scar on his neck and his slippery ways. I have been a fool. I knew I must not get caught. I watched carefully everywhere we went. But I was asleep under those Bethlehem stars. Now I pay."

"Can you understand their conversation?"

"Most of it. There is someone else involved, someone with much authority. I'm not sure who. It could be a Jew. It could be your American Mafia with large sums of money for the cause. The Serpent does not act alone. He is under orders. These orders are keeping us alive for now. Not for long, I am sorry to say."

Paulo thought that over. Roberto would not be above using any means to get back at him. Not only had his pride been hurt but his business as well. The mob was not kind to informers. It seemed unlikely to Paulo that a high-level Jew might want him dead. There was too much to be lost. After a few minutes, Paulo addressed the problem at hand. "Any bright ideas on how we can help ourselves?"

"Just one. In the lining of my robe, midway up my chest, there is a razor blade. I will fall against your back and be unconscious. Your hands can reach me if I am very close. Work the cloth until the razor cuts it. Then you can cut the ropes if you are careful. Above all, you must not be caught."

Abdul slumped against Paulo's back. The two men had five more minutes before the voices outside stopped and Frankel reappeared. The ropes binding Abdul's wrists were slashed almost through, but the prisoners lay silent, hoping for more time.

Time was all they had. It had been almost two day since they had eaten. Neither man was inclined to ask anything of their kidnapper. Paulo's mouth felt like cotton, and he knew they couldn't go much longer without water. "The Serpent" sat at the table stewing over his own hatred, his pistol by his hand.

Minutes turned into hours. Paulo didn't dare doze. If the man left even for a few moments, they must work on the ankle ropes and the ropes on Paulo's own wrists. Hours later, Frankel pulled a chunk of bread and two pieces of fruit and cheese from his pack. After eating silently, he tucked his pistol in to his trousers and left the room while he went to relieve himself in another part of the warehouse. Swiftly, Abdul and Paulo turned, and the razor began its work on the Arab's ankle ropes. The work was barely finished when footsteps approached.

Levi Frankel pushed through the door, his pistol drawn and determination etched on his face. He took a step toward his prisoners, but a voice called his name and he stopped. It was a woman's voice. He turned toward the open door and saw a woman in the dimness of the warehouse cavity. She was dressed in fatigues of the Israeli army. Her voice was soft but firm, and she called him by name. Levi was known to all his friends by his nickname, "the Serpent." Few knew his given name.

"Frankel! Levi Frankel, these men are to be delivered to army headquarters." She spoke in Hebrew, but she didn't seem like a sabra. Levi took a step toward her, peering through the shadows. Then quickly he dropped his eyes. Her face was too beautiful. He was ashamed, and he didn't know why. It wasn't only that he was ragged and dirty; he was embarrassed over what he was, who he was. He was gruff because of his shame.

"Who says this?"

"The commander."

"That's not good enough. I obey only one man."

"That is the commander I speak of."

"What is the password?" Frankel asked sullenly.

"'The Mosque.' He says you are not to endanger the greater mission. Return the prisoners tonight."

Levi stole another glace at her face. It was fair, glowing with health and an inner light. A fierce passion caught the terrorist. She should be worshipping in the synagogue, not interfering with his business.

"I will not return them! They will die, and the greater mission will start immediately!" Frankel was deliberately insolent and jerked his pistol from his belt.

At that moment, Abdul sprang. Frankel reacted swiftly, but the pistol was knocked from his hand. Frantically, Paulo worked the razor, cutting his fingers and cursing his impediment. Frankel shouted and dove for the pistol. Two shots rang out, and immediately Paulo heard the dull clang of the warehouse metal door. Heavy footsteps came running through storeroom. Paulo jerked himself to a kneeling position, then looked up straight into the sparkling, gray-green eyes of the woman. Strands of burnished copper escaped her military hat. Her lips formed his name, and familiar warmth flooded him.

"The ropes are loosed. Come quickly."

Paulo glanced down. The ropes were scorched and burned and lying beside him on the floor. But he had no time to wonder. He jumped up and reached for her hand, but she ran before him. He planted a foot in Frankel's midsection and pushed Abdul through the door, and they both dove as bullets splattered the wall. A sharp, tearing pain told Paulo he was hit in the arm.

Suddenly, a blinding light seared the musty old storehouse, stunning the kidnappers. Paulo and Abdul scrambled to their feet and dashed toward the boxes stacked on their right. They ran directly toward the light, or, rather, the light moved before them, and in the center of it, the woman in the army fatigues waved them on.

Still gunfire erupted. Guns were emptied into the blinding light, even as the two assailants held up their arms to protect their eyes. The woman's face was alive with excitement, and her eyes flashed fire. Now her hat was gone, and coppery golden hair fanned out around her shoulders.

"This way," Paulo heard her call. "Come this way, love."

He followed, heedless of the bullets zinging through the warehouse. Abdul was on his heels, low and dodging as he ran. Then the door. It was closed. Paulo reached for the lever, but the door was suddenly open. It seemed to move without moving. Barrier became freedom. Fresh air and sunlight welcomed them, and the door banged shut behind them. Still they ran, following the slight figure of the woman who was always ahead, looking for danger. As they tired, she paused and smiled and coaxed them on. Paulo was weak from two days of no food and from loss of blood. The wound was oozing blood with every step he took. Abdul called out to him. "We have to stop and bandage that."

"I know. I know. But where?"

Twilight obscured the alleys and row upon row of industrial warehouse. Paulo leaned against one building. Abdul tore a strip from the bottom of his robe to staunch

110

the flow. Paulo panted but kept his eyes only on the woman. She stood barely four feet away. He knew her now. She had haunted his life, starting with his vision of her when he was a youth. His life had been spent searching, loving, grieving for her, and now he did not count the cost. The vision, the dreams, the panic-stricken moment when he had seen her portrait in Shielah's room — none of those brief brushes had done justice to the woman herself. To say she was beautiful undershot the mark. To say she was glorious was a puny compliment. Abdul could scarcely bring himself to look at her. Paulo could see nothing else.

He didn't care about the wounds or Abdul's fussing over him. His hunger to touch her was so great, he knew only that one thing. "Charlotte," he called hoarsely, "stay with me."

Her smile was brilliant. Light flashed from her person and she called to him quietly, "Paulo, I'm here. I'm always here."

"Don't go," he pleaded.

"I have to. You will be all right now."

"Dear Lord, I can't lose you again."

"You won't. I'll see you again. It won't be long. Next time it will be in a holy place. Next time. Next time . . ." She seemed to grow very distant. Paulo felt as though he were fainting. He heard his own voice calling, "Charlotte, Charlotte," and her whispers echoed in his head, "I'm always here, Paulo. Always, always."

Then she was gone. Paulo looked at Abdul. The Arab was turned to the spot where Charlotte had vanished. His face was a picture of astonishment. He looked into Paulo's eyes with disbelief.

"What . . . ? Who . . . ? How did she . . . leave?"

Paulo choked. "She's still here. We just can't see her."

"What is that? What do you mean? How do you know she is here if we can't see her?"

Paulo pushed himself away from the building and began to trudge down the alley. "I just know. I . . . I can feel her. We go this way."

The Arab looked doubtful. "Are you certain?"

"I am certain. If we get lost, she will come again. But we will not get lost."

Paulo was right. They didn't get lost in the alleys.

111

Eventually a military jeep stopped and picked them up. Paulo lapsed into deep sleep while Abdul explained who they were and two Israeli soldiers took them to headquarters.

Paulo awoke in the hospital to the smiling blue eyes of David Cohen. For the first time, he was disappointed in seeing the young Jew. He wanted the green eyes of the red-haired Charlotte. But he managed a tiny smile.

"Welcome back. The whole city has been looking for you."

"Great. Thanks," Paulo replied with a grunt.

"In fact the whole world is asking the question, 'What happened to the American and Saudi negotiators?' Israel is publicly embarrassed."

"Good. Let her sign the treaty."

"The Knesset has voted to do so. Now it is no longer the Arabs who bear public shame. You have provided the Jews with a black eye and a need to negotiate the treaty."

"Is Schleger willing?"

"Reluctant but willing."

"And you? You must sign also."

"I will sign. I have spoken to Omar and pledged my personal friendship and help."

Paulo's face was ashen but calm. "How is Abdul?"

The deep voice of the Arab came from the corner of the room. "I am well. I will not be so well when I return to Saudi. Omar is already angry with me for letting you be taken."

"Tell Omar to come himself next time," Paulo replied.

"Abdul won't tell me how you got away from the terrorists. What happened?" David asked.

Paulo sighed. "She was beautiful, a real angel. Remind me to tell you about the woman of my dreams. But later. I'm going back to sleep now."

Abdul returned to Saudi Arabia after the signing of the treaty. Paulo stayed on for another week to recuperate from the flesh wound and to finish the photography he had promised himself. Everywhere he went he looked for Charlotte. He called himself a fool. He knew he would not see her, but he couldn't help it. She had said "in a holy place." This was a holy place. He visited every shrine, the Dome of the Rock and, finally, Mount Sinai. David warned him it was a hard climb, and Paulo was not yet fully recovered. He urged Paulo to come back another time and climb Sinai, but Paulo was immovable. He would go alone if necessary, but he must go.

One night, David drove him to Sinai. The mountain loomed dark and immense above them. It was 2:30 when the two friends started the climb. Paulo could scarcely see the path. The flicker of flashlights of other pilgrims was both ahead of him and behind him. The desert moon was bright, and they trudged along, climbing slowly. Sometimes, when the path doubled back on the north side of the hill, David had to use his flashlight for a short way. They passed others on the trail, moaning over their aching sides, but there was no complaint in Paulo's heart. This brought back memories of trekking with Omar in the Himalayas, and he looked upward at the top of the mountain, hoping against hope that Charlotte would meet him there.

How ironic, he thought, that I should go to Nepal just when I did. One week more or less and I would never have met Omar. I would certainly not be here, and the world might be plunged into war. David is right. Nothing happens accidentally.

The path stopped abruptly, and Paulo looked up. One thousand steps were carved into the mountainside. He looked straight down. Two thousand steps descended to the base of the mountain. They were all the result of the lifetime work of one monk! The moon was beginning to fade. The deep black of the sky had turned to charcoal gray, and the eastern sky was even lighter. Sinai was ruggedly cast in varying hues of brown and gray. David carried the camera case and fold-up tripod. Paulo had protested, but it was evident that he could never make the climb with all his photographic equipment. Seasoned as he was in trekking and climbing, the strain of the last few weeks had taken its toll. By the time he reached the last fifty steps, he could hardly bear the jabs of pain in his side. He kept watching the sky grow lighter and lighter, knowing that any minute the sun would break over the horizon.

"Hurry," he encouraged David.

113

"You punish me, my friend," David panted.

Paulo had come this far, and he couldn't miss that picture. So he stepped up the pace and promised his body that he wouldn't push it like this again. "We must beat the sun. To almost get the sunrise won't do any good. I have to have the first ray or the climb will be for nothing. We're almost there. Just a little farther, David."

The heights of Mount Sinai were dizzying. The distance to the horizon was so vast that one had the sensation of being on the very verge of heaven. Paulo reached the top and stood still, breathing heavily and searching among the fellow climbers for a woman with red-gold hair and the face of an angel.

David sensed his solitary mood and left him alone, quietly setting up the tripod. After a few minutes, Paulo turned to look out across the desert floor. Mile upon mile of the Negev desert stretched to the east. Far, far beyond the expanse of desert were the gray layers of the hills of Saudi Arabia. The morning air was so clear that he could actually see the dim outline of the mountains of Saudi Arabia in the distance. He was not disappointed. Who could be disappointed at the top of this mountain? But something was missing. He hadn't realized just how much he had hoped she would be here.

He adjusted his tripod and camera on the eastern edge of the mountaintop. David stood back. Behind them, a tour group settled down to listen to a narration of the importance of this spot to the Jewish tradition. The man recited the Ten Commandments that Moses received on the mountain. Paulo continued adjusting his equipment, trying several filters. Not more than five minutes later, the tip of the sun peeked over the far horizon. It glimmered; it shimmered; it poked its rim over the crest of the earth. And within another three minutes, the sun rose over Saudi Arabia, topping its layered mountains with crimson and gold. The dust particles from the desert magnified the orange ball until it seemed to have left its own orbit and fallen into the earth's atmosphere.

The group behind him began to stand, as one stands in respect for royalty. Then they sang a song he had never heard before, yet the words struck him to the heart.

"The spirit of God like a fire is burning; the latter-day glory begins to come forth. The visions and blessings of old

114

are returning, and angels are coming to visit the earth."

Paulo turned and stared at them. His spirit agreed with every word. He recognized it as the same feeling he had had each time he had seen Charlotte — a sense of spiritual blessing.

He sat down and watched the small group. Elderly men and women had climbed that path. Younger men and women stood with arms around each other or white-haired parents. Suddenly, Paulo was envious. He wished for Carmella, to share the moment. David was also intent upon the group and the song of their hearts. When they had finished the song, Paulo drew close to a man about his own age and asked, "What group is this? Are you on a tour?"

Friendly and ready to talk, the man answered. "We are a tour group from Utah. We are Mormons. Where do you come from? I see you're a photographer. Did you get a good picture of the sun? I'd sure like to see it! That was a spectacular sight."

Paulo heard only the first two sentences. Disappointment fell over him as though darkness had returned. He made some excuse and moved away. Disinterested now in photography, he took down his equipment and walked away. The beauty and magic had gone from the whole experience. Mormons! He had felt such identity with their jubilant song, but he could never have any kinship with them. The deepest sorrow he had ever experienced had come because of the Mormon church. Shielah's church had brought him nothing but grief.

"Are you ready to go?" he asked David.

"What did you think of those people? They are Mormons. I have heard of them. They build temples. Did you get the pictures you wanted?"

"Yes. I think there are some good shots here. I can go home now."

"I'll be sorry to have you go," David said sincerely, looking at his friend. "I'm afraid you will not remember us with pleasure. I wish it had been different."

Paulo smiled and shook his head. "I don't. And I will remember Israel with more pleasure than you can know."

They walked down the mountain talking quietly, but Paulo's mind was on something else. It was a comment he had overheard from the Mormons on Sinai. At the bottom, he asked David, "Do you think we're just God's creations, like the hills and rocks and animals? Have you ever thought that you and I might be sons of Deity?"

"What a unique thought," David mused. "I'll have to see what the Rabbis say. It seems blasphemous at first. But, on the other hand, what if it were true? That is an idea I might adopt."

"Behold, it is my will that all they who call on my name and worship me according to mine everlasting gospel, should gather together and stand in holy places." (Doctrine and Covenants 101:13-14, 22.)

Chapter Six

Three snowmobiles were racing toward the log cabin wedged into a grove of douglas firs. The smallest of the three was in the lead, carrying two people. A twelve-year-old boy was flying the snow rocket, jouncing over moguls and snow mounds with careless abandon. He was completely covered by a navy blue nylon snowsuit and a black helmet with a visor. Only his nose and mouth were uncovered, and his cries of victory rang through the frigid afternoon air. Clinging with both arms to his waist was a smaller child — a little girl. She was also cocooned in nylon and screaming with the delight of fright.

As they approached the clearing in front of the house, a man gunned the second snowmobile and shot around the lead vehicle. He paused to yell his own victory cry at his children. While he paused that brief moment, the last snowmobile came unnoticed from behind, whizzed by on the opposite side, and skidded to a snow-sprayed stop.

"Mother wins again! Up with woman power! Come on Kristin, we'll beat them into the house too!" Shielah Sorensen Gailbraith grabbed her little daughter and made a dash for the house.

She didn't quite make the step. "Hah!" Stephen shouted and tackled her. "Beat me at my own game, huh? The race is not to the swiftest." He began to roll his wife

117

in the snow. "The race is to the strongest!"

"Let me go!" she shouted. "Help, Kristin, help!"

"Let Mommy go!" the little girl pounded on her father's back.

"So, you want to be a snow angel too. Okay for you!" Her father pulled the little girl down into the foray and soon had her as covered with snow as her mother was.

"I give! I give! Let me go, you're getting snow in my collar," Shielah protested.

"Good!" he shouted. "Serves you right. What a sneaky way to win."

"What do you mean, sneaky? I just copied you."

"I know, and it was sneaky."

Stephen scooped his daughter up into his arms and helped Shielah to her feet. Just as they stood up, the cabin door was bolted shut. The triumphant voice of their son, Ben, declared, "I won! I won! The race is not to the swiftest or the strongest, it's to the house. And I won."

Stephen set Kristin on her feet and dashed for the back door. But again his son was quicker than he. That door was also bolted.

Stephen pounded on the door. "Little piggy, little piggy, let me come in."

Ben hooted in glee. "I've got the house. I'm king of the mountain!"

From the front porch, Shielah called out. "Okay, king of the mountain, if you want dinner, you'd better open up. Pronto!"

There was a pause of consideration. Then the front door opened and the conquering general walked in. "Food conquers all!"

Stephen had built his family a large, comfortable long home in the mountains behind Kamas, Utah. Carpentry had turned into general contracting for him in the Eighties. They had lived in Salt Lake City while he developed his business, and two years ago he and his family decided to start a new venture, building a resort retreat in the Uintah mountains. During the summer, he and Shielah had explored the region and fallen in love with the seclusion and the scenic beauty. For three years they had taken their children camping in the mountain

118

wilderness, and, finally, he had negotiated with the state to buy a hundred acres of land.

It didn't take a lot of coaxing to convince Shielah's brother, Buck Sorensen, and his wife, Bridget, to join them. Buck had settled into a teaching position in archaeology at the University in Salt Lake, spending his summers in South America on various digs. He had a wandering spirit and could hardly endure the confinement of any one place for long. Urban life had begun to oppress him.

The city had crept higher and higher up the mountain sides. The valley was filling with thousands of families moving in every year. They came, not for prosperity's sake, but for refuge and safety. Gradually, the cities of the east and west coast had devolved into beds of violence and sexual abuse. It was common for the youths to band together in gangs, murdering, raping, stealing. Once only the ghettos had been subject to that practice. Now it had become widespread, and drugs were the common denominator. Suspicion and fear forced even the children to carry weapons and to use them when they were threatened.

Drought had stricken the United States for four years. The great reserves of wheat and grain of America were depleted, and though fresh fruits and vegetables were available, they were outlandishly priced. Anger seemed to be everywhere. People who had become fat and lazy with easy prosperity were forced to tighten their belts and deny themselves their luxuries. Still they satiated themselves with television, movies, and video films that reflected the rich, sumptuous lifestyle they could no longer enjoy. The mood of the country became ugly.

Decent, hardworking people began to fear for their safety and started to look around for a better way of living. Latter-day Saints seemed to respond to an inner call to return to Utah. In droves they sold their homes, often at a great loss. These families arrived in the Great Salt Lake Basin with little money and few provisions but with a great need to work. Business and services sprang up overnight. The Church provided and provided. Tithing and donations were tripled to help the homeless and needy. At the same time, Utah's financial policy of refusing the World Wide Monetary System infuriated the non-Mormons,

119

and they left the state as interstate commerce began showing the strain of the noncooperation policy.

Buck and Bridget sold their six-bedroom home in Salt Lake City to two families who felt they could adapt the upper and lower floors into separate living quarters. The Sorensens took their five children and literally camped out with Shielah and Stephen one summer while they built a log home two miles from the Gailbraiths. It was a summer they would all remember, with cousins sleeping together like little cubs side by side on the back porch, and Shielah and Bridget both pregnant and laughing at each other as they bent to garden. For Buck and Stephen, it was a return to their youth. Working and sweating together, they kidded each other, challenged each other, and fell into exhausted sleep at the end of a day.

"Hey, Boss," Buck once shouted at Stephen as they doggedly hammered sheetrock. "You never told me that being a carpenter was so hard." He held up a blistered palm. "If Jesus did this for a living, I could make him a better offer. Now me, I like digging in the dirt."

Both babies were born in the Sorensen cabin. Bridget called Shielah one November night when a sudden snow storm had closed the mountain passes between Kamas and Salt Lake City. Buck was trapped at the university until the storm subsided. Bridget was in labor.

Shielah had gone to nursing school after she and Stephen married. The first few years of marriage, she had not been able to conceive, so she devoted her time to getting a degree in nursing. After she had three miscarriages, the doctor said she would probably never have children because of the angle at which her uterus was tilted. But the forth pregnancy went full term, and Ben was born healthy and squalling, to his parents great delight. Five years and another miscarriage later, Kristin was born. Now Shielah was due with her third child and Bridget with her sixth.

Stephen and Shielah took the truck to Bridget's and found her frantically calling the Heber City hospital. But snow had closed the roads both into and out of Kamas, and she was close to delivery. A half hour later, Shielah delivered her brother's child, a black-haired, red-faced baby boy. The next morning at daybreak, Shielah awoke to labor pains of her own. Stephen was worried. Babies

120

had never come easy for her. Her back pain was intense. He sat beside her, rubbing the small of her back and asking directions. His pride in himself was immense when he finally helped his little son, Justin, into life.

Shielah's great love was genealogy work. It seemed to be her calling in the Church. She taught Sunday School classes in it and drove once a week to Salt Lake City to pore over records in the genealogy library. One name haunted her, demanding to be found. But Charlotte O'Neill had no records anywhere.

Shielah sat at her kitchen table looking out over the snowy hills and read the letter once again. The clerk of the court in Shoal County, Illinois, regretfully informed her that there was no birth or death record of her great-great-grandmother. She crossed Shoal County off her list and sat staring at the map of Illinois. This was where Charlotte had lived, but where had she been born? Where had she died? Some knowledge of their family history had been passed down from Shielah's grandmother, Grace. She told Shielah the stories that her mother, Annie, had told her about Charlotte O'Neill. The beautiful portrait of her mother that Annie had done from memory now hung in Shielah's family room. She was a beautiful young woman with red-gold hair and soft, gray eyes. She wore a blue gown and stood with regal bearing, challenging the viewer with a mysterious look of happiness and pain intertwined.

Grace thought Charlotte had been born in Lawrenceville, and tradition said that her family had joined the Church when she was twelve. Shielah had searched the state for records, all to no avail, and the death certificate was just as impossible. One problem was that they had never known their grandfather's name. Annie never spoke of her father to Grace, and the family presumed that he must have died while Annie was very young and that Charlotte had resumed her maiden name. It must have been a short marriage, Shielah supposed, probably just long enough to give her one child.

Shielah had worked on this one name for five years, growing more and more discouraged as letter after letter came back with no information. She had often fretted and fumed over the stubborn problem. She had heard so many stories that she felt as though she knew this great-great-grandmother of hers. Once she had a dream of being a

121

small girl and sitting on a hillside, watching a huge fire, and Charlotte came to her. Such a feeling of comfort and peace had come over her that she awoke saddened at never having known the woman. She often told Stephen she could hardly wait to meet Charlotte on the other side and find out all about her life.

Great-grandmother Annie had often petted Shielah and said she looked like Charlotte. When Annie Partridge died, Grace had sat and held her mother's hand, and the last night, she whispered strange things from time to time. The last thing she said before she slipped away was, "The stars look just the same, Mother, a thousand miles away."

Paulo served Jim a drink and settled back into his leather chair, watching his friend with amusement. Jim Polanski was in love. It was a miracle. The two of them had been confirmed bachelors for years. More than a few models, actresses, and artists, and many a shapely secretary had dabbled in and out of Jim's life. Jim was no more conservative with his money than with his carefree, good-time version of love. Both were to be used as long as they held out, and he spent them both wildly, but now he had narrowed the field down to one unique red rose.

Jim introduced her to Paulo on his third evening with her. Cherri was an artist and did lovely things on canvas with a palate knife. She was five foot five and boyishly slim. They looked good together, Paulo observed to himself — Jim with his blonde hair and cockeyed, angular face, and Cherri with her slanted green eyes and light brown hair, bobbed and swinging free. She was comfortable in any situation. Most of the time she preferred jeans and a casual sweatshirt, but she astounded Jim in a clinging red dinner dress for an evening at Sardi's. She had the simple curiosity of a child and asked eager questions about the Vista Color. The two men showed her their offices like a couple of little boys doing handstands after school.

Jim and Cherri became constant companions for a year, and everyone warned Cherri it couldn't be done. Jim give up his independence, break his record at forty-five, and settle down? Never! But he actually began to find that idea appealing. He simply grew tired of living at two places, his and hers.

All his weeks of wrestling with a decision were useless because she turned him down.

"Nope, you're too young for me." Cherri went on peeling potatoes for dinner.

"You've got to be kidding," Jim said in disbelief. "I've got better than ten years on you."

She sighed, like someone explaining a simple concept to a small child." I don't care how old you are. You're too young for marriage. You just never grew up emotionally. I adore you, Jim. You're really a love, but I wouldn't marry you on a bet. My mom and dad have been married for thirty-five years next January, and when I do it, I intend to follow their example. Love comes and goes many times in a person's life, but marriage is forever.

"Cherri, I love you. I wouldn't ask you if I didn't think I could stick with it."

"I know. I believe you — that you're sincere, I mean." She kissed his cheek lightly and turned back to the stove. "But I have zero confidence in your staying power. There is absolutely no evidence to support you."

He threw up his hands. "For crying out loud. So that's your real opinion of me, huh? Well, I'm glad to find out now. You really think I'm a kid!"

"No, love, I don't think that. But you do have a formidable reputation. Tell me, have you ever really loved anyone?"

"Just ask half the women in New York," he grinned impishly.

"Exactly what I mean," she responded coolly and dismissed the subject.

But Jim couldn't dismiss it. It haunted him at night. He couldn't sleep for wanting her to be his, permanently his. Now he confessed to Paulo that she wouldn't marry him.

"Serves you right," Paulo laughed. "I'm glad someone's on to your game. Cherri's probably the smartest girl you've ever had. I don't blame her. I wouldn't marry you either, given your track record."

"So who's asking you?" Jim pouted. "Quit laughing, before your nose sees the other side of your face!"

"Shut up, or I won't take you to dinner tonight."

"That's right, it's your turn. Mind if I bring Cherri?"

"Nope. I want to be the first to congratulate her — that

she's not getting married."

It was a frosty February evening when the three friends finished dinner and tried to hail a cab.

"Oh, come on," Cherri said. "You guys don't have broken legs. It's just a couple of blocks. Let's walk."

When they reached the door of Cherri's apartment building, two young men were standing beside the elevator, rubbing red, chilled hands.

"How was your day?" Cherri asked them. "Find any 'golden contacts'?"

"Nope," the shorter one answered. "Just you. When are we going to teach you the first discussion?"

Cherri introduced Jim and Paulo to two Mormon missionaries. They lived just below her on the third floor and had tried several times to make an appointment for a discussion. Impulsively, Cherri invited them to join her little party. Paulo became suddenly reserved and silent.

Jim sat on the couch with his arm around Cherri. Paulo sat gingerly in the matching wing-back chair. He was wary and refused to participate in the discussion. He could see the young men's faces brighten as they began their discussion of the social conditions around them and then moved to the scriptures. Within a few minutes they had related the Joseph Smith story and asked what the group thought of it.

Cherri was enthralled. Jim was amused. Paulo couldn't help remembering his experiences on Sinai two years before, but he would contribute nothing. After a few minutes, he was restless and so uncomfortable that he went and stood by the window with his back turned to the others, pretending not to hear. He wanted to leave and almost excused himself twice, but some curiosity —some fascination — held him there.

When the young men looked at their watches and said they had to be in their quarters by ten, Cherri saw them to the door. They gave her some pamphlets with a brief explanation of what they were about and asked for another appointment. She glanced quickly at Jim, then smiled and said, "On Thursday night I'll be home all evening."

Cherri couldn't read fast enough to satisfy her thirst. She felt as though she had been hungry for a long time and a feast was before her. She read voraciously and soon knew the details of Joseph Smith's life, as well much about the Book of Mormon. Within three weeks she had had all the lessons. The missionaries were challenging her to baptism.

Sometimes the discussions between Jim and Paulo and Cherri lasted late into the night. Cherri defended her newfound faith passionately. Jim only kidded her about it. He couldn't take any of it seriously. To him, it was completely academic as to whether or not God appeared to Joseph Smith or if there were a true church. Once he told her it didn't matter to him because, even if it were true, he didn't choose to live that way. He liked his life. He liked smoking. He liked drinking and partying, and he wouldn't change for anyone.

Paulo was different. To him it mattered a great deal, and he was torn. Jerusalem had changed him. He craved the touch of the spirit he had felt there. He looked for Charlotte everywhere he went, and he dreamed many times of a woman he could see but not touch. He had no explanation for what he had experienced, for the being he had seen and heard. The Bible spoke of angels, but those were ancient, unreliable stories, and certainly his mysterious lady of light had no wings or halo. She was visible, tangible proof to Paulo that life existed on another plane. Was it life after death? Life before life? He didn't know. Neither did his boyhood priest. He didn't know how to pray about such things, but there were fleeting moments when he seemed to feel the closeness to God he sought. Then the veil would drop, and he would be shut out again. Paulo and Cherri argued across the dinner table almost every night. He disagreed with her new religion, but he was continually drawn back into discussing it. She was very new to the gospel and didn't have all the answers. But she knew one thing — the Holy Spirit had entered and filled her whole soul with a burning knowledge that it was true. Paulo envied her, but he could not and would not accept the Mormon Church.

Jim liked to needle her, and he did it quite cheerfully. "How can you talk about loving God when you can't see him? You can't talk to him. How can you love a mystery?"

Cherri grabbed his hand. "He's not a mystery! I can't see him, that's true, but I can talk to him. And he talks back. It's just as real as when you tell me you love me. But when God tells me, I just feel this tremendous bright, warm blanket of light flow over me. I don't know how else to describe it."

Jim tolerated her new interest with easy amusement. He was sure it would die away soon enough. She still made him his coffee and served him his drinks, though now she would not join him. He privately thought she would get over that. Then one night, she asked him not to stay. She didn't like their arrangement anymore. It didn't feel right to her.

"So, why don't you take me up on my offer. Offer still goes. Marry me and I won't have to go home."

"I don't know, Jim. I'm still afraid you'll love me for a while and then you'll meet someone else and it'll be all over."

"Hey, little girl, I'm here to stay. I guarantee it. You'll leave me before I leave you."

"Never," she whispered as he kissed her. The next Monday morning, Cherri became Mrs. Polanski in front of a busy clerk of the New York court. Paulo was the only witness to the news event of the decade. Jim Polanski had met his match.

"Paulo, it's the only smart thing to do." Zimmerman had called his stubborn vice president into the oversized office and now sat behind the expanse of his oak desk, employing all his reasoning ability. "Banks are closing everywhere. Of course, our assets are with Chase Manhattan, and we're not in any danger. But they are going with the system, and if we want to do business with them, we have to have their number. It's inevitable. The whole country is going to be with the World Wide Monetary System soon. And why not? Three of the men who sit on the board are our own men."

Paulo was intractable. "So?"

"So, they're Americans, and they know banking. Every bank president I've talked to, every congressman and senator — they all think it is the only way to save our financial structure. Where have you been? America is on the verge of collapse. Or don't you read the papers?"

"Get off it, Izzie." Paulo was impatient. "If America is on the verge of financial collapse, it's because it was planned that way. They've been devaluing our money for years.

Take the silver out! Take the gold out! Print more money; raise the debt limit so we spend tomorrow's dollars before we make them. Come on, wake up! You're too smart to be hoodwinked by this! Can't you see how carefully it has been planned? The bankers have manipulated world events too long. They invest our money in irresponsible leaders of third-world countries and let our own farmers and small-business owners go whistle. They loan our money to the Communists so they can use it to finance their armaments against us. That can't be mere stupidity! They encourage farmers to overspend and overbuy; then they bankrupt their farms when the farmer can't pay. The picture is very clear. Once the financial structure is in shambles, then they'll declare a worldwide system of slavery. And this is it. Omar is right! Can't you see that?"

"I can see we're going to damned well lose our shirts unless we join the system. Rabinski says it will be mandatory by year's end. Everyone will join and be assigned a number or they will not be able to buy or sell anything."

Paulo shuddered. Rachael sat silently in a chair in the corner. She watched the two men. Paulo's face was drawn, the lines deeper in his forehead. His dark eyes were troubled. And it was more than just the impending threat of the money system. For months he had forced his smiles. Often she would walk into his office to find him staring absent-mindedly out the window.

"Who's leading the show? Figured that one out yet?" Paulo asked.

"I told you, the whole world is behind it. Ralph Schleger is the most independent thinker I know, and he is ready to sign too."

"But Israel hasn't yet?"

"No, not yet. It's just a matter of time. The Knesset has to vote on it, and young Cohen is muddying the water."

Paulo smiled wryly. "I'll bet he is. David and Omar don't agree on many things, but they do on that. You didn't answer me, Izzie. Vladimoscov is leading the show. Ever since they joined the common market, they've grabbed the reins. They've got the most muscle. I wouldn't trust the system for that reason alone. Since when has the Soviet doctrine ever been cooperation? It is domination."

Rachael said softly, "One problem it raises for us is

127

with our employees. Already they are beginning to have a hard time cashing their payroll checks. The banks ask them for their number and ours."

Paulo passed his hand over his face. "Yeah, I know. They've told me."

Zimmerman slapped both hands down on his desk with finality. "Well, Paulo, I'm afraid the decision's out of our hands anyway. The board of directors will vote on it this month."

"I have a voice on that board."

"Yes, you do. But there are eleven others." His pudgy face had an uncharacteristically hard look, and his voice carried a clear warning.

Paulo stood up and leaned over the polished oak desk. "I won't have a number tattooed on my hand like a concentration camp prisoner. I won't do it, Izzie!" He held Zimmerman's gaze for a minute, then turned and walked out, slamming the door behind him.

Rachael didn't say a word to her uncle; she hurried after Paulo. "Wait. Paulo, can we have dinner? I want to talk to you."

He put his anger aside and looked at her. Rachael was a problem. She was in love with him. It showed in her look, in her smile. And he was no fool. She was a beautiful woman, ten years younger than he. He was flattered by her obvious devotion. He was tempted by the unspoken offer of herself. But he didn't love her. He had met the woman he loved, and he would be satisfied with no one else.

Suddenly, his resolve broke, and he reached out for her, pulling her into his arms. The office was empty. The last person gone. He buried his face in her fragrant hair. "Everything is wrong, Rachael! Everything is wrong. What am I going to do?"

"Let's talk. Tell me, Paulo. Let me help. Even if it's just by listening. I'm a good listener."

"I know. You're always a good listener. But I'm not a good talker. The words are all garbled up inside. I don't know exactly what's wrong. It's just something I feel. It's a terrible, heavy depression, like something is vastly, horribly wrong with New York, with the world, with me."

"Everybody feels that way sometimes — everyone. Come on, let's go home. I'll cook for you tonight. Let's just go and talk. Maybe it'll help."

He helped her with her coat, then grabbed his, and they took the elevator down. It was cold and windy in late February. Did he just imagine that the street noises seemed harsher, angrier? They hailed a taxi and drove past figure after figure lying or sitting on the sidewalk. The homeless had crept into the financial district. Pathetically, they waited with their hats out, hoping for some small offering. The didn't get many. At nightfall, they took their few coins and bought liquor and a few bites of food to ward off the cold. Then they huddled in doorways and slept.

The cabby rattled on. "A fella could freeze to death out here, and do ya think anybody'd help? Nope! I tell you, people don't care anymore. Used to be people helped other people, know what I mean? Other day I see'd a woman no older than my missus, curled up in the middle of the day on the sidewalk. I went over to her and shook her. Her eyes popped open, and I said, 'Git in lady, I'll take you home.' And ya know what she said? 'No thank ya.' Polite as can be, ya know. Just 'No thank ya. My family can eat for two more weeks without me. They're better off,' she said!"

"So what did you do?" Rachael asked.

"What could I do? I got in the cab and drove off. Lady wants to die, what can ya do? Me, I'm just thankful I got a job."

"There are organizations to help people like that," Paulo said.

The cabby looked back in surprise. "Where you been, mister? Them organizations long gone. Overspent themselves. Nobody bankrolls them anymore — too busy trying to keep food on the table. This drought'll kill us all. Jees, it feels like 1929 around here. My ol' lady waits twenty minutes in line just to get coffee."

Rachael looked at Paulo through the shadows. Fear was communicable. No one spoke until they stopped in front of Rachael's building. Paulo tipped the man forty dollars and waved away his thank-you's.

In the crushed velvet easy chair in Rachael's front room, Paulo waited while Rachael brought hot coffee to break their chill.

"I'm really not very hungry," he said.

"Me neither. It is getting pretty sobering. I never thought it could happen here."

He gave a short laugh. "Right. The land of plenty. The promised land. The breadbasket of the world. America has never known hunger like the rest of the world has. I guess it's our turn."

"Why is it happening? I don't understand."

He sighed. "Lots of reasons. We've been messing up our atmosphere for decades with nuclear testing, fluorocarbons, fossil fuels, all that. The scientists have warned us, but no one paid much attention. Last year, the rain forest in South America had shrunk to one fourth of it's original size. They've been cutting at it for years. Now the forest is dying, and with it, the natural evaporation process that brings rain to the whole world. The gap in the ionosphere doubled its size last year. We've known for a long time that the fumes from plastic production and automobile waste was destroying our ionosphere, but we won't change. What, go back to bicycles and horses? Heaven forbid! So now, we have less and less protection against the sun. And maybe, just maybe, God is sick of us all."

Rachael sat on the carpet beside his chair, watching him silently. There was no light in his face or eyes now. The silver strands that laced his black hair had become white patches at his temples. She rose to her knees and gently touched the lines of his forehead and beside his mouth. The bitterness that sharpened his voice pained her.

"Rachael, maybe the ice age will come again, as it did once. Maybe man has outsmarted himself with all of his inventions and destroyed his own planet. Somehow, I can't shake the feeling that it won't be long. And I'm sick. I feel nauseated, depressed. It's as though a huge, dark beast is hovering over us, over the city, over the world. I keep looking up, expecting to see the jaws of the dragon above me in the sky. It's a nightmare. I feel like I'm living in a nightmare."

She wrapped her arms around him and held him close to her. She stroked his hair and murmured comforting words. But he didn't respond.

At last he shook his head. "Am I crazy? I think I must be going crazy."

"No, you're not crazy. But it won't come to that. We're in a slump now. It's bad, but it'll get better."

"Rachael, did you ever wonder where you came from? What you're doing here? And what comes after? Have you ever wondered if you are just another one of God's creations, or if you're his child?" He searched her face for some shred of answer that he could make his own.

She would have said anything he wanted to hear, but she didn't know what it was. "Moses wrote that God created the world," she ventured. "And he created man in his own image. But I don't know what that means exactly. Whether it means we are just a creation, or whether we actually look like him. But that can't be, since he isn't a real man. I've never thought a lot about it. It's one of the mysteries of God. I've always thought the references to us being children of God — all brothers, things like that — I always thought it was just metaphoric."

"So did I. But Cherri has been baptized a Mormon, and she says it is to be taken literally — that we are created in his image and are his children. She talks about a spiritual pre-existence before earth. She believes that our reason for being here is to become perfect and earn a resurrected life with God and Christ. I wish I could believe it!"

"What is holding you back? If it helps, then accept it. You can't be any more miserable than you are now."

"But it's the Mormon Church! The Mormon Church! I swore I'd never have anything to do with it again."

"Again?"

He sighed and explained briefly about Shielah. "It was the Church, plain and simple. I would have married her and been happy, with children of my own. But the Mormon Church had such a hold on her. It stole everything — my ability to love, my sense of purpose in life."

"Paulo, darling! That was twenty years ago! You can't go on loving a memory."

"I don't. It's not Shielah anymore. I left her years ago in my heart. But I'm so lonely inside. There is such a hole." He shook his head. "Such a hole as can't be filled."

"Let me try," Rachael whispered, bending down to kiss him.

Her lips were soft and full, and so tender it took his

breath away. The warmth of the room, the dim gold light of the lamps, the sweet smell of her perfume — somehow it seemed to soothe his anguish. He held her and deliberately banished thoughts of the red-haired Charlotte. He had long since realized that she was the woman in Shielah's painting. Charlotte O'Neill was Shielah's great-great-grandmother, and she had lived a full century ago. He recognized her face, and her spirit, as well. How could you love a woman from another century? He couldn't even tell his best friends — they would think he was insane!

Rachael looked at him with her heart in her eyes. He kissed the corners of her eyes, the tip of her nose, the full lips barely parted. She loved him. And in a way, he loved her too. She was good. She was lovely and kind. Together they could shut the world away. With her, there would be peace.

He stayed with her that night, and they fell asleep, curled up together on the couch like two children. It was his first night of peaceful sleep in month.

At 4:00 a.m., the telephone rang. It was Jim. "Cherri's in the hospital! Cops found her this morning on the street. Can you come?"

Paulo sat straight up. "Of course. Where?"

"Holy Cross. Make it quick!"

When Paulo and Rachael rushed into the Holy Cross emergency waiting room, Jim was pacing like a caged animal. The nurses watched him apprehensively. He told the story bitterly and briefly.

Cherri had taken a job with the welfare services six months before. True to her nature, she couldn't see need without responding. People were hungry, cold, homeless. She felt she had to help, to do her part. Jim had tried to talk her out of it.

"What can you do, go in and hold their hands and tell them there will be a job tomorrow? The drought will end? You know it won't."

"I know it could. And there might be a job tomorrow. Are you God, to know that there won't be a job for a hungry man? That's the problem — people are giving up. No one has confidence anymore. The only way to help is to restore confidence and a sense of caring. I can do that."

It was useless to argue. "Well, you be careful. I grew up on the east side of town, and it isn't your average Sunday church meeting over there. A wop will knife you as fast as a black or Chicano will. I don't want you going down there without somebody else with you, preferably a man."

"Not to worry," and she kissed his cheek. "I have pre-set appointments with certain families. They all like me. The office knows where I am at all times and when to expect me back, and for good measure I carry meal tickets with me. That's the best insurance."

Jim was supposed to meet her at the grill downstairs when he got off work. At seven-thirty she was still not there, and he began to feel that something was wrong. He called the police station on the east side. His childhood friend Mike O'Daniels had just come in from patrol, and Jim asked a special favor of him — to check out the Cuban sector. Normally, O'Daniels would have waited until morning. Patrol officers had been taken out of that sector at night. Eight had been shot in the last year. But it was Jim Polanski asking, and he was a friend.

O'Daniels and his buddy Frank turned on the searchlight on the squad car and cruised the dark streets. Bands of teens blocked the roads and shouted at the police car. Several beer cans were thrown from the darkness. The smell of marijuana was thick, and some of the kids sat on the curb in a drugged stupor. At the very back of a dirty, smelly alley, their searchlight picked up the pale blue of her overcoat. Her body lay beside it. They got out to check for a pulse. It was erratic but still fairly strong. Cherri was a mess. Her blouse was torn almost off and her underclothing ripped. The navy slacks she had worn were nowhere to be seen. Her shoes had been lost well before they had cornered her in the alley. O'Daniels knelt beside her while Frank called for an ambulance and a police escort. She was battered, bloody, her jaw broken, and she was mercifully unconscious. She was lucky only in one respect — the gang had not cut her up, though all five had knives and had taunted her with them throughout the whole nightmare. The conquests were chalked up on the alley wall — five marks.

Cherri was cleaned up as much as possible by the time Jim reached the hospital and saw her. Only one thing

133

was in operation for Jim — his hatred. Even his love for Cherri was numbed beside the onslaught of hate and vengeance.

Paulo asked gently, "What do the doctors say?"

"What do they know? They stitch her up and prescribe some medicine and say we can hope it does not scar her too badly emotionally. What kind of useless crap is that? What's she supposed to do, get up tomorrow and say, 'Oh well, another day, another dollar?' If she can ever look another Cuban in the face again without going into hysterics, she'll have a pretty good recovery in my book. Right now, I'd like to walk down that neighborhood and take out every punk on the street. If I knew — if I only knew who they were — New York would have five less . . ." His voice broke, and he turned away. He stubbed a cigarette out in the ashtray with shaky hands.

Paulo was at a loss to comfort him. He felt the same helpless anger, and the desolate feeling of the night before had taken him again. He put an arm around his friend's shoulder. "I know. I know." They sat down with their heads bowed, staring at the bright linoleum floor. After an hour, a nurse came in and said Cherri was awake. They could see her.

Her eyes were closed when they went in. Jim sat down on one side of the bed, Paulo on the other. Her face was turned toward Paulo when she opened her eyes a few minutes later. Both eyes were swollen and black. No recognition registered. She turned her head slowly and found Jim. Then tears began to ooze quietly from beneath thick lids. She didn't make a sound, but Jim did. He put his head down on her bedcover and sobbed.

When he regained his composure, he sat holding her hand. It lay limp in his. Her jaw was wired shut, so she couldn't talk, but no one wanted to talk anyway.

Much later in the day, she motioned that she wanted to write something. Paulo found a pencil and paper, and she wrote, "Please take me away from here. I want to go to Utah."

At the end of March, Zimmerman called Paulo into his office. He sat behind his desk with his feet up. His hands were folded serenely across his belly. He was grinning broadly, his eyes bright behind his glasses. Paulo was suddenly wary.

"How does the title of President Paulo J. D'Agosta sound to you? I sent in my resignation to the chairman of the board last night and recommended you to replace me. I'm going to Israel. My old friend Ralph Schleger has made me an offer I can't refuse — secretary of education! The business is yours, my friend. I guess the old Jewish blood can't be denied forever."

Izzie grinned up at him. Paulo stood stock still. "You can't do that! The board just announced their decision to go with the World Wide Monetary System. I won't run this business under those conditions." He slammed his fist down on Izzie's desk and swore. "You're the one who wanted this; now you stay and deal with it. I won't throw in with them."

Zimmerman was alarmed at his vehemence. "Hey, calm down. Haven't you ever heard, 'If you can't beat 'em, join 'em?' Be practical, Paulo. You can't do business unless you join. Vista Color will go under."

"Yes, and so will the whole American democratic society! They'll have to hold me down to tatoo that number on my wrist! I can't be president. I won't be. I quit!"

Rachael looked up, startled, as he stalked out of the office and into his own. He yanked open the desk drawer, drew out a piece of company letterhead, and, with a shaking hand, wrote out his resignation. This he took out to Rachael and threw it down on her desk.

"Send this to the chairman of the board."

"What is it?" she asked as she looked up into his angry eyes.

"My resignation," he said, and he turned and walked back into his office.

When Rachael entered a minute later, Paulo sat with his back to the door, leaning forward in the leather swivel chair and looking out his fifteenth-story window. New York City lay below. It still looked much as it always had, busy, prosperous — the Big Apple. But now the polish was gone. He knew if he walked down to the street, he would not see the signs of prosperity. He would see fear, hunger, and anger.

She spoke softly behind him. "What will you do? Vista Color has been your life."

"Go home, I guess. I've neglected Mother lately. She isn't well, you know. She wants me to go over her papers with her. After that, I don't know." He shook his head.

She had known it would eventually come to this, and that he would not think of her at all when it was time to make a decision. Tears sprang up readily. She had failed. She had hoped to win his love by her love. But it hadn't worked. There was something Paulo D'Agosta needed that she couldn't give him. Until that was filled, she doubted he would love anyone.

"Put a call through to Riyadh, will you? I want to talk to Omar."

An hour later, she announced, "Your call is through. His Majesty's Royal Highness is on the line." Paulo smiled at the wry, bitter expression on her face. He picked up the phone. "Is there room in the royal palace?"

"Ah, so you are ready to give it up, my friend?" Omar sounded light years away.

"I have. I wrote out my resignation today."

"I wondered how long you would last. All of Europe, Russia, Canada are already under the system. America won't last much longer."

"My company voted to go with them two nights ago. I've had it. Now I'm a beggar. Are you generous to beggars? Need another palace servant?"

Omar laughed. "No, but I always need a friend. Many servants, few friends. Are you coming really?"

Paulo had started to relax during the conversation. Omar was a breath of fresh air to him. "Well, not right away. I have some things to do first. Mama is not well. She wants me to go through her papers."

"Ah, Mama! Your mama is a great lady. Bring her too. The desert air will be good for her. We'll put her on a camel. She'll like that, no?"

Paulo laughed. "No. But I will. We'll talk again when I get things straightened out here. Shalom to Jordan — and to you." With that, they both chuckled and hung up.

He sat looking at Rachael. Dear Rachael. She was the only good thing that had come to him in a long time. She wore a royal blue dress that clung to her shapely figure. He got up and walked around the desk. Pulling her to her feet, he held her — not speaking, for there were simply no words. Good-bye would not do. Yet, the fondness between

136

them was not what either of them needed. She deserved better than that. Somewhere a man would be willing to die for those beautiful eyes and tender lips.

"I'll be back," he whispered at last. "It's not forever. I'll come back."

But she shook her head no and ran out of the room.

"Oh my boy! My boy!" Carmella greeted him joyfully as Paulo came to her bedside. She no longer worried about her best silk dress. She rarely dressed now. It was only a matter of time until she would join Papa.

"How are you, Mama?" he asked, kissing her gnarled hand.

"Fine! I am fine. Better so than you. You look terrible. Paulo, you are too young to look so old. You are not sleeping good. I see it beneath your eyes."

"I quit Vista Color, Mama."

"Oh . . . " she breathed in amazement. "You quit your job? Paulo, are you sure you do the right thing? So many men search for some good job, and you are quitting."

He patted her hand. "It's just time for other things, Mama. I've been there too long. I want to be free to do my photography and to travel. I have many friends, and there are lots of interesting places yet to be photographed. I won't lack for work."

She was easily reassured. Paulo was a smart boy. He knew what he was doing. Paulo she trusted.

"How long will you stay? I am lonely without you. Ruth and the children, they come every day. But still, the time is long. I read a little. I sleep, and sometimes I watch television. But I don't understand what is on that thing now. Such terrible things. Gangs shooting. Murder, rape, little children hurting. I do not like what I see. Is it really that bad, Paulo?" she asked anxiously.

"No, no. It's just TV. They like to be sensational. You mustn't take them too seriously."

She relaxed again and patted his cheek. "You will stay now a long time?"

"Yes," he smiled. "I will stay now a long time."

"Sweet boy," she smiled back at him. "Always you tease me. It means you love me, yes?"

"Yes," Paulo answered fondly.

Weeks later, Paulo sat in the library, dutifully going through the papers his mother had given him. He came to the sale of the family home to the D'Agosta corporation. She had signed that a year ago. He read through the provisions. Everything was in order. Then, in the third to the last paragraph, after pages of other provisions, was one paragraph that jumped out at him. He read it again.

"I, the undersigned, do hereby agree to transfer all executive privileges appertaining to the execution of stocks, bonds, and deeds of property to D'Agosta Furs, Inc., to be administered by the president of the company, Roberto Dante D'Agosta."

He had it! So that was what Roberto was after with this transfer of the house to the corporation. He didn't want the house. He wanted voting privileges of Carmella's controlling stock. He knew it would go to Paulo unless he found a way to steal it. Paulo sat with his head resting on the back of the chair. Months ago he would have been angry. He would have challenged Roberto. But now, somehow, it didn't seem to matter. There was something infinitely bigger at stake against which he had already conceded defeat. D'Agosta Furs would also have to accept the number of the WWMS. He was curious. Would Roberto do that?

He had not spoken to his brother since that violent night two years ago. Now he called New York City.

"Roberto? I have the papers for the transfer of the house. Congratulations. That was a clever touch, burying the stock provision."

There was silence for a minute. Then Roberto couldn't help gloating. "Thanks. I thought of it myself."

"I'm sure. Late at night while you lay awake, right?"

"That's right!"

"Well, I'm curious. Have you joined the WWMS?"

"Hell no!" The answer was explosive.

"No? What will you do when the Federal Reserve puts all the banks on the system in December?"

"Fight it. I'm not joining that system. No stinking Frenchie or Bloke or American banker is gonna control me. I'll show them whether I can buy and sell without their permission!"

Paulo smiled in spite of himself. "Mess up your business, would it?"

"Yeah. I guess it would! Instead of us raking off the profits, they would. And you can bet the goods would still come in. Anywhere there's money to be made, somebody's gonna make it. Nothing will change, only the hands that take the money. My hands are gonna hold on to every dime! There'll be blood before we give in."

"I believe it," Paulo replied and hung up. So, the Mafia was just as adamantly opposed as he was to the plan, but for different reasons.

On Saturday, Paulo drove back to New York. He had to close up his apartment for good and settle the lease. In eight months he wouldn't be able to rent it without the number of the WWMS on his hand. He made arrangements with the landlord to store his furniture until he could sell it or move it to upstate New York. He refused to deal with the question of where he would live when the country went totally WWMS. Maybe Riyadh didn't look so bad. He took a few precious mementos and his clothing and loaded the back of his car.

Jim's was the last stop. A strange sense of peace had come to Paulo in the weeks since he had left Vista Color. Today he felt almost as though he had begun a long journey, and every omen was good. He was in good spirits when he rang the buzzer to Cherri and Jim's apartment. Before the buzzer rang in return to let him in, the door opened and a young couple walked out. He slipped in through the open door. He took the elevator up to the fourth floor and knocked on the Polanski door.

Cherri opened it, her face registering surprise. Just to the side of the door stood two large suitcases.

"Paulo! What are you doing here?"

"Came to say good-bye. Looks like you are, too. Where are you going?"

"To Utah," she answered, determination edging her voice.

"So, you're really going. Jim going too?" Paulo was incredulous.

Now she looked away. "No. He won't go. At least, not yet. I'm hoping he'll come later. Things will get worse before they get better in this city, and I can't stay here any longer."

Cherri's face was smooth and pretty as ever now. Only a slight irregular line of her jaw on the left side betrayed the beating she had endured months before. But the scars on her mind and heart had not healed. She was frightened of her shadow. She would not go to the store. She wouldn't go shopping or to a movie after dark. She was becoming a recluse, and she and Jim had begun to argue about it every night.

Jim was implacable. He loved Cherri more than he had ever loved anyone, but he couldn't change his way of life. He would never fit into the Mormon culture that she had completely embraced. She understood, but she also knew she had an obligation to herself. She had an impending sense of doom that was robbing her of all will to live. She had to get out. Today was the day she had picked. Jim was to be gone all day to the races. He would not be back until late. She would be gone when he arrived.

It was torture for her to walk out of the safety of the apartment alone. She had prayed all morning for the strength to go. Her airplane ticket was for 3:18 p.m. On Friday, she had ventured out as far as her bank and drawn out all her savings. She had written a letter expressing her love for Jim and her hope that he would soon follow her. Now, it only remained for her to go. But she couldn't. She seemed rooted to the spot. She had been standing in front of the door for ten minutes before Paulo came.

"Cherri, are you sure you want to do this?" he asked.

"Oh yes, I'm sure. Very sure. But I'm so scared, Paulo. What if . . . what if someone else . . . " She couldn't utter the unthinkable.

He put an arm around her. "Don't say it. Don't think it. It's over. Someday it'll fade and you'll hardly remember it. But I'm concerned for you, going to a strange city alone."

"Oh, don't be. I'm not worried. I have the name of a bishop in Salt Lake. Once I get there, I'll be all right. If I can just get there safely."

She became curious about him. "Why are you here?"

"To say good-bye. I closed up my apartment. I guess Jim told you I quit Vista Color."

She nodded. "Yes, he told me. It's too bad. I know how you loved it."

"Everything changes, Cherri. I can't stay on there once it changes over to the system. It's against my principles."

"I know. The Prophet is advising all of us against it too."

"What!" Paulo was astounded.

"The General Authorities say it is one of the signs of the last days. We are not to accept the tatoo. None of us are. All the Mormons are gathering back to Utah rather than join the system."

Paulo stared at her. All at once, Cherri's face brightened, and she grabbed his arm. "Paulo, come with me."

Rejection was immediate. "No! I can't."

"Yes you can. You're one of us, but you don't know it yet. You believe almost everything we do. You fight it, but I can tell you believe it. That is where your battle comes from, feeling one thing in your heart and not accepting it with your mind. Come with me! You have nothing to lose. Look at the Church up close. You can always come back. Please, Paulo. I need you. I'm afraid to go alone. But I'm terrified to stay. I'll die if I stay here! Please come with me and help me. I need a friend."

So it was that Paulo D'Agosta went once more to Utah.

*"But if from thence thou shalt seek the Lord thy
God, thou shalt find him, if thou seek him with
all thy heart and with all thy soul. When thou
art in tribulation, and all these things are come
upon thee, even in the latter days, if thou turn
to the Lord thy God, and shall be obedient unto
his voice, he will not forsake thee."*
(Deuteronomy 4:29, 30.)

Chapter Seven

Like a horse being dragged to water, Paulo went to Salt
Lake City. Reluctantly, he looked out the airplane window
at the city built between the mountains. Who stepped on
this place? he thought. With the exception of a few tall
buildings downtown, the entire valley was a residential
sprawl. It had a certain loveliness though, he grudgingly
admitted — a sense of repose, of peace, of normalcy. The
mountains were neither as rugged as the Himalayas nor
as gentle as the Appalachians. At the first of May they
were still white-tipped and formed a bowl about the city,
much as the mountains at Katmandu.

They found Bishop Roy Quinn that night as he was
leaving to visit three families recently moved in. His
resources were stretched as far as they could go. Cherri
was only one of dozens who needed assistance. He was a
man about sixty-five, with thinning white hair and a
weathered face. He was polite; he was kind. He offered
temporary living quarters with his own family. But jobs
were one to every three people who applied.

"The best advice I can give you is to try places outside
the valley. I know another area back up in the mountains
behind Salt Lake. I was raised in Kamas. It's a little town,
but it's booming right now. Gold was discovered two years
ago, and it's taking a lot of our overflow. Why don't you

143

take a look? I think we could get you some work over there. Salt Lake is saturated."

The next day, Bishop Quinn loaned them his car, and Paulo drove Cherri into the mountains. They wound through the growing resort town of Park City and then on around the loop to Heber City. Construction was going on everywhere. The buildings were most often condominiums and small houses. Some people had even moved into the basement part of a house, living there until they could afford the upper story. Cherri loved the small towns. They seemed like quaint mountain villages after living in New York for twelve years.

They missed the inconspicuous turnoff to Kamas and had to go back from Heber City to find it. In Europe, this would have been called a hamlet, Paulo thought. The man at the gas station regaled them with stories of the gold mine and the boom it had brought to his sleepy little town. He chewed a piece of gum, snapping it every few minutes, and rattled on about the rich history of Kamas with its Black Hawk wars in the Indian days and the Rough Riders.

Paved roads quickly turned into gravel back in the mountains behind Kamas. In some places, there were only tents for temporary accommodations for mine workers. Heavy modern equipment was seen everywhere, trying to keep up with the demand for housing, roads, and mining. Around another bend, they drove through untouched mountain meadows and saw sparkling streams and horses grazing in the fields. Cherri was enthralled.

The next day, Cherri and Paul visited Roy Quinn again. "You said you could offer me a job in Kamas. I accept. Anything you can find is all right," Cherri said. "We drove through there yesterday, and I lost my heart. Do you really think I could get work and a room there?"

Quinn was pleased with her response with his birthplace. "You bet. Let me make a few calls, and I'll let you know tonight. The room won't be a problem. I have a cousin, Ida McCormick, who had a small motel she has turned into permanent rentals. I know she has one empty on the end. Just talked to her yesterday." His eyes twinkled as he said, "Now let's talk about work. What can you do?"

Cherri was nervous. "My training is in art. I have a

degree in art from Indiana State College, but that is probably not a very salable talent right now. I have also done some social work with the New York welfare board, but . . . but I'd rather not get back into that." She glanced at Paulo and said in a smaller voice, "It wasn't a very good experience."

"Well, it might take a few calls, but I'll get back to you. Have you two walked through Temple Square?"

"Not yet! Maybe we can today." Cherri looked at Paulo for approval.

His face was set. Memories of standing across the street and seeing Shielah come out into the temple grounds, dressed all in white, were too vivid.

"Come on, I'll take you. It's about time for lunch. We'll just take a quick turn through." Quinn was out of his chair and ushering them toward the door. Paulo started to protest but Cherri's face was so bright. "Please, let's just go for a minute," she pleaded.

As they walked, Paulo commented, "I haven't seen a single person with the number of the World Wide Monetary System on his hand? Why is that?"

"Our people have all refused to be part of the system. That's why we've grown so suddenly here. Utah has refused to cooperate with the Federal Reserve mandate that we change over to the new system. There's a lot of pressure being exerted right now. Banks are closing here faster than anywhere else in the country. But they are reopening with their own independent state charter. Money is harder to get because they don't lend out as much on the dollar in fractionalized spending. But we think it will make for more stability in the long run. We intend to be self-sufficient. You'll find a lively bartering and trading system here — all kinds of goods and services are traded between people. That's been growing for years. We recognize that it won't be long before we won't be able to buy and sell anything with the rest of the country, and the state is converting as quickly as possible to using materials that can be produced here."

Paulo was fascinated. "Do you think you can do it? Become completely self-sufficient? You're talking about seceding from the union!"

"Only financially. We are the most avid patriots you'll ever find. We love our country, but we won't be slaves.

145

The original colonists were self-sufficient. Our pioneer ancestors were self-sufficient. We've become a little more spoiled than they were with federal programs, but we're still Americans. We've always had an independent streak. We'll do what we have to."

Paulo had relaxed his guard and was thinking about the society Quinn had painted. There was a challenge to it that excited him. Could he make a business thrive here, starting from scratch, what about materials. . . ? He stopped his runaway thoughts. He was crazy. This was Utah, Mormon country. He had no place here.

Tour groups were walking around the temple grounds. Guides were explaining the statues and recounting the Joseph Smith story, which Paulo already knew and had tucked into a nice skeptical place in his mind.

Roy Quinn guided them along, pausing briefly to give a background on the buildings. He gave a short history of the graceful, old-fashioned Assembly Hall with its stained glass windows; the museum; and the tabernacle with its astounding natural acoustics. But his major objective was the modern visitors' center. Paulo kept looking up a the classic temple with its spires rising above him. It was not as spectacular as the Dome of the Rock, or the cathedrals of Europe, or the Buddhist temples of Nepal. But it possessed a singular beauty. It was distinctly American in heritage. It had been built at great sacrifice by American pioneers as a monument of their devotion to their God. It was impossible not to stare up at the soaring spires and the golden, shining angel at the top.

Bishop Quinn spoke to him. "I see you enjoy our temple. It is our pride, I suppose, if we are guilty of pride. This is where we join families together for eternity. Our young people are encouraged to marry here for time and all eternity. And we do baptisms and other sacred ordinance work for the dead here."

He couldn't know that every word was a torture to Paulo. They went into the visitors' center and walked about, looking at the beautiful murals, hearing snatches of conversations about ancient Indians on this continent and pioneers settling the valley. They wound upward on a spiral ramp. The walls were all painted with a dark, night view of the heavens — stars, galaxies, planets. Then they stood before the Christus. The statue was pure white, its

146

head slightly bowed, looking down on them with an expression of love and concern. The hands of the statue were outstretched, beckoning.

"Why don't you go on without me," Paulo said to Cherri. "I think I'll stay here a moment."

He sat on the cushioned bench and gave himself up to the wash of sensations. In Jerusalem he had felt this spirit. Today, it seemed as though this statue might actually speak to him. But what would he say? Paulo asked himself, What would he want with me? I'm just a reprobate, an unfulfilled priest, too weak to live for him even though I crave his love. Depression deepened as he sat there, staring so long at the Christus that the statue seemed alive.

Roy Quinn came back after half an hour. "Do you want to stay longer?" he asked gently.

Paulo looked up, "No. No. I should go."

"You seem troubled. Can I help you?" the older man asked.

"I don't think so. I just don't know what to do next. I have searched for a long time for the answers to my life — what I'm supposed to do with it, who God is, and who I am to him. I guess the key must be understanding myself."

Quinn sat down and put his hand on Paulo's knee. Unerringly he went to the heart of the problem. "I'll answer your questions. Who is God? He is your Heavenly Father. You are his son. It is that simple. No mystery, no complex contradictions. Spiritually, you were born as his child. Physically, you are half divine, for your spirit is immortal and divine, and your body is created in his image. That means he is a man, like you. A Man of Holiness, a Man of Perfection, eternal, omniscient, all powerful. And your Father. Paulo, you have felt his presence, haven't you?"

Paulo nodded yes. The Bishop continued, "There is only one thing preventing you from accepting all that you know — your stubbornness. Like Paul of old, you kick against the pricks. You don't want the LDS Church to be true. Somehow you have been hurt, and you blame it on the Church. Perhaps you even have good cause. The Church is not perfect. The LDS people are not perfect, but the gospel of Jesus Christ is. We are just like you, trying to find out what our Father in Heaven wants us to do, and

147

trying to be strong enough to live for it. You are a blessed man. I felt the strength of your spirit when we first met, and I tell you that the Lord has a great mission for you. But you have to lay aside old hurts and grievances. You have to be humble and meek and search your heart for the truth. The Lord has prompted you many times to accept the truth, but you have held back. You have been miserable and will continue to be until you follow the promptings of the Spirit."

Paulo was amazed to watch the man's face. It had taken on a youthful vitality, a kind of glow. He spoke prophetically, looking into Paulo's heart and mind. A vibration hung between them like electricity.

A tour group came up the ramp and interrupted their communion. The men stood up and walked in silence back to the front door, where Cherri waited.

That night, Paulo said goodnight to Cherri at Bishop Quinn's house and took a bus back to the hotel. He sat alone on the bed in his room, thinking about the day. After an hour, the silence and solitude seemed to close in on him. His mind became more and more cloudy, unable to focus on anything. He looked around almost in a daze. He shook his head, but that didn't help. The room began to seem very small, and he shivered. Even with the heat turned up, he was still cold. He got up and put on his jacket and paced around the room. By now Paulo felt jittery and fragmented and then began to hear voices. They seemed to be down the hall. No, wait. They were behind him! He spun around. No one. Still the voices babbled, and there was laughter, high and shrill. The door rattled. The windows creaked. He heard a tapping like a fingernail on the windowpane. He threw back the curtain. Only blackness. No one was there. Was he a child again, imagining things in the darkness? He felt foolish and went to wash his face in the bathroom. His mind was becoming confused, unable to settle on any one thought. Why was he at the sink with a washcloth? Was he feverish? No. He was cold, in fact.

The more he paced the room, jumping at strange noises, the more he became disoriented. Can't stay here. No room. Too close, too dark. No lights in here. Get out. Get out. Which one is the door. Can't find the door handle. Closet door. No, bathroom door. Get out! Run!

148

Run!

Paulo stumbled through a long hallway, dimly aware of a green exit sign. He pushed his way out, breathing heavily now. He stood still a moment, looking up, trying to catch a deep breath. Were there stars? He didn't see them. City lights seemed foggy and far away. He had withdrawn from physical surroundings and curled up into a tiny ball in the center of his soul. And he was hurting. That small core was aching and stinging and radiating a bone-chilling misery throughout him. His breath was short and difficult. He could hardly see the sidewalk beneath him, and he stumbled like a drunkard crossing the street. But something propelled him onward.

Paulo looked up. There was no light in the universe, only darkness. He felt as though he were going blind, and he began to panic. Terror seized him. He wiped his eyes but it didn't help. A dark veil clouded his vision, and the panic grew. Forever sightless, forever dark! Forever lost and alone. Oh, the loneliness! It crushed him. Always, always alone. No love, no kindness, no one to care, no one to be with, no soul to touch his own. Alone forever. Shut off from every other spirit. No sound, no voice, no human touch. A vast expanse of empty blackness, and he the only consciousness! Charlotte, where are you now? his mind called out to her. Come now, come now. Now is when I need you most!

Fear and anguish wrenched a deep cry of pain from him and threw him backward against a wall. Paulo hung there almost suspended, pinned against the wall by a black force and pain too great for him to bear. His hands gripped the stones as he tried to keep from falling to his knees. Suffering with an intensity he had never before known, he writhed, trying to draw breath, afraid of dying, afraid of living. Finally, as he lay pressed against the wall in agony, some small voice inside him cried out, "O thou Jesus, Son of God, deliver me!"

Searing pain shot through his body. A high screeching pierced his ears. An unseen force attacked him until he was convulsed with agony. He shook uncontrollably and folded his body against the pain. He felt space begin to turn about him and the blackness suffocate him. Still he cried again from the furthest depths of his soul, "O God, have pity on me. I die! I die!"

149

Again his body was racked with pain, contorting him. His teeth were chattering. He was wrenched by the grip of some terrible thing that shook him like a rag doll. And a sense of horrible anger and wickedness stunned his mind. He was every murderer, every hateful sinner, controlled by murderous anger and hatred. It twisted his mind and spirit for what seemed an eternity, until he was sickened with lusty thirst for blood. After a time it was followed by weakness, then a slackening of the grip it had on his soul. In that weakness he called again from his heart, "Father, please help me. And I will be thy son."

There was a sudden tightening of terrible pain and despair, like the final twist of a great, torturous screw. He shook in the spasms of the horrible wrenching. . . and then, then it was gone. The fear and the pain, the despair and agony ebbed from him like water. He could almost see it go, flooding from his fingertips and shoes, and he was left weak and tired. But free! He was free and he was alive; just a moment before, he had been painfully close to death. Paulo's mind was stunned with the experience. It would take a long time to search through what had happened and to understand it. One thing he understood — the monstrous force had been replaced with the most tender serenity. Exhaustion left him weak in body, but his spirit seemed to be covered with a soft, warm blanket. He experienced a sense of benediction as sweet as the pain had been bitter.

Looking up, he saw the top of a gray wall, and over the top rose the glowing spires of the temple. A light rain was falling. He became aware that his face was wet — rain or tears, he didn't know. No one was on the sidewalk, and only a few cars passed on the adjacent street. A rush of warmth through his body counteracted the spring rains, and he lifted his face to the sky for the baptism of the heavens.

Paulo sat on the sidewalk, resting against the wall for several minutes. He was still trembling from the trauma he had been through, but he was no longer afraid. Then, like a sleepwalker, he walked around the dark corner and up the sidewalk to the gates of Temple Square. A guard was just locking up the visitors' center, but seeing his face and responding to the desperation in his voice, the man opened back up for him.

He went straight to the Christus and knelt. Tears flooded his cheeks, sobs broke from his chest, and total submission filled him. I have sinned, he confessed before the Champion of sinners. I have refused to see. I have refused to hear. I have wanted the truth to be my own way. Forgive me, O Lord. Forgive me and I will be yours. Without you, my life is empty. Without you, I wander. I wander and am never filled. No more — I promise you; I will kick against the pricks no more.

The next day he walked to the Church Administration Building to request baptism. On the steps, he saw the blonde hair, broad shoulders, and characteristic white shirt of David ben Cohen.

Sheilah and Bridget sat poring over the genealogy records and letters on the dining-room table. Years ago, Sheilah had found in her grandmother's trunk a yellow receipt for a casket. For years, it had meant nothing to Sheilah, but two months ago in the genealogy library in Salt Lake City, as she was studying the microfiche records for St. Louis, Missouri, she came upon a household of women. In 1882, the head of the house was listed as Elberta Longstroth, and numbered under her was Victoria Palmerly, Susanna Peterson, and Annie Peterson, a girl of fourteen. The names seemed to stand out in bold relief before her eyes. She paused and looked at the names for several minutes but then decided the boldness must be her imagination and turned the film. But curiosity wouldn't let go. She turned back. Again the names seemed twice the size of the others.

I wonder who they are, she thought. I haven't any relatives by those names. She tried to turn the handle, but the film was stuck. It wouldn't turn. At last, she took out a pencil and copied the names. When she finished, she tried the handle of the microfilm machine. It turned easily.

At home, she went straight to her old trunk and at the bottom found the yellow receipt. Susanna Peterson's casket was paid for by Elberta Longstroth. Why would Grace have this receipt? It was dated 1886. Annie, Grace's mother, would have been eighteen. She looked again at the names she had copied. Elberta, Susanna, and Annie. Annie

Peterson, Annie Partridge. A glimmer of hope began. On the receipt was faintly written, "Body shipped to Camilla Co., Iowa."

She had dashed off a letter to the clerk of the court in Camilla County. Today she had received her verification and more. This clerk was also a genealogy buff and read of Sheilah's search with interest. She had driven to the site of the grave and photographed the headstone. The photograph clearly showed "Susanna Peterson, died September 21, 1886." Underneath it was written in small letters, "Charlotte O'Neill Boughtman." Sheilah could scarcely believe her eyes. She held the picture close to her heart and cried. Charlotte had haunted her for years like a familiar ghost. Sheilah had even fancied hearing her great-great-grandmother's spirit call her at times. Now, here it was, the information necessary for Charlotte's work. She called Bridget, and her friend came right over. They laid out the receipt, the court records, the photograph, and the lovely letter the clerk had sent her.

"I can't believe it! I have waited so long. I can't believe that I can really do Charlotte's work at last. Look at the picture, Bridget!" and she pointed to the painting on the far wall. "That's Charlotte! That's my grandmother! Isn't she beautiful? She is waiting for this too. I know it. I've felt her prodding me, trying to get me to hurry. Why in the world did she take the name Peterson — Susanna Peterson? Her married name was Boughtman! I never knew that. Peterson can't even be a married name, or she wouldn't have taken a different first name. What a puzzle it all is."

She walked over to the portrait. "I'll have you baptized properly, and I'll do the work for you myself," she promised Charlotte. Turning back to Bridget, Shielah sat down at the table.

"You said you dreamed about her one night." Bridget said.

"I did. Only it was so real, I'm not sure it was a dream. But I was just a little girl, about ten, and I was sitting on a hillside watching a fire. I looked up and saw this woman walking across the hillside to me. She was wearing a long, old-fashioned dress, and she had luscious reddish-gold hair. She sat beside me and comforted me for a long time. I knew it was Charlotte. And you know something else

152

that I had forgotten until just now? Paulo recognized Charlotte. He saw this picture once and wanted to know all about her. He said he had dreamed about a woman who looked just like this. Isn't that funny?"

Bridget studied her friend. "Do you think you'll ever hear from him again?"

Sheilah's eyes were steady. "No. It's over. I've never looked back."

"Never?" Bridget asked. "Never think about him? That's unusual. Sometimes I still remember old boy friends. And you loved him so much."

"I did. No one knows how much. But I knew he'd pull me away from the Church. So, I don't think about him. I try very hard not to."

"It's probably just as well," Bridget said. "Why do you think it happened, meeting him, falling in love, having to choose between him and Stephen?"

"I don't know. But I learned a lot from him. He is the one who really taught me about forgiveness. It was the greatest lesson of my life. I owe a lot to him. I hope he's happy."

Cherri took the little kitchenette motel room from Ida McCormick. Bishop Quinn had found her an interview for a teaching job in the crowded, pre-fab building that served as school quickly erected for the influx of new families. It was little more than army quonset huts. The insulation was bad, the rooms small and drab, but the children were bright and fun to be with. Cherri and Jim had not had children. He wasn't interested. Now she found herself charmed by the beautiful young faces before her. They were so desperate for help that she started the very day they hired her, which was the same day she moved into her motel room. She taught not only art but general math, English, music, and social studies. With no visual aids and no experience, she had a lot of at-home preparation. She decided to decorate the room with paintings — the children's and her own.

One Saturday she put on her hiking shoes, and took her artist's supplies and a sack lunch. She headed into the hills to paint. The day was glorious. It was May. The mountains were greening for summer. She sang as she walked along, never minding that she was frequently off key.

She had called Jim when she had found her place. It had been an unsatisfying talk. He was remote, disinterested in her adventure. All he wanted to know was when she was coming back. She wanted to tell him the truth, "never." But she just said, "Not for a while. Won't you come? Come just for a visit. You might be surprised and find out you like it."

"Not me," he replied. "I'm no mountain man. Just a city boy. When you get ready to come home, just let me know. I'm awfully lonesome without you."

She was lonely without him, too. His silly grin still made her smile. She even missed the teasing. It would be a while before she made new friends and had someone to talk to. But today, she was not lonely. Today, she was next to heaven. It was perfectly quiet, and the solitude was inviting. She was not afraid here. The mountains carried no sense of threat as the city did. She sat down to sketch the opposite mountain with the clouds puffing up behind it.

Up the hillside and behind some evergreens, Buck sat talking with Stephen. They had ward business to discuss, and it was too nice a day to do it in the bishop's office. Stephen was the bishop of the ward, wrestling with the same people problems that all the Utah bishops now had — not enough housing, not enough jobs. He had called Buck as his counselor. The friendship between the two men was stronger than ever, since they shared spiritual experiences as well as sleeve-rolling work.

"Who's that?" Buck pointed curiously.

"Looks like someone painting. I don't blame her," Stephen said. "I wish I were an artist sometimes."

They sat idly watching Cherri for a few minutes. She was obviously doing the opposite mountain. After a while, Buck said, "Let's go see her stuff. Maybe it's good. Maybe I can get a free picture if I play my cards right." And he grinned mischievously.

They scrambled down the slope. Rocks started rolling and skipping as their shoes knocked them loose. Cherri glanced over her shoulder. Two men were coming toward her in a hurry. She jumped to her feet, fear choking her. Her palette tumbled to the ground and skidded a few feet.

154

She grabbed at her canvas, hoping to salvage it, but in her haste she knocked it down too. She was almost tied in knots, she was so frightened. They were coming fast. Her movements were quick and confused. Leaving her materials behind, she ran down the rugged hillside toward the trail at the bottom. Panic took her breath away.

"Hey, wait a minute," Buck called out. "We're not going to hurt you. Wait!"

But Cherri couldn't hear the words. She only knew that he was shouting at her and quickly catching up. Everything had changed now. The May sunshine had darkened. Memories of shouts and a long alley blacked out the world around her. Terrified, she ran faster, taking great steps as she leaped over rocks in her way. But the pace was too fast. She stumbled and fell, wrenching her ankle. She was shaking and wide-eyed when they reached her.

"Here, let me help you. I'm sure sorry. We didn't mean to scare you off. We just wanted to see what you were painting. Are you hurt?"

She shook her head, not daring to look up at them. Her voice was shaky as she protested. "No. No, I'm not hurt. Please leave me alone."

Stephen had stopped to pick up her canvas and held it out to her. "Here you go. Sorry. I guess we scared you, running like a couple of moose down the hill." He knelt beside her. "That ankle doesn't look good. I think you hurt it."

She shook her head, desperate to keep them from knowing she was helpless. "No. It's okay. Just leave me alone, please, please!"

Stephen looked up at Buck. They both sensed she was terribly frightened.

"Looks like a good picture," Buck said lamely. "I feel like a fool scaring you to death. Let us help you back up to your spot and maybe you can still finish this."

Cherri looked up at him. Slowly the air was clearing and she became aware of her real surroundings. These were not young Cuban toughs. These men were dressed in slacks and pullover shirts, and they were not threatening her. Her panic began to subside. The brown-haired man reached down to help her up. Now she had to acknowledge to herself — and them — that her ankle really was hurt.

She had scarcely been aware of the pain before, but now it was very sharp. Cherri tried to get up by herself. Her head scarf slipped down around her shoulders, and shiny brown hair swung down around her face.

Stephen smiled reassuringly, "Looks like you might need some help after all. I'm Bishop Gailbraith. This jerk over here who hollered at you and scared you to death is Buck Sorensen. I'm going to have to speak severely to him. This is no way to approach a lady."

Cherri could see the good-humored kindness in his face. She felt silly. She glanced at Buck. Obviously, they were friends. Obviously, she had overreacted.

"No," she said. It's my own fault. You startled me, that's all. I didn't think. I just ran like a kid, spooky in the dark."

Buck could see she was wincing. "You think it might be broken?"

"Oh, no. I'm sure not."

"Let me take a look. I'm very good with things broken — arms, legs, plates, promises, anything at all."

She smiled as he hoped she would, and he knelt and touched her ankle. His fingers probed gently, and she jerked back. He stood up. "Probably not broken if you can step on it. But it's going to swell up. I hope you're not going anywhere important tonight. You'll need to keep that elevated and iced."

Stephen teased him. "Watch it, Buck. You make it sound like a bottle of wine."

"Looks like you're going to have to accept our help," Buck prodded her. "I don't think you'll make it down the hill without it. Where's your car?"

"I . . . I don't have one. I walked. I just moved into the Valley. Just last week."

"Where are you from?"

"New York."

"Good decision." Buck grinned.

"I think so too." Cherri had to look up at him. He had brown eyes, laughing and bold, with lashes too long for any man. Brown hair had fallen across his forehead and gave him a rakish appearance. She found herself smiling at him. It was impossible not to.

Stephen walked back up the hillside, collected her materials, and rejoined them. They each put an arm under

156

hers and half-carried her down the mountain. They helped her into the back seat and drove her home.

Buck made her comfortable with her foot propped up. Stephen made an ice pack for her. When Buck brought some hot chocolate for her to drink, he sat down beside her.

"Well, we did a good job of spoiling your day and we don't even know your name."

"It's Cherri. Cherri Polanski."

"Will you forgive us?" he asked, only half contrite.

"I'm not sure you deserve it." She cocked her head and teased him back now.

"I don't. I never have. Peck's bad boy, Dad used to call me. But I promise I won't run at you and wave my arms and holler anymore." He raised his hand. "Boy Scout's honor. Now, are you going to be all right here alone?"

"I'll be fine. My ankle is feeling better already."

"If you need any help — groceries, butter, fetch and carry, anything, just let me know. I do penance well. I'm very practiced."

She couldn't resist his smile. "I'll remember that. But I think I'll be all right."

Buck stood up. Stephen had already gone out. Buck looked down on her shiny, smooth hair and into wide green eyes, slanted just a little. Suddenly, he was lost for words. He grew self-conscious. It had been a long time since he had reacted so much to a woman. Bridget was his only love. But there was a kittenish, adorable quality about this woman. He pushed back his hair. "Guess I'll go then. Good-bye."

"Good-bye," she said, smiling up at him.

Their awkwardness hung in the air. "Maybe I'll see you sometime." he said.

"It's a small town. Maybe."

She still smiled at him, very much like a waif just in from the cold. A rush of protectiveness came over him, and he realized he didn't want to leave. He wanted to stay and learn everything about Cherri Polanski.

"Well, good-bye. I'll see you." He opened the door and went out with the whisper of her name on his lips.

The day Paulo was baptized, an earthquake shook the

great San Andreas fault. It started in Canada and traveled down the California coast, jumped central America, and sliced South America like a huge knife. Satellite pictures were horrifying. The dead littered the city streets. Cities lay smoldering under massive tons of concrete; fires ran rampant; mountains had slipped and buried wealthy Americans and poor Chileans alike. Pictures of the destruction, taken from army relief planes, were akin to photos taken in Germany after the war. They also showed the gigantic, jagged trough cut through the earth's crust when the platelets of the continent slid. Thousands of unwary Americans had built homes right down to the edge of the ocean. These simply disappeared in the tidal waves that scoured the coastal cities, flinging ships up onto dry land and beating the cities with their own debris. National relief began immediately in America. In South America, there was little relief. Tremors continued for weeks. It was a natural disaster of worldwide proportions.

Paulo and David had spent a week together. David was in Utah for a particular purpose. He was on special assignment from Prime Minister Schleger to study the Mormon temples. His was to be the delicate job of preparing to build a Jewish temple — on Mount Moriah. The ancient scripture spelled out the dimensions of the temple, the courtyards, even the rooms. But there were some rooms for which they did not know the purpose.

David's letter from Schleger took him right into the office of the president of LDS Church. He didn't know exactly what he had expected — perhaps the white, flowing ceremonial robes of a pope. He knew this man was recognized by his church as a prophet of God. But the Mormon prophet was dressed in a dark business suit with a white shirt and tie. He was a gentle man about eighty years old. His white hair was thinning, but his handshake was solid and firm. Graciousness seemed natural to him.

He merely glanced at the letter and placed it carefully aside. "Mr. Cohen, I'm Jesse Taylor. I hope I can be of some help to you."

"I'm not sure exactly what I need to learn from you, if anything. But you are the only ones who build temples at all like the Torah describes. I hope to tour one of them and discuss the practical purposes. Our directions in the scriptures are merely measurements, with little said about

158

the purpose. We are willing to build it as the Lord has commanded, but then what, we're not sure."

President Taylor leaned back in his chair, his old, wise eyes crinkled in gentle amusement. He answered, "We could tell you a lot. You may not accept everything we say, but you'll find it interesting. We've been watching you in Israel with great interest. We know, for instance, that your building materials are all ready, and that only the knotty problem of the Dome of the Rock stands in your way."

"That's right. The Dome is a problem. Even if it weren't the Moslem holy mosque, we'd be reluctant to tear down such a beautiful edifice. It is the focal point of all Jerusalem. I'm still not sure how we will solve the problem. Maybe Jehovah will solve it for us. He has a way of doing that."

The older man was curious. "Tell me a little about yourself. You're a young man to have such a heavy task laid on you. Are you Israeli born? What is your heritage?"

"I guess youth is no protection." David smiled. "I'm not really sure how I came to be in government. Yes, I am Israeli born. I never suffered as many of my people did. Before the university, I served in our army as all of us do. Then after college, my father's friend, Prime Minister Schleger, asked me to be his aide. One assignment led to another. He had to make me a member of his cabinet to have a good excuse to give me so much work. Now, here I am. I'm not sure I like the job."

The president chuckled. "I don't blame you. It will take another Solomon to unravel this problem. Well, we'll do what we can to help you. You do understand, of course, that our temples are used for Christian ordinances. Jesus Christ is our focus. We baptize in his name, we pray in his name, our sacred ordinances all point to him."

"I thought as much. Tell me, why do you focus so much on him? I know you consider Jesus divine. But, after all, he only claimed to be the son of God, not God himself."

The prophet's eyes were bright and intense as they watched the face of the handsome young Jew. "He is Jehovah, the God you worship. It was Christ who spoke to your fathers. It was Christ who created this world, under his eternal Father's direction. And when the world is destroyed, it will be for this reason — that mankind has not honored their God. That is the great sin of the world — the disrespect, the blasphemy of our own Creator."

David Cohen held his gaze. "He claimed only to be the Messiah, not the Creator."

"Who could deliver that which he had not first created? And who would create a world and not redeem it? His work would then be lost. Christ was the only one who could redeem it eternally, for he was the one who created it. It is completely consistent with your law."

David watched the older man with quickened interest. He saw the prophetic quality come suddenly to the man. Power had come into his voice, the power of conviction, and the power to convince. When he spoke of Christ, all equivocations were stripped away. Only pure logic and principle remained.

Then President Taylor relaxed. "I have arranged a meeting with our temple building committee for you tomorrow. You'll be able to see our plans, our dimensions, and our designs, and you'll be able to ask anything you want to about them."

"Thank you. Thank you very much."

"My counselors and I would be very glad if you'd join us for dinner tonight," the older man offered. "It's not every day we get to meet the temple builder of Jerusalem."

David stood to go. President Taylor walked with him to the door, his hand on the younger man's shoulder. "Thank you, but no," David said. "I have a friend here. In fact, I was unaware that he was even in Utah, but I met him only an hour ago in front of your building. Paulo D'Agosta and I have been friends for three years. We toured Jerusalem together, and now it looks like we will tour Salt Lake together. I think he is your newest convert, and I am happy for him. I admire your principles, even though I'm Jewish instead of Christian."

Slightly stooped, the once-tall frame of the elderly prophet was almost the same height as the younger man. Warmth from his hands seemed to penetrate David's shoulder. His eyes were once more amused and kind. "You are from Judah, we are from Ephraim. The Lord is gathering the house of Israel in many ways." He cocked his head and asked, "What is your full name?"

Curiously, David answered, "David Cyrus ben Cohen."

"Such a heritage! A Levite, and from the stem of

Jesse." President Taylor smiled broadly. "David and Jesse — we make a good team."

David shook his hand warmly, almost regretting that he must leave. But there was always tomorrow.

Paulo waited downstairs, absorbed in reading the Book of Mormon he had obtained from the visitors' center. He looked up. David looked older, more mature than three years ago in Jerusalem. And he was more reflective.

They had so much to talk about, so much to tell each other, and when the time was right, Paulo wanted to take him to the Christus. Unquestionably, David must be here for his baptism.

They spent the rest of the afternoon and night talking. Dinner was mechanical. They discussed world events, the earthquake, the nuclear testing in China, the treaty with the Arabs, the continued terrorist attacks, the relations between the Soviet Union and the United States, and, most of all, the World Wide Monetary System. Starvation was stalking the world. The news media carried hundreds of pictures and reports on the hunger in Africa, India, even in Russia, as the early winter and bitter cold had stolen their crops and destroyed their wheat.

"You might be interested to know," Paulo said, "that I spoke to Omar a couple of months ago. He has invited me to come back to Riyadh. He says he wants me to ride in the camel races."

"That I would like to see. Do you think they would stone a Jew?"

"You could always pass for a Christian," Paulo kidded.

"It might not be such a far stretch. That is one of my problems. My mind is too open. I should be like Schleger, decisive and committed to my own way. Instead, I see all sides of a question, and that can be confusing."

"Yes, but it is a better trait. That is why Omar trusted you."

"Speaking of friends," David brightened. "I have met two of yours. Isaac Zimmerman has joined us in the cabinet, and has brought with him his very pretty niece, Rachael."

Paulo was taken aback. "Rachael, in Israel?"

"Yes. And apparently to stay. It wasn't hard to talk her into it. She is very American, but she found she was also very much a Jew. Like you, she was captured by the

161

magic of Jerusalem, and now she is our prisoner."

Paulo mulled that over. "I hope she finds what she is looking for. I think I have found mine. I want her to be happy."

"So do I." Paulo looked at David. The younger man was grinning broadly. "So, tell me. You think you will stay in Salt Lake?"

"Back up just a minute! Let's not change the subject so fast. You sound as though you personally intend to see that Rachael is happy."

"I'm trying."

"Oh, you are?" Paulo's eyebrows were raised.

"Government doesn't leave much time for personal life. I haven't thought too much about it until now. But my mother is reminding me of the old customs. A man must marry. A grandmother has a right to grandchildren."

"You sound like me." Paulo laughed. "That's my story."

David clapped a hand over Paulo's arm. "Well, my friend, you ought to listen. Marriage cannot be all bad. Look at all the people who have tried it."

"And tried it. And tried it."

"For me, only once," David said with conviction.

"Me too. Can you believe I'm still looking for the right one?"

"You are too choosy. I consider myself lucky you didn't choose Rachael."

"She was too young for me."

"And too old for me, so she says. But I am trying to convince her otherwise. You see, I'm quite mature for my age." He was trying to hold back a mischievous smile.

"Get out! Mature? You're just in love." Then Paulo sobered. "Are you in love with Rachael Feldman?"

David's smile disappeared also. "I think I am. Do I have your blessing?"

Paulo nodded his head soberly. "You do."

In the next three days, David pored over the temple plans with thoroughness, pointing out similarities between his scriptural mandate and the Mormon construction. He talked with the architects about materials, construction time, stress factors of the buildings, and foundation problems on the mountainside. When David had asked every technical question he had, he sat back and mused over all his information. Unconsciously, he spoke aloud,

162

wondering. "But for what purpose? It would be easier if I knew that."

President Taylor stood in the back of the room. He gave the answer. "Isaiah said the Lord will come suddenly to his temple. That is the purpose. You are building it for him."

It was the middle of May, and Paulo asked to be baptized in a mountain stream. He had no regular meeting house. He had no bishop. Roy Quinn agreed to baptize him in the Provo River in Kamas. They dammed it off the day before, and by the morning of his baptism, the cold mountain water was deep enough for the two men. Paulo and Bishop Quinn picked up Cherri. Cherri was ecstatic over his conversion. He had called her and told her about his conversion night. She was amazed. She had not struggled so for a testimony. It had been as natural as breathing for her. Her greatest struggle had come after, in deciding to come here.

Just a few people attended Paulo's baptism — Cherri, David, Roy Quinn, Albert Swensen — a portly, middle-aged guide from Temple Square who had answered Paulo's questions — and President Jesse Taylor with his first counselor, Elias Stark.

Paulo stepped down into the water. It stung his feet and legs with its chill. But he was not cold. He looked up. The sun shone warmly through the newly greened cottonwood and aspen trees. Birds were trilling back and forth with the joy of living on a bright spring day. When he held out his hand to help President Snow into the water, Paulo's face shone as with a bright light. Looking at him, David Cohen recognized the immense capacity for devotion that his friend had. Years seemed to lift from his face. He seemed almost a young man again. Cherri saw it too and was amazed. She had always thought Paulo D'Agosta exceptionally handsome, but now his physical beauty was overshadowed by his radiance. Quick tears sprang to her eyes. This was the light of Christ.

Roy Quinn said in a strong voice, "I baptize you in the name of the Father and of the Son and of the Holy Ghost." He leaned forward, swiftly plunging Paulo under the icy water. The two men stood up shaking. Paulo was dripping

163

wet and laughing. He put his arms around the older man, and they stood together in a wet embrace. Then they walked back up on the bank, and Paulo turned to his other friends. Cherri ran forward and hugged him hard. David came next and put both hands on his friend's shoulders. Solemnly, he kissed one cheek then the other. Then they embraced for several minutes. David could feel Paulo shaking, but he knew it was not because of the cold. In fact, his body was far from cold. It was warm, very warm. The tour guide shook his hand vigorously and hugged him briefly.

President Taylor had watched all of it with satisfaction and a growing sense of something important happening. He looked frequently toward the sun overhead. He looked back to the man's face. Paulo D'Agosta seemed to be shining with a very perceptible light. A bulb might have been lit within his skull. And the President could feel a vibration in the air, radiating from the man. Steadily, he looked at Paulo. Silently, he prayed to understand. Then an inward vision broke before him. He saw two temples rising. One was in the old world, and one was in the new. Now he understood. He embraced Paulo, looking full into his eyes. This was not a young man. He had come to the gospel of Jesus Christ after some price. He was a mature man in his middle years, and Taylor knew his devotion was deep and rich. He was a man who had loved God all his life and had only just discovered the religious potential within him.

President Taylor said softly, "I wish to bless you, and confirm you."

Paulo knelt on the grassy bank of the river. His clothing was still damp, but he was unaware. The sun shone down on his head and warmed him. Then President Taylor placed his hands on Paulo's head and began the confirmation. "Receive the Holy Ghost." It was a commandment, and it was instantly fulfilled. The Holy Spirit entered his soul and filled the empty places that had so long been aching. Then President Taylor looked up. David ben Cohen stood beside him watching. The prophet knew his thoughts and placed one hand on the younger man's head. "There is also a blessing for you."

Then the white-haired prophet began to tell his vision. With one hand on Paulo's head, he blessed him to fulfill

164

the work of the last days — the building of the temple in the New Jerusalem. With his other hand on David's head, he blessed him to fulfill the work of the ancient scriptures — the building of the temple in old Jerusalem. Power drained from his hands and entered the souls of both men, and the Holy Spirit witnessed to both hearts; they were the Lord's anointed!

*"For as in Adam all die, even so in Christ shall
all be made alive. Else what shall they do
which are baptized for the dead, if the dead
rise not at all? why are they then baptized for
the dead?"*
(1 Corinthians 15:19-20, 22, 29.)

Chapter Eight

Summer in Kamas, Utah, was lazy. School was out,
and Cherri had only her painting to keep her busy. She
grew to consider herself a loner, and that was unusual for
her. She had always been a social person. Here, activities
were family oriented, though the Church tried to help the
divorcees and singles with various activities. So,
consequently, when the ward got together for a dinner or
a picnic, she usually sat next to one of her Sunday School
girls. That was easy to do; they all clustered around her,
and she delighted them by drawing their portraits. One of
the few women she did relate to was Shielah Gailbraith.

Shielah had heard about her twisted ankle and had
brought a hot dinner to her, though Cherri had protested.
Shielah had grown up a very quiet, withdrawn girl because
she had been hurt by life as Cherri had been. At ten years
old, Shielah had witnessed the destruction of her home by
fire — and the death of her parents. It had left her very
alone and frightened. She recognized the same
vulnerabilities in another soul and reached out to comfort.

Shielah caught Cherri one day sitting on the grass in
front of the motel, sketching a dilapidated, ancient tractor
in an adjacent field. The relic sported a jaunty young boy
on its seat. "Did you know Buck Sorensen was my
brother? He says you're a terrific artist."

167

"You don't look at all alike."

"No, not much I guess. Family tradition says there are two strains in our family, dark and light. I'd like to see your art sometime."

"I'm almost finished with this. You can look through it if you like, but I warn you, your brother exaggerates."

Shielah turned the pages slowly. "I don't think so. These are wonderful. There's Buck! Cherri, you captured it all in the eyes and the jawline. It's so . . . so . . . better than real!"

"Well, thanks. Would you like that one of your brother?"

"Oh, yes — if you'd part with it."

"Sure. It's good to make a friend."

Shielah put her hand over Cherri's, "I think so too. Can I come watch you draw sometime?"

"I'd like that."

Shielah rose to go. "Oh, Buck said to tell you that you're doing a great job on the scenery for the ward play."

"Your brother is very nice," Cherri said. "Is he always so friendly to everyone?"

Shielah laughed. "Almost. He's been like that ever since I can remember. Buck is everyone's friend — never meets a stranger."

Cherri could see that in the brief encounter they had had. But she couldn't afford a friendship with a man like Buck Sorensen. He was too appealing. She guessed he was as old as Jim, but mature in a way Jim was not. More than anything, Buck had a quality that invited immediate intimacy. It was what she needed most and what she feared most. She was still very much married. Cherri promised herself she would never be alone with Buck Sorensen. It was the mouth and the eyes — that funny, tender smile. There, she had it right now. Quickly, she sketched in the hair and the narrow nostrils, then looked up from her sketch pad and, for no reason, blushed.

Several weeks later, she was working on scenery and lighting for the ward play.

Buck stayed away from Cherri, deliberately disciplining himself, until one night during play rehearsal he threw restraint to the winds and walked around the stage and found her at the lighting box.

"So, they got you in up to your ankles. I'm not

surprised."

"Hi," Cherri responded, glancing quickly at him, then right back to the switches.

"Hi yourself. I haven't seen much of you lately. You're hard to catch. Don't teachers stay after school anymore?"

"Nope. Too busy painting scenery."

"Shielah showed me your sketch. I'd like to see more."

Cherri deliberately kept her face turned away so she couldn't look into his eyes. He brushed against her elbow, and she was intensely aware of a tingling sensation running through her. This was silly, she told herself. She was thirty-five years old and had no business being excited by any man besides her own husband. She closed her eyes and called Jim's face to mind. All she saw was Buck's laughing eyes.

"Could I see your work sometime?"

"Sure, sometime,.." she replied haltingly. "Do you draw?"

"Me!" he laughed, "No. Not at all. What talent I have could be put under your fingernail."

"I don't believe it."

"It's true."

Behind the heavy curtains, they stood talking in the dim light. There was silence for a moment while she kept one eye on the director and switched on the red and yellow lights on cue.

"Have you had a chance to do much painting? Are you into oils?" Buck asked after the pause.

"A little. Actually I mostly wander around, daydreaming or soaking up the sun."

"What a life. Wish I could join you. I could use a little daydreaming."

She dared a glance at him. "Working too hard?"

"No, just not playing enough."

After a minute, he asked, "Where do you wander, little girl?"

She kept her eyes studiously on the director out front. "Oh, everywhere, I guess."

"Not a very informative answer."

She shrugged.

"Hey, Cherri Polanski, have I done something to offend you? I thought we were friends. Was I wrong? You won't give me the time of day."

169

She answered him quickly, though still not meeting his eyes, "Oh no, you haven't done anything. We're still friends. You saved my ankle once, you know."

He put his hand on her shoulder and turned her to him. "Then how about looking at me when we talk."

Cherri was not given to blushing, but she did then. Even in the semi-darkness, he knew her face had turned color, and she was very uncomfortable, "I, uh, well, I can't. I'm supposed to be running the lights."

"That's an excuse. You look right past me every time we meet."

"I . . . I don't mean to. That's one of my faults — being shy, I mean." She looked up at him then, and when their eyes met, neither of them could look away. Neither could say what they really felt. Both saw the truth plainly, and both knew the intense attraction was impossible. This time it was Buck who looked away, and moved away — afraid of a powerful impulse to take her in his arms.

"Good night, Cherri." He backed away.

"Good night, my friend."

The next night, Buck proposed a trip to Bridget — a trip to Hawaii, her home. They had met there, twenty-three years before and married in the Hawaiian temple.

"Come on, Honey. We deserve a vacation. It's been a long time, and I . . . well, I need it. Shielah will keep the kids,I'm sure. We'll just go for a week."

"They'd hate us if we didn't take them too. We couldn't go off and leave them."

"Sure we could. They'd be disappointed, but their day will come, and we need a vacation."

"Can we fly without the WWMS number on our hands?"

"Probably not for much longer. It will soon be mandatory nationwide, but right now they are still accepting cash. That's why I think we should go now. Even my gold coins won't be accepted outside Utah beyond the end of the year."

Bridget smiled playfully at him. "Who knows, maybe you'll never get me back here, if we go."

"Listen, I dragged you off once, I can do it again."

They planned a vacation for the last week in August. The vacation was more than either of them hoped for. Just visiting their favorite spots would have been enough. They went surfing three days and spent almost every night with parents or old friends. The day before they left, they arranged to spend the morning with Bridget's parents, Thelma and Donald, in the temple.

The temple brought back time-sweetened memories of their wedding. This time, they were chosen to be witnesses in their session. As they knelt at the altar, Buck kept his eyes on his wife's face. She was still the lovely, dark-eyed girl he had fallen in love with many years ago. Bridget had always been first class, and as she had grown in maturity, her graciousness was almost queenly. Soft-spoken, sweet-tempered, gentle even with his faults, she was truly everything a woman should be. Over the altar, their hands clasped in strong affirmation of all their temple vows, their hearts and souls were united as never before. All conflicting emotions that had plagued Buck recently were swept away by a confirmation of the Holy Spirit that this soft and loving woman at his side was his eternal mate. Love for her flooded his whole soul as they knelt side by side. He wanted to shout and laugh for joy. He looked at her and saw not just the physical person he knew, but also a soft, filmy, radiant shadow, as though it were superimposed on her body. The testimony of eternal sealing was burned upon his mind.

That night, he took her in his arms and stroked her dark hair. She held him close and murmured love words in his ear. After a long while, he asked, "Do you know what happened in the temple today?"

She was careful. "I'm not sure what you mean."

"Didn't you feel what I felt?"

"Do you mean at the altar?"

"Yes."

"It was very special. I've never felt the Spirit so strong."

"Did it tell you anything?"

She leaned away from him and looked him directly in the eye. "I'm not sure I'm supposed to talk about it."

"I know, and we shouldn't to anyone else. But I think we should both know that we know."

A soft smile started, then spread until her whole face was alive. She ventured, "The Spirit told me that our marriage is sealed before God and you are mine forever. Just think, stuck with me for eternity."

Buck pressed her fiercely to him. He choked out,

"That's just what it told me. I saw your spirit, Bridgie! I saw you — the real essence of you, superimposed on your body. You were a queen, my queen. I love you — only you," he vowed. And at that moment, it was true.

Weeks later in his mountain home, Buck lay wide awake at 2:25 a.m. Bridget was sound asleep beside him, one arm flung back behind her head. Occasionally he looked at her, asleep and breathing deeply. He reached out and picked up one heavy strand of hair, rubbing it gently between his fingers, then lifting it to his lips. As he studied that face, so familiar now, another face glazed over his mind's eye, and he lay back against the pillow.

It was Cherri's face, small-boned and delicate, with her green eyes and waif-like quality. He had awakened from a deep sleep and a disturbing dream. In his dream, he was again in the temple kneeling beside Bridget, but now Cherri was led into the room by a temple worker. She knelt on the other side of him and smiled through a haze of brilliant light. He took her hand and heard the officiator's voice, "Sealed for time and all eternity." Electricity seemed to jolt his body, and he was instantly awake. Now he lay still, quietly and frighteningly alone with that thought. The realization of all it implied made him plead with God to take it away. Yes, he had been playing with flirtation. He was abjectly contrite. He vowed in the darkness to put all thoughts of Cherri away. No sooner did he begin that vow than the same feeling of electricity drove its force through him. A profound touching of spirits overpowered him and seemed to blend Cherri's spirit with his very soul. His dream returned vividly to his mind, and again he saw Bridget beside him on his right hand and Cherri shyly standing on his left.

It was daybreak before Buck slept again. He awoke with a heavy heart and spent the morning helping Bridget around the house. He had been retyping a treatise on archaeology in preparation for the new school year, but that could wait. He was unusually tender and stopped Bridget several times just to nuzzle her. He stringently allowed no thought of Cherri to intrude on that day with his wife.

The next day, Cherri was walking home at five o'clock.

He saw her a block away. She had a bunch of posters under her arm and a small brown kit with her art supplies. Dressed simply in jeans and a T-shirt, she looked almost like a teenager. He parked the car at the curb and got out just a little ahead of her.

They stood looking at each other for a minute. He looked down first, then asked, "Whatcha got there?"

"Oh, these! Some posters the kids made. The drugstore is having a poster contest. The best ones will be in the window. I've got one here by Wayne Sorensen. Want to see?" She smiled.

"Yeah, let's see what he can do. Is he very good?"

"You want the truth?"

He laughed. "Oh, that bad, huh?"

"Well, not bad, but not exactly original. He copied one of the girls."

"I see," Buck said. "He's a rascal, like his dad." There was silence between them. "Can I give you a lift home?" he asked, looking into her wistful eyes.

She considered a moment, then answered, "I think I can make it. Actually, I need the exercise."

"Actually, the answer is just plain no." he said.

"Jim always warned me to be careful," she said quietly.

"If he's so concerned about you, where is he?"

She looked away. Her eyes came to rest at the top of the mountain behind Buck's shoulder. "He's in New York. I've been trying to convince him to come out."

"So, are you going to stay, even if he doesn't come?"

"Yes. This is where the Lord told me to go, and I can't do anything else. I . . . I had a bad experience in New York. I'm afraid to live there, afraid of the people, of the city itself."

He couldn't look away from her face. She was in pain. "He's a fool," he said shaking his head. "A man with a beautiful wife like you should never let her go."

"He never would have. That's why I left when he was gone one day. Things just don't mean the same to him as they do to me. I used to hope he would join the Church, but lately I've pretty well reconciled myself to the fact that he meant what he always said. It doesn't matter to him whether it's true or not; he just doesn't want it."

He wanted to touch her, to comfort her, but he couldn't. He just stood there, hurting for her and because

173

of her.

"I got a letter from him last week. He is asking if I want a divorce."

"Do you?"

"No! I want a husband. I want him to come join me. I hate being alone. It hurts." Tears sprang instantly to her eyes and streaked down her cheek. She jerked her arm to brush them away, and the armload of posters scattered over the sidewalk. Buck knelt to gather them up. Cherri knelt and reached for the posters. Then they were both immobile, their hands and arms touching.

Buck clenched his teeth and brushed the tears from her cheek. "It'll be all right. Everything works out for the best. You're not alone, Cherri. I'm always here."

"Stop it! That's worst of all. I can't lean on you." She grasped the posters and backed away. "Especially not you."

The memory of his dream was a curse. It knotted his stomach, and he couldn't bear to look at her. After a moment, he tapped the posters. "Say, you don't accept bribes from proud fathers do you?"

She moved away. "What do you think?"

"Okay, okay. Sure I can't give you a lift?"

"No!" She glared at him, then seeing the hurt on his face, she drew in her breath and slowly let it out. "Thank you, but no. I'd better go on alone. Say hello to Wayne for me."

He started to speak, but she broke in. "I'll be all right. You just caught me at a bad time. I'm okay, really. I'll get used to it — being alone, I mean. Lots of people are . . . even when they're married."

She backed away from him, and Buck watched her until she turned the corner.

At 11:00 p.m. on November 8th, Paulo's telephone rang. It was Ruth. She sounded very far away, and she was crying.

"Paulo, Mama made me promise to call you. Can you come home?"

"Is she all right? What's wrong?"

"She died yesterday. I wanted to . . . I haven't had a minute to call, until now."

Ruth's voice was muffled. It was either a bad connection or she was whispering. Paulo looked at his watch. In New York, it would be two o'clock in the morning. His mother had died the day before, and Ruth was only just now calling. He tried to control the rising anger.

"Why didn't Roberto call?" His voice was ice cold.

"He . . . he wasn't sure you'd want to come this far. It's a long way just for a funeral," Ruth finished lamely.

"In other words, he wouldn't have even let me know," Paulo interjected bitterly.

"I have to go." Her voice was anxious and still muffled. "The funeral is Friday morning at eleven in Father Santino's church where Mama used to worship. She put it in her will."

"I'll be there."

"Paulo!" She interrupted sharply. "Don't say I called you."

"I won't," he said and hung up, fuming.

Ruth crept back to bed. Her room was quite dark, but she knew her way here, after so many years of walking quietly so as not to bother her husband. Roberto lay on his side, his back to her as she gingerly lowered her weight onto the bed. Just as she was about to relax against the pillow, his hand shot out and grabbed her wrist. In the dark, his voice was a knife.

"Where did you go?"

"Just to check on the children," Ruth answered haltingly. "I . . . I was afraid . . . they might have bad dreams, because . . . of Mama's death."

"You're lying!" he twisted her wrist harshly. "What else did you do?"

"No! Nothing else. Just the children . . . I . . . I did go to the bathroom. Roberto, you're hurting me!"

He had turned over, and even through the darkness she could feel him staring into her eyes, searching for the truth. "Don't lie to me, Ruth. I hate people who lie to me. You called him, didn't you?"

"No!" she cried out. "I just went to the children."

He slapped her and swore. "I knew you'd call him. I listened on the phone. 'He wasn't sure you'd want to come this far.' You're such a mealy mouthed little liar. You knew I didn't want him here. He doesn't even deserve to know, always running around the world. I'm the one who has stayed by Mama's side. I'm the one who took care of her in her old age. Damn you, you disobeyed me!"

Roberto's rage filled his head, pounding and blocking out all sense of proportion. His hatred of Paulo possessed him, and he turned it on her. He began to shake her, and the back of her head hit the headboard. Ruth cried out in pain and instinctively raised her knee, catching him in the groin. He relaxed his grip on her, roaring. She jumped up and tried to dart out of the room. She had never seen him like this, even though she knew he could be cruel. She had overheard enough conversations to know he was a harsh master when it came to people who worked for him. He had hit her once before — the night he had staggered in from a fight with Paulo. Battered and bloody, he had been in a black rage while she tried to clean up his face. He had picked up the telephone and called New York City as she swabbed his cuts with hydrogen peroxide. She had heard him say, "Connect with D'Agosta. He's hot." What he meant exactly she didn't know — didn't want to know. But she had tried to soothe his anger with gentle words. "Brothers sometimes fight. All brothers do. For Mama's sake, you must try to work things out." Coldly, viciously, he had knocked her back against the bathroom wall, then opened the door and walked out.

Now Ruth dashed through the bedroom doorway, but he was too quick and caught her by the hair. She stumbled backward, and he crushed her within his arms, carrying her back and throwing her onto the bed. Then came a shocked voice: "Daddy, what are you doing? Don't hit Mama!"

Roberto was kneeling astride his wife on the bed. His head jerked around to the doorway. His fourteen-year-old son, Mark, was staring in horror from the hallway. Slowly, Roberto stood up, shielding Ruth from sight.

"Go back to your room, Son!"

"But, Dad, you're hurting — "

"It's all right. I . . . I..was angry. I'm . . . sorry. She's okay. Go back to bed. It'll be all right."

Reluctantly, the boy backed away until he was out of sight down the hall. Roberto looked at his wife. She was curled up into a tiny ball, weeping into her pillow. He was still angry with her, but had regained his sense of balance. Because of her, Paulo was coming, intruding on what should have been his time with his mother and family. Because of her, even this time of death would not belong to him alone. Ruth was still trembling when he walked out of the room and went to the guest room to sleep.

Paulo took the morning flight from Salt Lake to New York at 5:00 a.m. So many of the large airlines had failed in the past two years that only the largest remained to connect west and east. Even those would close their Salt Lake City offices at the end of the year when the WWMS number became mandatory. Businesses and banks had closed all over the country, putting a tight squeeze on the credit of even the larger banks. The ripple effect had torn through the economy, closing down small businesses, suppliers, farmers, grocery chains, and transportation.

Paulo sat in the airport thinking about all the times he had driven home and his mother had greeted him. "So, my boy is come home!" He had known it would not be long for Mama, but still, the knowledge that she was truly gone was almost unbearable. She had been his deepest anchor.

From Kennedy Airport, Paulo called Vista Color. Jim would want to know. Carmella had been like a second mother to him. But Mr. Polanski was not in. He was on a business trip to Paris for a week, and his secretary volunteered to take a message. Paulo ate a late lunch, feeling very much alone. He noticed the wide halls, the huge expanded facilities, and the few people who now used them. Airport traffic was cut in half, even in New York City. And almost everyone who passed him had a number tattooed on the wrist. They looked like concentration camp refugees, he thought. He gave his money to the cashier and asked, "You do still take money?" She glanced behind her at the manager and hesitantly nodded. But cash register change was sparse, Paulo noticed.

He took a small, fifty-passenger airplane to Albany at 6:00 p.m. He had expected Ruth or Robbie, the oldest nephew, to meet him. Coming into the terminal, he glanced around for one of them. No one he knew was there, so he headed for the rental car counter. As he

177

stepped up to the counter, an arm slipped around him, and a woman's voice interrupted.

"You won't be needing a car this time."

Paulo looked into Elaina'a face. He hadn't seen her for two years. It had taken some conscious effort and several excuses to stay out of her way. This time there was nothing he could do. She drew him away from the rental counter, entreating him with wide eyes and honied voice.

"Come on. I came to save you the trouble. I have my Ferrari outside. You'll love driving it. It's an exact duplicate of the one you had." She tugged on his tie and cocked her head, using her most winsome, innocent expression.

He laughed over her obvious ploy. "Okay. You talked me into it. Where's Ruth?"

She brushed away the question. "Oh, she's not feeling well. All the funeral stuff, you know! But I needed to get away, so here I am. I'd like to spirit you off to a wonderful little ski chalet about an hour and a half from here. In the summer, it is quiet — almost deserted. Perfect for introspection, quiet walks and talks. Care to go see?"

Paulo put his bag in the trunk of the red Ferrari and slid into the seat. "Nope. Don't have time. Funeral is tomorrow." He backed out and turned the car toward the exit sign. It was almost dark. He turned on the headlights and swung into traffic headed for Albany.

"Well, naturally I don't mean right now. But after the funeral we could — "

Paulo interrupted, "Is Ed going to be here?"

"Ed? Who knows? Who knows where Ed is going to be? Last week he was in London. He belongs to some kind of an international business group. They think they're going to run the business of the world someday. Rabinski's in the group, a top KGB man and bankers of other nationalities. Ed's the only one with real business experience. I tell him they're trying to pick his brain."

"Are they a part of the World Wide Monetary System?" Paulo asked.

"Everyone is, silly. We all have the tatoo — see!" Elaina held up her left hand on which a dark blue tatoo stood out against the white skin of her wrist. "It looks terrible now, but the color will fade in a few months. Then it will only be seen by the infrared scanner. Ours is the first family to join. Roberto's holding out. He can't see the

178

future. The WWMS is the only way to save the banking system of America. We're in the worst depression since 1929."

"You think the WWMS will solve that?"

"It's our only hope. The world has to band together. Countries can't survive in isolation. If we don't join with Europe, we'll go under. We have to work together."

Paulo looked at her quickly. She was perfectly serious. He laughed. "Prosperity can't be restored without food. The Monetary System may be able to prop up the banks for a while, but it can't end the drought. Only God can do that."

She looked at him from veiled eyes. Her jet-black hair was tousled fashionably about her face. Paulo thought she looked as inviting as a cobra. She challenged him. "Are you still sure God knows or cares about us? I thought you had grown up, Paulo."

He continued looking out the windshield and smiled. "I have."

They pulled up in front of a small hotel in downtown Albany. "Why are you staying here?" she asked.

"I didn't want to inconvenience Ruth. She has a lot on her mind and a lot of details to handle."

"That's bull! You just don't want to stay in the house with Roberto. He's furious that you're here," Elaina said gleefully. "He wouldn't let Ruth come, so she called me. You always try to smooth things over. Well, you could have stayed with me. I hoped you would. It's closer, and we do have a guest room, you know."

"I know. You don't have to come get me tomorrow. I'll rent a car."

Elaina pouted like a four-year-old. "I want to."

"Well, don't," he said firmly.

Her dark eyes narrowed as she pouted. "Paulo, we haven't spent any time together in years. You are always gone or unavailable. You don't even know me anymore. I've changed. Really I have. I've been going to church with Anthony. I can see where you got your religious faith. There's a beautiful mystery to the church."

Paulo chuckled in spite of himself. He was almost tender and spoke to her as though she were a child. "Elaina, it won't work. We have nothing in common anymore. Nothing at all. We had our childhood, but that's

179

long past. Go home to your son and husband."

In a whisper she said, "I want to stay with you. For old times' sake."

"No," he said softly.

"We do too have something in common." She hit upon her last, brilliant idea.

"What?"

She turned from him, sat straight up in her seat, folded her hands in her lap resolutely, and stared out the windshield. "Anthony."

"Tony?" Paulo puzzled. "What do you mean?"

With her smallest, trembling voice Elaina said. "Tony isn't Edward's son." Quickly, she glanced at Paulo. His face was impassive. "Tony is . . . your son."

"What!" Paulo jumped as though he'd been shot. "What are you saying! You're crazy, Elaina! Tony can't be my son, and you know it. And you'd better not let Ed hear you say that, or we'll both be dead. Ed dotes on that boy."

But she was stubborn. Shaking her black hair, she repeated. "Tony is your son."

He grabbed her shoulders and turned her to face him. "Cut the bull! You know that's not true. It's impossible. It's been too many years. Once, maybe twice, when we were hardly more than kids. I haven't touched you for at least twenty years." Paulo was angry now — angry that she would lie about something as important as that, that she would do anything to get a hold over him, and that she would use her only son to do it. He was also angry at the flood of emotions that swept him at the mere mention of having a son. His eyes were neither soft nor gentle now. She had the morality of a cat. He jerked her so that her head flew back and she looked into his eyes.

Elaina laughed inside. Now she had truly touched him. His face was set and hard, his eyes were fierce. Now he was the most handsome she had ever seen him. She had watched the boy turn into a man, many years before, and she had loved him desperately, wanted him unreasonably, and almost given him up to God. But she had fought bitterly. At fifteen she had offered her young body to him and had taken his innocence beneath the trees of the forest. Even then she was not innocent. She knew exactly what she was doing and what she hoped to accomplish. She wanted to bind him to her so that he would never leave her. But even youthful chemistry couldn't mask the differences between them. Paulo had been a serious, spiritual youth, strikingly handsome with his dark hair and sensual lips. But he was filled with visions and thoughts of the priesthood. He had experienced immediate guilt and done months of penance for her. She pretended the same, but Elaina had never felt anything for Paulo except the torture of longing to be with him, to touch him, to read love in his eyes. Next best was the anger and burning desire for a son that she now saw.

"You forget," she said, reaching delicately to touch the silver threads at his temples. "Remember Vermont that January? We were all there, Jim Polanski, Roberto, Ruth, Mama, even Maria. We all went up for a ski trip, and we got snowed in. You were making eyes at a blonde waitress and got so dead drunk Jim and I had to help you to your room. Jim left and I undressed you. You told me that you loved me, you wanted to marry me. I believed you, even though you were drunk. Often people say what they really feel when they are drunk. That was the night it happened. You swore you loved me and I wanted to believe you. Afterwards, when you were sober and still would not admit to how you really felt about me, I finally accepted Ed's offer. I needed someone to take care of my child. But it was you I loved. It's always been you."

Disbelief and anger still gripped Paulo. "You lie! Why didn't you tell me then, if you were pregnant with my baby?"

Tears welled up in her eyes and spilled over. She was the very picture of wounded grief. "I was proud. I didn't want your love out of duty. Besides, I was mad at you. You had made such tender love to me, then told me to get lost. I did it out of spite as much as anything. But oh, I'm sorry now, Paulo! I'm so sorry. All these years, you should have had your son to love. He's such a sweet boy. So much like you." Then she tempted him. "I would give you another child, if you wanted."

"Shut up!" He shook her and pushed her away from him. She stayed in the dark corner of the car. His arm across the steering wheel, he rested his head on his forearm. "Shut up, Elaina. You're . . . you're a . . . I don't believe it. You'd lie to Saint Peter. Don't say anything now, or so help me, I'll strangle you."

181

After a moment, he jerked open the door and got out. He lifted his bag out of the trunk and handed the keys through the window to her. "Go home. Don't ever say anything like this again. You're crazy. You know Ed would kill you if he ever heard that lie."

She grabbed his hand. "Paulo, I know you don't want to believe it, and I will never tell Ed. It would hurt him too much. But please, please don't hate Tony, even . . . even if you hate me."

He pulled away from her. "You're such a damned good actress. Get out of here." She watched him walk into the lobby of the hotel. Flushed from the excitement of touching him so profoundly, Elaina turned the key and smiled.

Carmella's funeral was long and dissatisfying. The small group of friends and family sat for a half hour before the priest came in, preceded by young boys bearing candles. He walked with measured step, fulfilling his priestly role. Latin prayers were said. Candles were lit. Deep, resonant tones of the Catholic liturgy filled the small church. Then he spoke a few words of comfort for the family. Nothing was said about resurrection. There was no hope given of a family life beyond the veil. Paulo listened to the beautiful, sonorous Latin prayers. It brought back his childhood, and watching Mama kneel in the quiet church. But now he had something more, and he felt the missionary spirit urging him to tell them all about life after death, families living together eternally, marriage for eternity. Tears stung his eyelids. Mama and Papa were together now at last. Maria and Jean Paul were beside them. For one brief moment, Paulo wished that he were also on the other side of the veil with his family. But life now held hope for him, more hope than he had had for many years.

Roberto was a model of decorum. This was his event. These were his friends who peopled the benches. Outside the church afterward, he moved among them like a perfect host at a summer party. Then they brought the casket out, and Roberto turned and saw Ruth walking beside it. They were taking it to the far end of the little cemetery for burial. He looked toward the open pit in the earth and back to his mother's casket which was moving slowly, inexorably, toward the hole. He pulled away from the conversation and went to Ruth, putting an arm around her and another around his son, Mark. Real grief broke with a flood of tears. Ruth's face was veiled to hide her bruises. Still, she comforted her husband. Paulo walked behind a few feet, on the other side of the casket. The little group stood at the edge of the burial hole. Roberto's head rested on his wife's shoulder. He was crying, and the tears were unaffected. He had loved his mother, and he felt he had somehow not measured up to what she had wanted from him. He had tried. His was the ingenuity that carried on the family business. So what if he had departed from hers and Papa's values? Survival was all that counted. But she had never understood that. None of it had been meant to hurt her. Paulo stood at the other end of the grave, not watching Roberto or Ruth or anyone else. He spoke in his heart to his mother. Mama, he prayed, I've always carried you in my heart, now it'll just be longer until we see each other again. I remember the little wishing pond you had Papa make for us, out behind the back door of the house. I believed in that wishing pond for so many years. And I remember your flower gardens. So beautiful, Mama, just like you.

But all he felt from the darkened grave was silence. Carmella was gone, and with her, his childhood, his youth. No one else knew him. No one else cared. Now he was truly and completely alone.

The first spade of dirt went in, in the old traditional custom, and Roberto let out a cry. They all turned away. Paulo walked back toward the church. His eyes were wet; he carried a great weight, but his heart carried the knowledge that he would see his mother again.

"I'm sorry, Paulo." A young voice spoke at his elbow. Young Tony Ciardi stood beside him. The boy was twelve years old now. He possessed his mother's striking good looks but a sweeter nature. Paulo studied his face, grief spurting through him. The young face was so pure, so beautiful in its childhood innocence. The question haunted him, could this boy be mine? The thought was pure torture. He tentatively put an arm around the boy's shoulder.

"I know. It's all right, Tony. You see, I believe in a life

after death. Do you believe that?"

"I don't know," the boy said, shaking his head. "The priest doesn't speak of that."

"I remember. Just of being good and doing penance for our sins, so we can escape hell, right?" Tony nodded. "But sometimes hell is with us right here on earth. Do you believe that?"

Tony nodded solemnly. "Yes. I feel that too. You were very close to your mother weren't you?"

Paulo choked up and couldn't answer. He just nodded yes. Tony said, "I wish I were that close to my mother." The boy looked across the small cemetery. Elaina was deep in conversation with friends. "I hardly ever see her."

"Does that hurt you?" Paulo asked him gently.

"Oh, yes," the boy responded.

"Do you see much of your . . . father?"

"Much more than her. Dad comes home almost every weekend. He takes me hunting and sometimes into New York. He says he has just the spot in his business for me when I am ready. Dad's a great guy. But he's gone a lot. I spend a lot of time at Ruth's and Roberto's."

Paulo studied Tony's face. Was it his imagination or was there a family resemblance around eyes and mouth? Carmella's mouth? His heart pounded so loudly he was afraid Tony would hear it.

"I want to travel, like you," the boy said. "I'd like to go with you on your trips and paint the things you photograph."

Paulo drew the boy swiftly to him with a brief hug. Feelings he never knew he had rose in him. Feelings of protectiveness and kinship flooded him.

"I'd like that," he said gruffly. "I'd like to show you all the places I've been. I've never shared them with anyone special. Maybe someday we could go together."

Roberto's voice was loud behind him. "You'd better ask Ed about that. He has other plans for his boy than trailing a penniless photographer, with no more ambition than to take pictures all his life."

Clearly, the gauntlet had been tossed. Paulo slowly relaxed his hug and patted the boy's shoulder, encouraging him to be on his way. He didn't turn to Roberto nor answer him; he simply began walking away. Roberto called after him, "Have you thought about that, brother? You're penniless now. The family home belongs to the family corporation, and I have controlling interest. You have nothing — no home, no business, no family. Even Vista Color is no longer yours. What will you do? Grab your little camera and run off to India to take pictures?"

He made the mistake of grabbing Paulo's sleeve. Paulo spun around, tense and ready to spring. Ruth jumped between them, her hand gripping Paulo's arm.

"Please don't! Please, both of you. Mama's funeral! How could you?"

At close range, Paulo could see that her face was puffy. Was it from crying? He brushed aside the veil in one quick movement and saw the black and blue bruises on her face and neck. He looked with disdain at Roberto.

"You got your revenge, I see. I don't care about your money. It'll soon be worthless. The Monetary System will own D'Agosta Furs just as it owns Vista Color and almost every other business in the country. I won't be a part of that system. Money is worthless now, but people aren't."

He spoke to his sister-in-law. "Ruth, I'm sorry."

She began to cry. Roberto shoved her roughly aside. "If you're so damned sorry, stay away. Stay away from my family. You turned your back on us three years ago when you betrayed us. You used me. You used the information I gave you to run to your Arab friends. You made me look like a fool and almost got me killed. It's taken a long time to rebuild trust. Now, I call the shots." He punched his forefinger into Paulo's jacket front. "Don't you come back!"

Ruth stood with her hands to her face. Her children crowded beside her. Others around the cemetery were not even aware of the confrontation. Only Elaina watched from a few feet away.

Paulo answered quietly, "I won't. There's no reason to. Good-bye Ruth. Take care of yourself." He walked back to the dark blue sedan he had rented and started the engine. Elaina came hurrying across the grass.

"Paulo, where can I reach you? I mean, if we need you?"

"You can't and you won't."

Still, she clung to the car door. "But, but . . . what about Tony?"

He was disgusted. "Tony is a beautiful boy. Try not to ruin him."

"Will you ever come back?" she asked in a shaky voice.

"No. It's done." The car started to move. She walked with it as long as she could.

"Paulo!"

"What?" he asked impatiently, anxious to be gone.

"I love you." she said. "I've always loved you."

This time there was no acting. But there was also no answer. The window came up automatically, and he drove away.

It was only a half hour into Albany. Paulo went into the hotel, changed quickly, and left for the airport. In the airport, he passed a television section. The screen was filled with the Slavic face of Soviet Premier Vladimoscov. He was newly named president of the board of directors for the World Wide Monetary System, and beside him was Pope Peter Carlucci. The two of them were talking of economic and religious unity for the world.

It was June in Utah, little more than one year from Paulo's baptism. He had liquidated all his assets in New York City and bought actual goods with the money — a truckload of automobiles, gold jewelry, silver dinnerware, and expensive electronic equipment. These things he sold in the highly inflationary economy of Utah. Two automobiles purchased him a tiny, one bedroom, seventy-year-old home in downtown Salt Lake City. It was scheduled to be torn down before the influx of families three years ago, but with paint, mortar, and decent furniture, it was suitable for his needs. He was close to the temple and to Church offices. Elias Stark had taken a genuine liking to him and constantly found projects for him as a Church photographer. For weeks at a time, Paulo would follow Elias or other General Authorities, recording Church history with his cameras. He established a small darkroom in his basement.

Paulo was taken through the temple the first time by Elias. It was a cleansing experience. In one day, his sense of unworthiness was wiped away. A new concept of himself as a son of God possessed his mind and kept him pondering the temple ceremony for months. Soon afterward, he was called to serve in the Salt Lake temple and trained as a veil worker. He went every Monday,

Tuesday, and Wednesday, and stayed from early morning until evening, taking meals in the temple cafeteria. Elias told him that his time was better spent here than in photography of Church leaders. In brief explanation, he once said, "This is your future."

This Wednesday morning, Paulo had watched the eastern sunrise with a strange sense of apprehension as he prepared to go. It was lovely but not unusual. In the temple, he asked one of the other workers, "Do you sense something unusual about today?"

Henry Hansen looked at him curiously. "No, don't believe I do. Do you?"

"I don't know. Maybe it's my imagination. I feel kind of strange, almost excited, but I don't know why. This isn't a special date, is it?"

"Can't think of a thing. It's July 19, but I don't know a single thing significant about that."

Paulo shook his head. "Oh well. My imagination, I guess."

On July 19, Shielah Gailbraith arose, conscious of a tremendous excitement. The day was circled in red on her calendar. While Stephen was shaving, she stood outside the bathroom door and called to him, "Are you going with me?"

"Where?" he asked innocently.

"Where?" she echoed. "You know where! To the temple. Today is the day my great-great-grandmother has been cleared for the ordinance work. You said you'd go."

"I know, Honey; but we're working so hard on that new development, and I need to be there!"

"No, you don't. Please, Honey. You promised me last January when I found all those records that you would go with me when I got to do her name."

He opened the door with a face half full of shaving cream. "Sure, if you'll give me a big ol' kiss." He lunged at her and bent her over backward. "Come on, now — isn't your grandma worth a big ol' kiss?"

"You let me go. I don't want to kiss you, mush face."

"Mush face! Boy, that's an unkind blow! Here, it's really soft and nice. Let me give you some!"

She began squealing, and Ben came running in with

Kristin right behind him. Ben was pulling at his father, and Justin had a death lock around his legs. The whole family was yelling at him to let her go.

"But she wants a kiss," Stephen bellowed.

"I do not!"

"She does not," the kids echoed.

"She doesn't?" Stephen said in surprise, straightening abruptly but still holding Shielah dangerously close. "Oh, I thought she wanted a kiss." While everyone was off-guard, expecting him to let her go, he swooped down and smeared her face with his wet, slippery lather.

She shoved him away. "Blech! Thanks, rat. See if I go to any temple with you"

"Oh, are you going to the temple today?" he asked in surprise. "In that temper? Tch, tch. Do you think you should?"

She wiped the shaving cream off her face with her hand and, quick as a wink, wiped it all over the thick hair on his forearm. "A rat! You're a rat. Go watch over your silly development."

She started out the door, but he held her back. "Now, don't be mad. I'm going down to the temple today. Want to go, beautiful?"

She wrenched away and yelled at him: "No!"

"Aw, come on. Don't be mad. Do you think she ought to be mad?" he asked Ben.

Ben looked from one from the other. "Naw, I don't think she ought to be mad. But I don't think she ought to give you any breakfast, either." He ducked and was gone at a dead run.

"Charlotte O'Neill Boughtman, May 16, 1843-1877" was the small white tag given to Shielah and pinned to the sleeve of her dress. Sheilah and Stephen came into the temple at 11:15 that morning, after a little more teasing and a lot of reassurance on his part that he had never intended to miss it. He kept his arm securely around her as they drove and listened again to her excited story. Elberta Longstroth was really the hero of the day. Elberta kept records of her dealings, and when Charlotte had died, she had sent to Annie the receipt of the burial casket. The body had been shipped back to Camilla County in Iowa,

188

and Victoria Palmerly had gone back to her old homestead in Montrose. The tombstone read 'Susanna Peterson' for a long time, but just before Victoria died, she had had the engraver inscribe "Charlotte O'Neill Boughtman" below it.

Shielah didn't know how Victoria had labored over that decision. Finally, she had put her trust in God to protect Charlotte's last remains from the tenacious, vicious Jack Boughtman. Victoria had told herself many times that even he wouldn't be so evil as to desecrate a grave. She had been right.

Jack had found the grave a few months after Victoria died. He had gone inquiring after Charlotte's location and had finally found the town where Victoria Palmerly had lived. Behind the old town church, with the flowers growing wild and the grass waving halfway up to his knees, he had found Charlotte's grave and could see that her true name had been inscribed there only a few months before. Jack had stood looking down at the stone. His beard was long and scraggly, his clothing ragged, and he walked stooped over — hardly the proud, swaggering man he had once been when he had wrestled the Prophet Joseph. Jack had turned rustler, scout, outlaw in some parts of the country, and whiskey had taken over his life. Jack was tired of all the moving, the running. He had one more wagon train to scout for as far as Fort Kearney, and then he would settle down. Maybe buy another ranch. He spoke to her grave.

"Too bad you ain't here to help me, Charly. Maybe you and me could learn to get along now. I've settled down a bit. I'll come see you sometimes, when I git back." But Jack Boughtman never came back. He was killed in an Indian raid just outside Fort Kearney, and they buried him in a shallow, unmarked grave which the wolves dug up the next night.

Shielah went through the washing and anointing procedure for Charlotte. Her sense of exhilaration heightened with every word of the covenant. She felt cleansed in a special way, and the Spirit seemed to fill her with intense joy. It was her own joy, but it was Charlotte's too. The endowment session took on an unusual meaning. Shielah felt as she had the first time she had heard it —

as though her heart could not drink in the meaning fast enough. Each vow was imprinted on her mind. With each step toward the final covenant, she grew more and more restless, more on edge, more cognizant of Charlotte's spirit beside her.

Paulo walked through the morning's duties, his expectation and restlessness building until he moved almost in a daze. He finished his lunch in the cafeteria. Two o'clock. Henry Hansen spotted him across the cafeteria.

"We have an extra-large session, and Brother Greer isn't feeling well. Can you take his place at the veil?"

"Sure," Paulo answered. He stood up, wiped his mouth, and tossed down his napkin. "I was just finished."

He and Henry made their way to the veil separating the terrestrial and celestial rooms.

"Do you still feel like something is going to happen today?" Hansen asked.

"More than ever. I can't shake it." Paulo looked around him. Hansen was dressed in white. All the temple workers were. Pure white — it was the color of the Lord's house. Looking down at himself, Paulo wondered that he had taken so long to come to this — this oasis of peace. Almost, one could shut out the world beyond the temple walls. Almost, one could forget the tensions and politics outside. Here, even his agonizing longing for a wife and family was assuaged, although he worked all day with families being sealed. Something here whispered hope.

Paulo stepped to the veil. There was one station not filled by a worker. It was at the very end. He heard the whisper of voices all around him. He took his place, and a female veil worker began the familiar questions. Several times, Paulo went through the ritual and welcomed women into the celestial world as they gave the correct responses. With each repetition of the covenants, Paulo felt a raising of spiritual awareness until his body was filled with an intense burning. Then the worker on the other side of the veil introduced the last woman. She gave the name of the woman for whom the work was being done. It was Charlotte O'Neill Boughtman, who was dead.

His heart stopped a moment, and he caught his breath. The vision of the portrait in Shielah's apartment passed before him, and then the vivid memory of

190

Charlotte, running before him out of the warehouse. He was shaking, remembering the intense longing as he had begged her, "Stay with me."

Then he heard another voice. It was a whisper, but he still recognized that voice. He had hoped never to be in this position, and yet had longed for it too. His memorization served him well. Mechanically, he gave the inquiries. Shielah's voice came soft and low, and Paulo hurt with every cell of his body for the bittersweet love he thought he had long since buried.

An all-enveloping spirit throbbed round about and through him. The feeling of great expectation grew until he was hard pressed to finish the ceremony. All the others had moved into the celestial room. They were the last two. The final words were spoken, and his hand reached for Shielah's to bring her through the veil. She came readily, and the veil parted with a silken swish. The face was still lovely, softer and more mature than he remembered it. The youthful fullness had disappeared and left the high cheek bones sculpting her heartshaped face, emphasizing those incredibly blue eyes. He saw it all at a glance, and had they alone, it might have been more than he could stand. But they were not alone.

When Paulo looked, expecting to see only Shielah, he saw two women. One he recognized as his only earthly love. But the other he knew to be his eternal companion — Charlotte! Charlotte stood in a pool of light. Surrounding her was the same radiance that had blinded his kidnappers, a glory brighter than anything on the earth, akin to the brilliant morning sun on a snowy bank. On her face was inexpressible joy.

Shielah had seen Paulo at the same moment his eyes had met hers, but, like him, she was too entranced by the personage standing by her side to speak to him. She knew the woman too. It was her great-great-grandmother. She recognized the spirit that had often haunted and hounded her to do the work. Tears started in Shielah's eyes, and she would have reached out to touch her; but before she could, Charlotte spoke.

"Thank you, my dear child. It's been a long road for you, and you didn't give up. Thank you for all these blessings of eternal life you've given me today."

Then Charlotte turned to Paulo. Could an angel cry?

Those beautiful, green eyes were misty, and her face was full of longing. She whispered words he had never thought he would hear. The warmth of her spirit enveloped him. It was as though she enclosed him within herself. He trembled with love so long unfulfilled.

"My only love," she whispered. "How long I have waited to see you again. The loneliness has been almost unbearable."

Tears started at the acknowledgement of the trial they had both endured. Centuries had separated their love. Only God could unite them again.

"I told you, I would always be with you," she reminded him. "And I have. I loved you my whole lifetime and yours. You were the one who saved me from the darkness of hell. It was only fitting that I save you that dark hour in Jerusalem. It is you who welcomed me back home to the spirit world, and now, today, you who has brought me into the celestial world. "

"How much longer?" he asked, vibrating with every pulse.

She smiled. "It has been hard for you, hasn't it? For me too. Being separated is the greatest trial either of us could endure. But time is growing short. How short we do not know. We are all prepared and waiting until the Lord gives the signal. Sometime after that, you and I will be husband and wife. Someday. Someday. Until then, remember I am always with you. Wait, my love. Wait for me."

Then she was gone. It had taken only a minute. Too fast, too fast. Paulo and Shielah stood staring at each other, tears streaming from each face. She stretched out her hand. He took it. He was no longer afraid of her and the love they had once known.

Stephen stepped around the corner and saw them like that, Paulo and Shielah holding hands and weeping. Stephen didn't recognize him at first. They seemed to be standing in an aura of light. Were the temple lights brighter in that spot? What was it that seemed to waver for a minute or two next to Shielah, casting its radiance on her hair? He walked toward his wife. Her face was shining. When the man looked up, Stephen stopped. It was Paulo D'Agosta.

"Howl ye; for the day of the Lord is at hand; it shall come as a destruction from the Almighty. Therefore shall all hands be faint, and every man's heart shall melt: Behold, the day of the Lord cometh, cruel both with wrath and fierce anger, to lay the land desolate:"
(Isaiah 13: 6-7, 9.)

Chapter Nine

Nuclear war was a Frankenstein in the closet. Few Americans believed it would happen. Few of them had ever seen the devastation of war that had blanketed Europe and Japan. It was fate's worst trick, because it emasculated their will to protect themselves.

On October 10, financial ruin for America was imminent. The World Bank, financial arm of the United Nations, had collapsed as impoverished nations reneged on massive loans. Arabs unloaded their stocks on the New York exchange. When the giant muscle man, the USSR, also declared itself unable to repay the hundreds of billions it had borrowed, the whole structure of international finance began to crumble. America was the heaviest backer of the World Bank, and U.S. banks began closing immediately. The Federal Reserve called on the World Wide Monetary System to administer financial stability by freezing all assets. Officials were alarmed. Stability must be returned to the United States or panic would overtake the world. World leaders banded together for moral support. The Soviet ambassador was televised with an arm around the United States president, expressing deep anguish over this difficult time. With world finances in tatters, Soviet-American relations were at their warmest point since World War II.

On a mild October morning, two hundred and fifty miles above the earth's atmosphere, Soviet satellites detonated three fifty megaton nuclear bombs, each with one hundred times the force that leveled Nagasaki. At 9:00 a.m., these bombs exploded over the North American continent. They emitted a powerful electro-magnetic pulse of such force that it formed a wall of electric shock producing fifty thousand volts per meter surging through all integrated electrical systems. It was like a wall of lightning, striking in the blink of an eye. The pulse was cumulative, collecting voltage as it flowed through electrical wires, but the time span was so brief it could only be measured in nanoseconds. In those split seconds, the voltage exceeded by forty times the surge protection of all commercial computers and was sufficient to destroy all control circuits and unprotected computers. An electrical America was instantly disarmed and dysfunctional.

Simultaneously, Soviet subs stationed 120 miles off east and west coasts released ballistic missiles in suppressed orbits that pummeled key military installations and shattered Washington, D.C. Relying on the mutually assured destruction theory popular for fifty years, there had been no anti-ballistic missile defense of the capital city. Surface-to-air missiles that were adequate defense against aircraft were capable of matching the velocity of the SLBMs. But more importantly, reaction time to interrupted communications was the weakest link in American defense. Within three minutes, the two men who could have given the launch commands for an American retaliatory strike — the president of the United States and the secretary of defense — both lay dead in the rubble. Compounding this, confusion prevailed as to the certainty of their death. Telephone communication was cut off. Top-level generals could not be reached for verification of the launch command.

Only America's submarines gave her a strategic nuclear deterrent force of SLBMs and protection from her enemies. What no one in American defense circles knew was that one month earlier the Soviets had perfected their efforts to make the oceans transparent to their tracking devices. While Soviet satellites detonated their nuclear bombs, their own submarines had homed in on the fifteen American nuclear subs below the surface, using a four-layered screening process for heat, light, sound, and current patterns. They destroyed the subs in the water and blew up the other twenty subs in port for crew changes.

Circling at ten thousand feet was the Strategic Air Command airborne command post, a 747 with highly sophisticated computerized instruments and weaponry. Lt. Colonel William Watkins was captain of the aircraft, trained for fifteen years to respond to an escalated nuclear situation. He had at his disposal the launch codes for all the missiles sites in the country. And he was perfectly prepared to use them in the event of an attack where all other lines of authority were destroyed. But Watkins never had the chance to send the launch codes. In fact, his aircraft went down over Ohio one minute before the SLBMs detonated on Washington, D.C. The massive electromagnetic pulse immobilized the computer controlled instruments of his aircraft, and it fell like a rock from the sky.

It was a perfectly timed operation. The Alaskan Air Command, trained for years to intercept an attack across the great expanse of the North Pole, was struck by SLBMs within seconds after the EMP. Air Force fighters, F-15s and B-52 bombers, were destroyed before they could leave sight of the base. Only one squadron of F-15s were in the air over the North Pole on a practice run when the bomb exploded. All communication with the ground was instantly cut. In perfect formation, they turned to fly into what they immediately knew was coming, Russian Bear H bombers. They were hurtling through Alaskan and Canadian airspace within minutes of the explosion. No more simulated runs against the U.S.; now it was the real thing. For years, Alaskan and Canadian fighter crews had intercepted Soviet bombers on practice runs and escorted them back to their own territory. Such practice maneuvers had lulled America into thinking it had capable deterrents. "Wolf, wolf!" had become such a constant alert that it no longer carried any sense of real danger. It had almost become a game. Whose fighters were the fastest? Who could bluff the best? Now it was not a game. Russian Bears and the newer Blackjacks carried live missiles destined for American military installations.

One lonely squadron went into the jaws of hell and attacked the beast. The F-15s had first to contend with the MIG-31 Foxhound fighter planes that protected the Bears. One by one the Americans engaged them. But the bombers flew away from the foray, carrying their precious cargo. And when the Americans shot down one Foxhound, another took its place, until the whole sky vibrated with the roar of hundreds of Soviet fighters and bombers, like migrating vultures heading south. Fifteen minutes after first contact, it was all over, as the American fighters died in fiery explosions. Those crew members able to eject lasted only three minutes in the icy Arctic waters.

Within thirty minutes, intercontinental ballistic missiles launched from Soviet bases completed the decapitation that the submarine-launched bombs had begun. A stunned America never launched a single missile in her own defense. This was what the Soviets had banked on. They well knew that America's defense was built on the premise of escalating tensions and a preparation period. They had carefully made sure there were no escalating tensions; the preemptive strike was totally unexpected. For years, terrorist attack had been the primary concern of the United States.

Also, the Soviets had watched Americans wrestle with a dwindling budget for defense. They had paid lavishly for propaganda to influence top U.S. government officials and popular media commentators in believing that the American military was self-serving and loved war maneuvers for their own sakes. Greedy traitors had sold the Soviets sensitive tactical and technical documents for high prices. Underworld connections like Roberto D'Agosta had kept them supplied with top-secret data and provided the hitmen for the KGB. America's own CIA was infiltrated and often played in the Soviet camp unawares. The American Congress had boondoggled defense spending, postponing the development of mobile missile basing and kinetic energy defense devices, and the military itself had compounded the problem by incompetence in managing its own budget.

While had America stumbled and mumbled about the high cost of the defense budget, the Soviet Union had stepped up its deployment schedule. Even while it spoke of peace and democratic change, practice missile runs over Alaska had tripled in frequency, Soviet bomb shelters had been completed, and their aircraft had been constantly updated. At the same time, the U.S. F-15s had become outdated and tactically incapable of combating the Blackjack-Cs and MIG 31s. American surveillance satellites had faithfully relayed pictures of Soviet practice war maneuvers, accepted now as merely routine. Only this time, the seemingly routine maneuvers had masked the real intent.

From sea to shining sea, America lay in ruins. Her military bases were obliterated; surrounding cities were destroyed or without power, fuel, water, and food; and her people were devastated by the surprise strike they had not believed in. Most American cities were not directly hit. It was not the Soviet plan to destroy the wealth of America — it was that very wealth they wanted. Their objective was defeat, not destruction. They had bankrupted their own economy for the first-strike military offensive, into which they poured over a trillion dollars, and a substantial portion of those billions spent on their offensive preparations were western world dollars. Unwary, materialistic western bankers had loaned the Soviet Government enough money to strangle America. Their entire military machinery was geared to this first-strike coup. Their goal was to decapitate the U.S. command structure and destroy the strategic nuclear force.

Thousands of midsized and smaller cities were virtually untouched, although the bomb's pulse knocked out all communications and electricity. However, cities built around military bases were obliterated by the attacks. SAC headquarters in eastern Nebraska was one of many prime targets. The base had been hardened during the previous decade to endure near misses, but the concrete and steel was not sufficient to withstand the newer, more accurate Soviet warheads that fell uncontested from the sky. All one thousand missile silos in America's five missile fields were pummelled. Nebraska, North and South Dakota, Wyoming, and Missouri were scoured when each silo was hit by multiple groundbursts each.

California, with her military bases and weapons stockpiles, was an easy target for the Soviet submarine launched missiles. It wasn't even a challenge. With dozens of warheads unloaded on the coast the tenuous stability of the subcontinental plates was jolted and the crust of the earth shifted for the second time in eighteen months.

Miles of rock, hills, and sand twisted and slid into the sea. The ocean rushed in to claim the low land, while new hills rose up, naked and rough, where there had once been green valleys. The ancient redwoods were wrested from the earth, toppling like matchsticks. The survivors of May's earthquake not killed outright in the thermonuclear blasts and the radiation pulse that followed the bombs cursed God and begged to die in this new terror.

Pearl Harbor had been among the first hit by concentrated submarine firepower. Only the Naval carriers in the Pacific offered any resistance. Their FA-18s were launched when sensors detected approaching threatening aircraft. The carrier battle groups were rendered ineffective by the air-launched cruise missiles that overwhelmed the defenses by sheer numbers alone.

New York City was not initially targeted. Most of the wealth-producing cities were not. They were simply held hostage. By way of warning, Russia detonated a one-megaton warhead ten thousand feet over New York City. Cooperate or be obliterated — that was the obvious message. Theirs was the ultimate power now, and they would use it. New York did not have to be directly hit. The atmospheric blast shook the giant buildings to the earth, burying thousands of men and women. Fantastic wind velocity shattered windows and disturbed delicate structural balance. Dozens of Babel's towers tumbled from that. The concussion of the bomb created tidal waves that ripped the harbor to shreds. With that warning blast, New York City was ravaged of half its people.

A few escaped — lucky New Yorkers who had taken vacations to the upstate mountains, or who lived away and simply worked in the city. Edward Ciardi and his family, along with Roberto D'Agosta and family, had spent all week in their homes in the Catskill mountains. With the early morning blast that shook their part of the world, both men had known immediately what was happening and hurried their families down into well-stocked cellars. Inside knowledge had been hastily delivered but, favor for favor, they were given early warning through their underworld chain. Military secrets they had funneled out of the country for years bought them their lives.

Jim Polanski was not so lucky. Vista Color was his only devotion since Cherri had left. He was at work by

7:00 a.m. and sometimes slept there. At 9:00, he was conducting a staff meeting with technical advisors. Equipment had been difficult to obtain lately while American business was adjusting to the World Wide Monetary System. When the electricity blinked off with an atmospheric jolt, they took it in stride and continued their discussion — for three more minutes. Then, in a shattering blast, Vista Color rocked, swayed — window glass spraying — and collapsed, floor upon floor. With the first deafening roar of concrete ripped apart, Jim stood up while others dove beneath the table. Glass flew around him; the floor began to give way; walls crumbled; the roaring filled his ears, and Jim smiled. Cherri, he thought, you were right! I knew it all along, but there's no place for me with you. I know it was only until death do us part, but I loved you, Cherri. I love . . . Vista Color took two thousand people — employees and street traffic — to their death. Jim died the way he wanted to, with Cherri's name in his heart.

Over the western United States, Denver and Colorado Springs were pummeled with missiles. The groundburst explosions set off an earthquake along the great Continental Divide. What the missiles did not destroy, the earthquake did. The Rocky Mountains shifted like a great giant yawning.

Hill Field, in the sleepy Ogden valley, was another target area. A Soviet submarine cruise missile detonated a mere six hundred feet above Ogden, and its thermonuclear blast shook the earth and skies for twenty miles around, as the infamous cloud of terror rose with hideous majesty like a gigantic mushroom, thousands of feet in the air. The city of Ogden blinked in the morning sun and vanished in a cloud. Within seconds another cruise missile exploded the Salt Lake City International Airport. All commercial runways over seven thousand feet long had to be destroyed to prevent American bombers from landing. An hour later, ten Russian Bear and Blackjack bombers came in from the devastated Alaskan frontier and dropped their loads on targeted Dugway and Tooele.

Only in one respect were the Russians not successful. For six years the ammunition dump at Tooele had been a decoy only. The outdated equipment and aged ammunition still remained stored there, but secretly, the real weapons — land mines, claymore mines that could be strung like clothesline, shoulder-fired Stinger and Red-eye missiles, machine guns, howitzers, rifles, and ammunition — were all concealed in subterranean vaults far back within the Wasatch mountains.

Paulo's life was spared, while thousands died, because he was some fifty miles away from the larger Ogden explosion and twelve miles from the airport. Since Ogden was an airburst rather than a groundburst, even the twenty-megaton warhead delivered over Ogden destroyed only the surrounding twenty-mile radius. Salt Lake City rocked in the concussion of the blasts. Tens of thousands of unprotected, unwary residents took the full shock of the nuclear pulse emitted from the airport bombing. Both bombs released only minor radiation into the stratosphere, mercifully saving the surviving cities the horrors of intense radioactive fallout. The mild northeasterly winds pushed the radiation over the mountains high above Morgan County. Aircraft bombs, although only one megaton each, had the most destructive effect since they were surface bursts. Buildings, vehicles, rocks — all were sucked up into the furnace of the blast, pulverized and thrown back to earth as radioactive particles. In the western part of the valley, few residents survived, and only those who had adeq·1ate concrete protection.

Paulo was shaving at 9:00 a.m. He had already taken his morning walk through the narrow, quaint avenues of residential Salt Lake City. Today he had an appointment with Elias Stark, first counselor to President Taylor. He had not been told what the meeting was about, only that there were some plans they wanted to go over with him. The fall chill made his morning walk delightful, even as the warmth of the sun promised another lovely day. Paulo was whistling as he opened the door to his old-fashioned brick home. It was tiny, with only one bedroom, but he felt lucky to have it with the city so crowded. He had lived for four months with another family, until his need for privacy made him desperate. This little nook had taken almost all the assets he had from the sale of his property in New

York, but the quiet privacy was worth it. Late summer petunias were still blooming. The fresh breeze ruffled his window curtain as he stood before the round porcelain sink, methodically removing his dark whiskers. He squinted and pulled his face to the right, then to the left. Clean. Not a shadow.

He reached for a towel, and the house rocked. Beyond the tiny bathroom window, a streak of light dimmed the morning sun. Then, a mammoth, gray, mushrooming cloud filled the sky. Its ghastly size overwhelmed everything else. Paulo dropped to his knees as the overblast shook plaster from the ceiling. In that same instant, he began scrambling through the bedroom and down the stairs that led to the concrete cellar below. Most of the old homes in Utah were built with them. Paulo had carefully put aside enough Army Meals Ready to Eat rations and gallons of water to last for a while. How long, he did not know. This tiny house saved his life. The cellar was able to be sealed off almost completely. He kept his emergency kit, blankets, and a sleeping bag down there as well.

Instinctively, Paulo knew what had happened. The nuclear blast left no question, and he didn't stop to wonder why. His first response was purely self-preservation — get out of the way of the nuclear pulse before the heat and radiation could hit. The pulse took only a minute to sweep the Avenues. The bricks and concrete of Paulo's home was the most convenient, immediate protection. Density and mass were the key. Had he been outside, a deep ditch would have served, since earth was excellent protection. Here, in his house, an interior room with no windows offered immediate shelter from the pulse, but the cellar was his long-term protection, and he headed straight down-stairs.

The roar of the holocaust shook the ground like an earthquake and terrorized northern Utah. The bombs were so immense that even the light from the Denver detonations could be seen. The gigantic cloud boiled up and over, swelling and swelling and belching radiation into the stratosphere. Fascination was fatal to hundreds of thousands of horrified residents. Mothers doing the morning household chores, children on playgrounds, men and women in automobiles or buses stopped and turned full face to the monstrous sight. Disbelief and amazement

201

were fatal, for, as they stood watching the spectacle, the deadly thermonuclear pulse flowed out from the bomb, burning and destroying the living cells in its path.

America was devastated more by ignorance than actual blast destruction. Across the food belt of the United States, farmers stood in their fields and watched hell encompass heaven as the awesome clouds billowed above. Had they known, had they been taught, had they prepared, millions of lives would have been preserved. But the government for the people and by the people had neglected to prepare its people to live through a nuclear strike, even though it had known for forty years that this possibility existed. In those forty years, every man, woman, and child could have been educated about how to save their lives, but there were no programs in the schools to teach nuclear survival, no courses offered in the colleges. Most people mistakenly believed that nuclear war would kill everyone and there was no need to prepare for survival. This falsehood had been issued by Soviet scientists in the fifties to mentally disarm Americans, while they, themselves, built extensive bomb shelters for the evacuation of their cities at risk. The falsehood was canonized by well-meaning Western scientists, and it completely discouraged civil defense in the United States.

After hours of hiding, huddled in the farthest corner of the cellar, Paulo felt the ground begin to tremble beneath him. The Wasatch Fault began to grumble against the atmospheric clashes. Would the mountains cave in on them? Would he be buried alive? There were no answers in the darkness of his shelter. He was alone, yet not alone. Sweet and clear, visions of a bright, beautiful, red-haired angel filled his mind. The sooner the end came, the sooner they would be together. Paulo did not fear death now. He feared only the years without her. His life had been so empty without love. The reassurance she had given him only a month ago had dispelled the loneliness that had tortured him, but he had no great desire to go on without her. Perhaps this was truly the end. Christ would come. Certainly, they were in the jaws of the beast. Only a merciful God could save them now.

Hours stretched into days. Paulo had enough sense to stay below ground, waiting for the radiation to disperse. Still, he expected the earth to go into convulsions at any moment and bring about the prophetic fulfillment of the coming of Jesus Christ. But after two minor tremblers, the fault lay quiet. Paulo slept and woke, slept and woke. Days passed in solitude, his hopes for a heavenly deliverance growing dimmer with each cycle.

Paulo's watch registered seven days. The suspense had become unbearable. At times during his seclusion, his will was almost overcome by the need to know the extent of the destruction, but he was determined to wait out the danger of radiation. After seven days, he cautiously opened the cellar door and crept to a broken window. At his shoulder level, it was ground level outside, and he peered out. Nothing moved on the street. It was eleven-thirty in the morning and no children were out riding bikes. No housewives drove to the stores. No dogs barked, no cats prowled, no birds chirped overhead. It was deadly quiet. Then he became aware of a low growling in the distance. As it grew closer, he made out the sound of a truck engine. Every so often it stopped. Finally, he saw the hood of the truck come into view as it turned the corner onto his small street in downtown Salt Lake City. It was a U.S. Army truck, and the two men inside wore fatigues. They also wore special gas masks. They stopped not far away. One man jumped out, testing the ground with a radar meter. Paulo called out to him from his little window. The young soldier jumped and spun around.

"Don't shoot! Don't shoot! I'm over here in the cellar. How many are alive? How bad is the radiation?"

Cautiously, the soldier approached the broken window. It was such a relief to Paulo to see another human face, and an American soldier at that. Then he noticed how young the boy was — just a kid, really.

"Don't know how many are alive. The ones that are dead ain't talking, and the ones that are alive are hiding, like you. Immediate radiation danger is passed in your neighborhood. The winds took most of it. What fell here has decayed to safe levels. Out by the airport, where the bomb hit, it's worse, and we don't know about Tooele or Ogden. More danger of natural gas leaks than anything else right now."

"Any Russian troops?" Paulo asked.

"We don't hear nothing about troops. Radios have got so much static we can't make out everything. We figure they'll occupy the coast cities first. It's probably only a matter of time before they git here. Are you in good shape? Can you help clean up?"

"Whenever you think it's safe. I'm fine. Scared, but otherwise fine."

The young soldier answered. "No different from the rest of us. The colonel said if we find anyone who'll help, who's not sick or dying, we start organizing to bury the dead. You game?"

"I'll help. Can you take me with you?"

The young man walked back to the truck to check with his companion, then called out to Paulo, "Come on. We're going back to our reserve unit at Fort Douglas right now to report in."

They rode through the paralyzed city. Animals lay dead on the streets and sidewalks, their bodies burned from the thermal pulse. A few cars were stopped in the middle of the roads, their doors flung open as occupants had raced for shelter. Downtown streets were blocked with rubble of old decayed buildings crumbled to the ground. Since the blast area extended only six miles from the airport, the newer buildings didn't suffer structural damage, but all the bright, slick window fronts had shattered with the concussion, making the streets treacherous. Fire had rampaged through the fallen buildings, and the smell of charred ruins and burned bodies was sickening. They found an old couple on a side street. The man was wandering incoherently, calling his dog, and his elderly wife was clinging to his sleeve, crying for him to come back inside. The truck stopped, collected them, and took them also to the fort. Otherwise, the city lay silent in the grip of death and fear.

Fort Douglas gave Paulo hope again. As a military center, it was greatly reduced from the previous decade, but it still functioned as a reserve center. Now the post struggled to cope with the aftermath of the Soviet preemptive strike. No communications were possible to call in the soldiers from their homes. Many were still entrenched in basements and other shelters, but reservists and full-time army personnel had started to trickle in. Army trucks were slowly fanning out all over the Valley, testing for radiation and natural gas leaks. People within twenty miles of the blast area were being advised to stay put for another day or two, unless gas leaks in their neighborhoods threatened their lives. The most serious problem was that of identifying and burying the dead. The task was hideous, with bodies blistered, burned, and decomposing. Where there was no immediate family to care for the dead, army personnel loaded them into trucks and took them to large excavation sites where they were dumped and covered with earth. Relatives would search in vain for loved ones dead and buried, after the initial shock wore off.

One whole building at Fort Douglas had been set aside for civilian accommodations. The governor's family, along with a few other local officials, were staying there. The governor himself had been at the airport and had not survived the blast. A few higher church authorities had been brought into the fort for consultation. When Paulo came in, Church leaders were meeting with government leaders, and a debate was under way. With no certainty as to when Soviet troops would come into the area, the decision had to be made to fight or to submit.

"How can you even ask the question?" the lieutenant governor shook his head in disbelief. "This is it, folks! There isn't anymore! We are now the U.S. of Russia. It's as simple as that. What d'ya mean 'fight or submit'?"

A big, beefy man in the corner spoke up. Paulo recognized him as John Oakley, second counselor in the First Presidency of the Church. "One always has that choice. The pioneers had the same choice. Admittedly, they didn't have to deal with nuclear bombs. But they had the same choice to fight or submit to Johnston's army. The dilemma goes back further than that, to the Nephites and Lamanites of the Book of Mormon. I think we have a more powerful enemy, but we also have greater resources with which to resist."

"How resist?" an air force colonel asked impatiently.

Oakley said, "Just the way our fathers did before us — make the place unprofitable for the Russians to occupy. Leave nothing growing, leave nothing standing, no one to work for them. No one to carry out their orders. No services of any kind, no labor to command."

"That's crazy! The people would never do it," Colonel Schiller argued. "Ask them to destroy their homes, their businesses? And what good would it do? If the Soviets

205

have planned this all out, they are here to stay! How long could we resist? How long could we live without shelter, without food? Winter is coming on. Be realistic, Oakley. We're not freedom fighters."

"Why not?" The question came from a man leaning against the wall. He was perhaps five-foot-eight, slight of build, hair thinning and deep lines in his forehead. But his dark eyes were bright and penetrating. His voice rang out in the room, and Paulo turned to see who had spoken. He stepped slightly forward, feet apart, determination etched into every line of his face. "My people are freedom fighters. We are Afghani. My brothers, my uncles, my own father vowed to fight the Soviets to the death rather than submit. And they died. But they won! The Soviets finally pulled out. Are we less men than they were? Brother Oakley is right. We have more resources here than the people of Afghanistan did. Besides, do you think the rest of the world will sit idly by and watch Russia swallow America? This country has been the world's breadbasket for decades. If Russia takes us over, that bread will go only into the mouths of their people. Believe me, the rest of the world may hate us and envy us for being the richest country in the world, but they know they depend on our food, our strength, to help them survive. The Moslem nations will not sit by and see the world taken over by infidels. China, Japan, Western Europe — the world will mobilize against the Reds. They can't physically control the globe."

He made a fist and jabbed it into the air before him. "Fight for your freedom!" he challenged from between clenched teeth. The men in the room looked from one face to another. The lieutenant governor stood up. "That is a decision for the people to make. For Brother Oakley's plan to work, everyone must be willing to join it. I don't think total destruction of our cities and homes would be necessary, but there would have to be total evacuation up and down the entire state. And how much time do we have? No one knows."

Colonel Schiller spoke up. "Soviet troops will move into the eastern cities and the west coast first, and our best guess is they won't all be Soviet. South American troops — Cuban, Nicaraguan, Chilean — will be the main contingents. Soviet troops will supervise. Of course, they could airlift troops into the Valley here any time they want, but our guess is that they will be concerned primarily with establishing control over the greater populated, industrial areas of the coasts."

Oakley spoke up. "Your trucks are covering the city. Let them ask the people what they want."

Young Lieutenant-Governor Oberg was derisive. "The people! The people are either dead or too stunned and scared to respond to that kind of question."

Gently, Oakley responded. "Let's see. They've had a week to meditate and to ask themselves hard questions. Let's see what they will do."

Paulo leaned against the wall, listening to the debate. Obviously, civil authorities didn't like Church interference. But this was more than a political or military question. A whole way of life had to be considered. Paulo spoke up, "Does the Church counsel us to fight?"

Oakley responded. "The quorum of the Twelve has not met. The president is unaccounted for. I'm afraid President Taylor may have been in Ogden with his daughter's family. It was his birthday last Monday. The Quorum hopes to meet tonight, but I can speak for myself — I would rather resist than submit. Freedom has come easily to us as modern-day Americans, but my forefathers fought and died in the Revolutionary war. They thought liberty was worth the price. So do I, and I also propose that we re-ratify our allegiance to the American constitution and the flag."

The Afghani strode over to Oakley's side and in an impassioned voice said, "I, Gibran, will be the first to pledge my allegiance. The flag, the constitution — they have been the hope of the world. Do they mean so little to us?"

The colonel stood up and started for the door. "You'd better consider the consequences. If you destroy this city, you commit yourselves to possibly a lifetime of living like outlaws or Indians in the mountains. And it's not just you, the men. It's your women and children too. You may not even survive the first winter. The Soviets have had lots of experience in combating freedom fighters. They have the means and no incentive to restrain themselves. Don't think you'll go unpunished!"

"Will you tell the army to ask the people?" Oakley pressed.

"Tomorrow. Today we are checking for gas and radiation. Then we'll compile a death count. Our estimate now is about 20 percent of the population of Salt Lake and Bountiful is either dead or dying. When we know it is safe, we will let the people come out, and we'll see if they want to leave their homes." The colonel strode out of the room.

Of the Quorum of the Twelve Apostles there were seven in town. They were located and brought, with their families, to the fort. The others had been either traveling abroad or living in Ogden or Layton. The entire area was massively destroyed. It was confirmed by one of the apostles that President Taylor had, in fact, been spending the week with his daughter in North Ogden at the time of the nuclear strike. The Quorum convened. Two men were almost disabled with radiation sickness. The oldest ranking member of the Quorum was not there. The second oldest had been on assignment to Chicago. The next in succession as president of the Quorum was Elias Stark who had taken Paulo under his wing. He was a man about eighty years old. He was bent, one shoulder slightly twisted because of arthritis, and one elbow unusable from the disease. His left eye squinted behind his glasses, and he was nearly bald, but Elias did not lack in fire.

After a fervent prayer, the meeting proceeded with Stark getting immediately to the issue. In a strong, almost nasal voice, he outlined the pros and cons of the situation and the decision. Of the one million Latter-day Saints who had crowded into the Salt Lake Valley, two hundred thousand were estimated dead. The numbers were not hard. Information was being gathered daily, and the final count might never be accurately known. Retirement homes were simply tombs for elderly people, too confused and incapable to protect themselves. Hospitals, with their windows and hundreds of patients, had also become houses of death. Those not killed in the initial blast, were, within a week, either dead or dying from the radiation dose of the thermonuclear pulse. Throughout the northern part of the city, thousands died within days from massive radiation taken as they cowered in their automobiles, stood by windows, stood on street corners, or shopped in supermarkets with large, lovely windows.

The question of resistance presented many

considerations. The children would be at risk. Medicine and food would be the first things to be stockpiled into hidden caches in the mountains. Families should take as many of their provisions as possible and be prepared to share with neighbors. They must look for years of resistance both active and passive. They must be prepared to die rather than cooperate.

The alternative was to bury their dead and try to resume their lives, waiting for the Communists to take over and rule. In this case, Americans would suffer the same fate as the Polish, East Europeans, Cambodians, and Vietnamese. All wealth would be taken from the country. Their freedoms would be abolished. Military rule would be harsh in order to subdue the country. The totalitarian system would turn the people into spies one against another. Their temples would surely be closed, and group meetings, religious or otherwise, would not be allowed. But, on the other hand, daily living conditions would not be as primitive as if they decided to resist.

It was a somber moment. With the alternatives clearly outlined, the men sat looking from one face to another. "What we recommend, the Latter-day Saints will most surely do," Stark warned sternly. "We must be united. And we must be sure that we speak for the Lord. That is the great question, finally — not what we will, but what he wills."

Silence prevailed. The men pondered in their hearts the unpleasant alternatives. Finally, one of the younger apostles broke the silence. "Well, Elias, have you still got that thirty-aught-six? You used to be a pretty fair shot when you and Dad went hunting." Joseph Kennison was obviously sick but he tried to smile. Then he said seriously. "The Lord has never meant his people to be slaves. And I don't think he means us to be now. He established temple work in these latter days, and it won't stop until the final end of the Millennium. Brothers, we seem to be in the last days. We've known it for a long time. We've said it for a long time. Now it seems to be undeniable. And we know what is coming — perhaps not how far away it is — but we know the Lord will come in glory. Surely we can trust his love enough to withstand our enemies as the Lord's people have always done."

Another man, mild-mannered and gentle, spoke the

reality. "True, but the Lord's people have been carried away into captivity several times, their cities burned, their people killed. And it has often taken centuries for the Lord to save them, and that not without sacrifice. Colonel Schiller projects that the occupying army will come from the south, from Las Vegas up through St. George. We have to consider the realities."

John Oakley countered. "Sacrifice is certain. We have no choice in that. The Russians have mandated sacrifice either way. But we don't have centuries left in the earth's timetable. Daniel prophesied that it would be a time, times and a half. John prophesied the same. In other words, one year plus two years plus a half — or three and a half years of tribulation. And then the great archangel Michael shall return to give the keys of the kingdom back to Jesus Christ." He spoke to men who had studied the prophecies as he had. No one challenged him. "And even if the time is longer, I feel the will of the Lord to trust him, to resist our enemies, to fight for the freedoms he gave us. Brethren, this is a cleansing process. Both the weak and the unprepared, and even many of the faithful, will die — there are no guarantees — but a remnant will be saved here, just as in Jerusalem. We too are of the house of Israel."

Elias Stark's sharp, powerful voice filled the room. " 'Thus saith the Lord concerning the King of Assyria, he shall not come into this city, nor shoot an arrow there, nor come before it with shields, nor cast a bank against it. By the way he came, by the same shall he return, and shall not come into this city.' (Isaiah 37:33.) That prophecy does not speak to Jerusalem in the old world. We know that it shall be overrun with enemies, to the taking of one half the city, before the Lord comes. That prophecy speaks to us."

Oakley voiced the real issue: "It comes to this — do we believe the scriptures, or do we not? It is easy to believe doctrine and principles. It's easy to look at history and say 'I can see how that prophecy was fulfilled.' But can we build our future on the scriptures? That is our decision. If we say yes, then the decision is easy. We resist and rely on the Lord to deliver us — and he will deliver us, for we are called to build the New Jerusalem one day. If we are afraid to build our future on the scriptures, then we admit

210

that our faith is of no consequence."

The words died away in the room. Nothing more was said for many minutes. Then Elias spoke with muffled, pain-stricken voice. "I can see now how Brigham Young must have felt facing the exodus from Nauvoo, setting off into an unknown wilderness. For myself, I don't fear death or hardship. But oh, the grief that awaits our people! That is hard! That is too hard to bear! My little grandchildren, my daughter! My sister has already died in a rest home! The trial is so great — almost too great!"

By now, tears were coursing down every cheek as the vision of the suffering of the Latter-day Saints was plainly impressed on their minds. Each man saw his own family and those of his friends in the long, fearsome days ahead. And they saw that in these times, there were no happy answers. The die was cast. There would be hardships either way, but with one path, they would at least hold on to their faith.

A vote was called. Kennison spoke first. "We must resist." And, one by one, the apostles agreed. When they finished, Stark called in Colonel Schiller and Lieutenant-Governor Oberg. As acting president of the Quorum, Elias made the announcement: "We will advise our people to resist, and we will organize an immediate evacuation into the mountains."

Oberg retorted, "You are dooming your people to certain death."

Colonel Schiller simply saluted. He couldn't speak.

It was neither the evacuation nor the radiation of the bombs that proved the greatest threat. It was starvation. Of all the Latter-day Saints in the Valley who had listened to their leaders beg them to store a year's supply of food, only 20 percent had done so. Many more had a few months' supply. But the great majority had only enough food for a few days. The long drought, as well as overcrowded conditions, had taken its toll.

Trucks with loudspeakers roamed the streets calling for bishops to surface, mayors and policeman to come forth. The farther from the actual blast area, the more people survived. Instinct drove most of them into their basements,

211

where the fallout danger was reduced by half to three-quarters. Within a few days, the word was passed from bishops to home teachers to every LDS family in the Valley — the Church leaders advised resistance. Most of the people were surprised to be alive. They had never considered surviving a nuclear attack. The rallying call was the only thing that now gave them hope. They were fiercely independent people who had already left the mainstream of America to live in Utah rather than submit to the Worldwide Monetary System. Now, would they leave their homes rather than submit to Russia? The decision was theirs. Their answer was a resounding yes!

They were told to combine as wards wherever possible, helping one another, pooling resources, evacuating quickly. In some areas of the city, there were hardly enough people left to form a ward. From the point of the mountain at the south end of the valley, through the tiny towns in central and southern Utah, as far as St. George, people were found and instructed to evacuate into the mountains. After the evacuation, mountain passes were to be closed off with dynamite wherever possible. Provisions were loaded into vehicles and taken far back into the mountains. Cars and trucks were used until the gasoline supply was exhausted. Then the exodus on foot began. Bicycles were used. Many people had horses, and they were used. The army dynamited passes north of Coalville that led into Wyoming, and the people melted into the valleys. Some refugees went east and south, beyond Price, into the southeast Utah desert. The total evacuation took five days. Army vehicles were used to transport medical supplies and food. The gasoline pumps would not work without electricity, so gasoline was pumped by hand from the stations until it was all gone.

It was a strange exodus. Campers and trailers lined the highways, bumper to bumper. Then, as gasoline gave out, they were abandoned beside the road. Many of them were driven back into the side trails of the Uintah Mountains and provided shelter for families who walked in. The Utahns felt as though they were reliving history, and family stories of pioneer ancestors were retold to keep up their courage. The children who had survived the nuclear blast were stunned into silent submissiveness. Those who had lived farther away were irrepressible. After the first few days of fear, it began to look like a grand adventure to them despite the tension that gripped the adults.

They were constantly chastised by the adults. Terror of the unknown and the now hideous "known" affected everyone differently. A family oriented society, the Mormons reeled under the impact of so many loved ones dead or lost. Some faced the future silently, too numb to speak. Others became so distraught that rational action was impossible. Men were impatient with those very loved ones they were trying to protect. Women frequently gave way to helpless, sporadic weeping. Thousands delayed their departure in order to bury children, parents, or mates. Death in such massive numbers staggered their ability to cope. Yet, through it all, the fabric of their lives held together with the thread of prayer.

Controlling America without destroying her wealth was proving a gigantic task for the Soviets. On the east and west coasts, massive destruction turned the survivors into animals. Disease from dead and wounded bodies ravaged the living. Rats were bold predators and spread disease among the survivors. No plan or organization existed to give them hope. Gangs scoured and plundered the remains of what had once been rich, consumer businesses, while couples and families hid from their more violent neighbors. Communist soldiers worked at securing key cities. It took massive infusions of troops — Soviet, South American, Cuban — to organize terrified, hungry people to start the business of burying the dead and running the industries that supported the country. Utah was of relatively little importance.

It was actually three weeks before troops started into Utah. Reconnaissance aircraft was sent in the third day. It reported Hill Field as a direct hit and the surrounding area as desolate. All seemed to be quiet in the sleepy Salt Lake Valley.

The women and children were moved back into the high Uintahs beyond the Kamas and Heber valleys or south to Price. Once they were safely settled, the men would return and patrol the first line of mountains, dynamiting passes, waiting for the enemy.

It had been suggested in the zeal of the resistance

effort that they destroy everything occupying troops could use. Burn their homes, businesses. Burn the fields and destroy the livestock. Leave nothing with which the Soviets could sustain an occupying force. But, wisely, the military leaders pointed out that probably only small numbers of troops would come in, and wholesale destruction of their cities would be more of a loss to the Utahns than help to the enemy. So they simply disabled the vehicles they left behind, emptied the stores of food and other goods, and left their cities sleeping in the mild October sun.

Paulo worked almost around the clock helping families prepare to evacuate. For the first time in his life, he was glad he had no family of his own. He gave his time entirely to the evacuation movement. On his back he packed most of his worldly goods — one change of clothing, two pair of garments, another pair of shoes, and a canteen of uncontaminated water. He had not shaved in two weeks, water being too precious to waste. A heavy, black beard obscured his face, and a dark mustache grew into it. His clothing was dirty, and his eyebrows were almost gray from the dust.

Paulo continued to work with the army-organized evacuation and then the resistance effort. As the evacuation was completed, they mined the main highway into Salt Lake City and all the canyon entrances. If the Soviets came, the canyons would be closed off and the highways impassible. Paulo was glad the decision to resist had been made. Sitting and waiting to be taken over would have been harder than this. Still, he did not delude himself — the hardship was only beginning.

Shielah stood at the back of her truck parked beside the gravel road that wound through Kamas into the Uintah mountains. Refugees trudged by her, heading they knew not where, only some place of safety in the mountains. The vehicles had come in earlier, driving as far as they could into the wilderness and then parking. Some fortunate people had campers or motor homes or trailers. Others came in cars packed with camping equipment. Shielah and other Kamas residents stood by, offering first aid, hot drinks, and sometimes a place to rest. The elderly were the main concern, and the mothers with young babies. Many of them ended up staying behind in the small, mountain towns, where strangers took them in, while their families went on deep into the mountains.

No one knew how far they should go. It was an individual matter. If enemy troops broke through the mountain passes or airlifted men into the Kamas and Heber valleys, they wanted to be as far into the wilderness as possible. Others, without the stamina or resources, opted to stay in the small towns until that should happen. Tents lined the fields, streams, and vacant lots of Kamas, Woodland, and Heber. Luckily, October weather held fair, even warm during the day.

Some of the weary refugees were weak with debilitating radiation sickness, which destroyed the body's immune system. Shielah worked from early dawn to after dark, visiting each camp and helping where she was needed. Often, it was just a broken blister that needed bandaging. Sometimes encouragement and comfort proved the best medicine. Then there were those who were truly ill, needing insulin, penicillin, and antibiotics, which were in short supply. A makeshift hospital was set up in the Kamas elementary school. Shielah spent almost every day there since she was a trained registered nurse. So did Cherri. Cherri had no nursing skills, but she was valuable help. She had no family demands to consider, no one to go home to. Often she slept at the hospital. She quickly learned the simple, routine things that made a patient comfortable, and she was excellent at holding a wrinkled hand and listening to stories of grandchildren or pioneer ancestors. Soon, she began to be as inordinately proud of those old pioneers as their own descendants. It was their courageous example that gave hope to this modern exodus.

As the late afternoon light began to grow dim, Shielah walked down the long hallway that led to the door. Cherri sat slumped in a chair, "Why don't you come home with me tonight?" Shielah said, putting her hand on Cherri's shoulder. "You look exhausted. I'll bet you were here all last night, weren't you?"

Cherri had sat down in a wooden student's desk and put her head down on the writing board. Now she opened her eyes and looked up. Shielah's hair was caught back into a ponytail. In jeans and sweatshirt, she hardly looked

215

like a nurse.

"No, that's all right. I'll probably go back to my room for a few hours."

"That's too lonely. It's not good for you to be alone so much. Come home with me," Shielah pressed.

Still, Cherri refused. "I know you. You've got half the Salt Lake Valley camping in your house. You don't need another body or mouth to feed. I'm okay. Just a few hours of sleep and I'll be back at it." Then she asked tentatively, "Have you seen the Sorensens? Wayne stopped in here day before yesterday and said something about trekking up into the high Uintahs."

Shielah buttoned her jacket. "He and Buck left yesterday. They are on horseback, taking first-aid supplies to the groups that have gone way back. I'm getting worried about them. It can't be much longer until snowfall. Bridget doesn't expect them back until the end of the week."

"Oh, I just wondered. Wayne is . . . well, he's one of my favorites, although I know teachers aren't supposed to have favorites."

"He's a good boy. I know he sure likes you. All summer long we heard 'Mrs. Polanski this' and 'Mrs. Polanski that.' I wonder if we'll ever have school again," she sighed. "Well, get some rest. You know you're always welcome if you get lonely."

Cherri pulled herself out of the little seat. "Maybe I would feel better if I got some sleep. Mind if I walk with you?"

"That would be nice." The two women walked along in the cool October air. In a vacant field, a young boy sat with a battered guitar, singing softly to himself.

"I wonder if anyone else is resisting." Cherri mused as they walked.

"I don't know. Our radios only pick up static and a little Russian gibberish. All we can do is to wait and see, and fight if we have to."

"Have you ever shot a gun?" Cherri asked.

"Yes, but I don't like to," Shielah answered. "Stephen takes me deer hunting with him sometimes. He makes me practice, and he makes me shoot for real."

"Do you think you could shoot a person — a man — if you had to?" Cherri spoke their worst fears.

"I don't know. Maybe. If he were threatening my

216

children. Heaven help us if it comes to that."

"I hope heaven helps us before that. We need it right now," Cherri observed wryly. "At least you've got a husband to help you and children to keep you going. What family I had must surely be dead by now."

"You are married, aren't you?" Shielah asked. "I heard that, but you've never mentioned a husband."

"I left him in New York. I knew I had to leave. I was . . . I was . . . attacked once, and it scared me so badly I had to leave. But Jim wouldn't come with me. I talked to him just a couple of days before the bomb. And now . . . who knows. Maybe he's alive. Maybe not." Tears sprang up into her eyes. Shielah put her arm around the younger woman, and Cherri brushed her face quickly. "Wondering every day if he is alive or dead is driving me crazy."

Shielah let her ramble on. As they stood together, a horse and rider came down the paved road like a ghost from the Old West. The man almost passed them, then abruptly reined the horse in and jumped down. It was Buck. He grabbed Shielah in a bear hug. "Hi, Sis. How do you like my hat? Wayne says I look like an outlaw. How are you? How's Stephen and the kids?"

Shielah couldn't help smiling at him. He was just what she needed right then. "Fine. We're all fine. Stephen is gone to Mt. Timpanogos. He calls it reconnaissance. He just can't stand to stay back here wondering if there may be real action going on."

"Hi Cherri," Buck said. "You all right?"

"I'm fine," Cherri said, tears all brushed away.

"She's okay," Shielah intervened for her friend. "She's just lonesome and tired and worried about her family back East."

"Have you heard anything at all?" Cherri asked him.

Buck looked into her hopeful eyes. "No. I'm sorry. Still no information about the rest of the country at all." He felt awkward, wanting to comfort her but not daring to. Turning to Shielah he asked, "You want to take my horse?. It's starting to get dark. You'll be a long time getting home if you walk. I'm not going home yet. I've got to stop at the sheriff's office and report on the families in the mountains."

"All right. If you're sure you don't need him."

"I'm sure. Here, I'll help you up."

Shielah had spent her childhood summers on her uncle's ranch in Birds Eye, Utah, learning to ride when she was only five years old. She patted the horse's neck. "He doesn't look good, Buck. Is he getting sick?"

"I hope not, but I'm afraid he may have drunk some contaminated water those first few days. Right now, he's just tired. We've been gone three days. Put him in with yours. Give him a rest tonight. Maybe he'll be better tomorrow."

His sister rode off toward the road through Woodland. "Let me walk you home," Buck said. Now that they were alone, he felt more awkward than he had expected.

"How are things at the hospital?" he asked.

"Getting worse. Medicine won't last forever. Choices are becoming terrible for the doctors. I'm glad I don't make them. I just comfort the patients, bathe them, feed them, and listen to their stories. I hope someone, somewhere, will do the same for my mother and father."

He wanted to put his arms around her, as Shielah had, to comfort her, but he knew he couldn't. "Look, I . . . I feel so helpless. I want to do something for you, but I don't know what. I can't stand it that you are alone. Come live with us, with my family, I mean. We already have another family living there and — "

But she shook her head violently. "No!" she said. "I couldn't live with you . . . with your family."

"Why not? You'd be a help to Bridget. Believe me, she has her hands full, what with the kids and every passing group that needs help. And I wouldn't worry about you so much. I find every excuse I can to ride in here to check on you."

Cherri was looking up into his face. Softly, she said, "I can't, because I'm in love with you."

She might as well have punched him in the stomach. "I don't want to be," she said. "But I am. I'm married. You're married. It's wrong and I know it. But I can't help it. I love you."

This was the time he should run. He should turn and run and never see her again. Every reasonable thought in his mind told him to leave, but her wounded eyes held him. "Oh, Cherri," was all he could say. And he took her in his arms and gave in to the longing they both had fought. He stayed for two hours. They were the happiest

218

— and unhappiest hours — either had each spent for months. When he left, they stood by the door a long time, not kissing, just holding each other.

"You know I love you, don't you?" he whispered.

"I thought. I hoped. But then, I can't hope. You aren't mine and you can't ever be. I shouldn't have said anything. I'm sorry. I'm afraid I've hurt us both."

"No," he lied. "It'll be all right. Somehow, it'll all work out. Be patient. Just knowing that you're here is enough for me. And I'll take care of you. I promise. You don't have to be alone. You don't have to be afraid. I'll take care of you. I love you." He kissed her gently. "I love you."

Buck didn't go back home that night. He slept in the sheriff's office in the back room. Tomorrow he would go home to Bridget.

In the mountains behind the American Fork canyon, a campfire lit the faces of the resistance committee. Two army officers were there, as well as a Cambodian who had seen the Communist tactics in Cambodia, a Vietnamese who had fought and escaped the Viet Cong on a tiny boat, the Afghani who had spoken so rousingly for resistance, Stephen Gailbraith, a green beret Marine, an Indian, and Paulo D'Agosta. Paulo had no experience in combat, but he had a cool head and no family to worry about. It was an unlikely crew to stop the Soviets, but that was their intent. They spent two days mining the narrow stretch of land between the point of the mountain on the east to the western mountains three miles across the valley. Now the entrance to the Salt Lake Valley was strung with explosives. How long they could resist, the men could not speculate. It all depended on the Soviets — how many troops they sent and how badly they wanted the land. Similar bands of men slept in the mountains, waiting for their chance at the enemy.

The campfire cast an eerie light on the haggard faces of the men.

"We'll depend a lot on the surprise," Colonel Alder said. "There can't be a shot fired as they come through Utah Valley. Let them think we are dead. When they reach the point of the mountain, just before they top the crest, that is when we detonate. The whole shebang goes up! If we've

219

done our job right, it'll blast a trough across the valley that they can't cross with road vehicles. It'll buy us some time at least."

"I want four men," he continued. "Two men to set off the dynamite and two men for backups. No goof-ups — no second chances."

Gailbraith spoke. "I'll go. I know these mountains like a book."

"I go," the tiny Vietnamese asserted. "This work I do before, many years ago in Viet Nam."

A young army lieutenant, broad-shouldered, strong, with hardly a shadow of a beard spoke up. "Don't leave me out. I've been trained in this." Tom Jackson looked more like a Boy Scout than a freedom fighter. "I know the delay factor, and I can get us back here in thirty minutes. I grew up in Alpine and played hide and seek in these trees."

Paulo spoke last. "I helped with all the mining along that entrance. I know what's supposed to blow. I'm going too."

Alder looked around. "That does it. The rest of us will stay here at the mouth of the canyon. If they turn up here, we close it off whether you four are back or not. We'll wait till the very last."

"If they shoot nerve gas, what you do?" the Cambodian asked quietly.

"Blow the canyon and seal ourselves off in the cave," Alder replied decisively. "This cave goes back into the mountain hundreds of feet. We can close that steel door and live in there for at least a couple of days. They wouldn't get through before that, with a thousand tons of rock on top of them." He stood up. "We're getting radio signals, weak ones, but they say a convoy of soldiers in trucks are moving through St. George. They could be here in the morning. Jackson, keep in touch with that radio. If they move through the night, we don't want to be surprised. We've got to give our men time to get to the dynamite."

Alder walked over to his own sleeping bag and lay down, only to stay awake all night listening. He was a career army man in peacetime. He had a wife and five children hidden in the Uintah mountains in a ten-foot camper. He had never thought he'd be here, defending his

220

own soil.

Tension and fatigue were heavy in the resistance camps — no laughter, no smiles, no good-natured joking. Not a man there had ever pictured the destruction of a nuclear bomb. Not one of them had ever dreamed of a savage life for his family and himself. Soberest of all were younger men who had served missions behind the Iron Curtain, for the brief time it was allowed. Their one purpose had been to teach love and Christ to the Soviets, not to shoot and kill.

The men sat around the fire, drinking a hot tea made from some sweet roots that Harry Never-Miss-a-Shot had dug from the soil. Harry was a man of few words. Tonight he listened to the Cambodian, the Vietnamese, and the Afghani trade war stories from their native lands. None would give up this last bastion of freedom without a fight. After this, there was nothing. Harry had never known war. His grandfathers had talked of old wars between their grandfathers and white men. Now here he was, fighting beside the white man, whom he despised as all his tribe did. It was funny, but he did not laugh. War makes strange tentmates.

After the talk died down, Paulo asked Gibran, the Afghani, if he had traveled the Himalayas.

"The Hindu Cush, yes. But that was before the Soviet invasion. I was a small boy then. My father took my mother and me and my four brothers and sisters out of Afghanistan and sent us to America with my uncle. My father knew what was coming. He was a great man! A Moslem, you know. He prayed with his whole soul, tears streaming down his face. A passionate man, I remember. He sent me out of Afghanistan, didn't want me to have to fight a war. Now look at me!"

"Now look at you," Paulo agreed. "You're trying to get yourself blown up."

"Perhaps, but my children are grown. My wife left me years ago — a strange woman, she couldn't live with me. I am too much like my father, too passionate, in many ways. I became a Mormon; she had no faith. I have spent these past few years playing in the stock market, starting businesses and then selling them. It began to be boring. There was no challenge to life! If we live through this, I will have endless stories to tell my grandchildren.

221

If not . . . well, I have lived it all! My father will be proud of me."

Gibran finished his hot drink, made a wry face, and said goodnight. The darkness was deep and quiet. There was just the sound of the fire crackling. Stephen Gailbraith and Paulo D'Agosta sat staring into the fire, listening to the sound of the mountain stream far below. Paulo was lost in thoughts of the weeks he had spent in the Himalayas with Omar. But it was very different tonight, the tension was almost palpable. Only a few short weeks had passed since the bombing, and the shock of wholesale death hung over them like a shroud.

"I never would have expected to see you here," Stephen said, at length.

Paulo glanced up. "Are you sorry?"

"I think so," Stephen replied honestly.

"For her sake and mine, you don't have to be." Paulo responded to the unspoken barrier between them. "She chose you. And it was right. I didn't understand it then, but I do now. There is someone else for me. Do you remember our meeting in the temple last summer? I realized it then." He stopped, wondering how much to tell Gailbraith.

"What did you realize?" Stephen asked coldly.

"There . . . there was another woman. I . . . I met her there, and so did Shielah."

Stephen watched Paulo across the dying campfire. "Haven't you ever married?" he asked curiously.

"No, I never have. I wanted to but never found the right woman. Until last summer, that is. You're a lucky man. You've had what I have wanted all these years, a wife and a family. On the other hand, I am free to risk myself without concern. You aren't," he said pointedly.

"I know. I don't intend to get killed."

"I don't intend to let you," Paulo said to his old rival. "Shielah needs you." He stood up and stuck out his hand.

Stephen stood also, and tossed the rest of his drink onto the embers. Then with sudden decision, he carefully put his hand into Paulo's. Soberly, he challenged D'Agosta, "I'll beat you to the point of the mountain."

A slight smile lit Paulo's eyes. "You're on." And they shook on that.

Morning came and there was no sign of a Soviet convoy. The hours stretched into noon. A light snow began to fall, the first of the season. Finally, after they had stamped around impatiently all day, the radio picked up a faint signal from Spanish Fork. A Soviet convoy! Eight trucks, three American cars for the bigwigs! That was it? With eight trucks of soldiers, they expected to secure all of Utah! The men looked at each other in astonishment. Then the young lieutenant whooped and threw his hat down on the ground. "Damn, we're gonna waste our dynamite! Come on, let's go!"

Down from the mountain they ran, through underbrush and trees, jumping over rocks, adrenalin pushing them on. The lieutenant led the party out of the mountain, then across the foothills. Each man had a map of the detonation points. There were two, one at the base of the rounded Widowmaker hill, and one further up, tucked into a crevice only a few feet from the top. They split up, Paulo and the Vietnamese, Lin Chung, took the high path. Lieutenant Jackson and Stephen took the lower. They reached their destination well before the convoy came out of Provo.

As expected, the convoy was mostly South Americans. Only a few Soviets commanded the unit. It was a reconnaissance convoy, continually stopping to inspect the land. They could not believe what they found. This Utah! It had been hit with only three bombs, and that far to the north. But the whole state was desolate. There were no people. It was a ghost town of immense proportions. They expected to subdue the civilians with a show of force, find a local stooge, leave a few men in the larger towns, and control with fear. But there was no one to subdue. They roamed through empty cities, homes locked and left, no animals, no food, no provisions. Wheels were off all vehicles. Tractors sat in the fields with no wheels or vital engine parts.

They eyed the mountains uneasily, but not a shot was fired. The land appeared totally deserted. Radio communication with the base in Nevada confirmed that this area should be relatively untouched. Their orders were to go into Salt Lake City and establish base camp there. Citizens were to be thoroughly intimidated with example executions, then normal business activities were to resume

223

as soon as possible. The land had resources in mining and steel refinery. It had not been properly exploited. They were to organize the population to do that and get rail traffic running again to move the ore and steel.

Dark-skinned Nicaraguan soldiers watched from the backs of trucks as they wound through the deserted streets of the small towns. They exclaimed in surprise. So far, they could not carry out a single order. The Russians shook their heads. This was the strangest of all. Mobs they could cope with. They had had brief, harsh battles with looters and rioters. But this! They had no response.

Straggling out of Provo, the convoy headed on northward toward Salt Lake City. Paulo and the others lay hidden at the point of the mountain, watching and waiting. Adrenalin pumped into his heart and stomach every minute and a half. The dynamite lines had been checked. The Vietnamese looked up at Paulo from a few feet below. His oriental face was impassive. I wonder if he's as antsy as I am? Paulo thought. The man seemed abnormally calm to him. Do I look like that? Paulo wondered inanely. Storm clouds had been gathering overhead. The sky was gray, and a light breeze had sprung up. The lights of the convoy went on as though perfectly timed.

Stephen had regressed to the jungles of Vietnam. All the better to see you with, my dears, he thought. Come on sweetcakes. Keep right on coming. We've got this great surprise party for you. Just another mile. Just another mile.

The red marker set up on the east bank of the road was the magic point. When the first truck cleared that, they would all be in range. And the Russians made it easier for them by traveling two abreast. Paulo held his breath. The headlights of the two lead trucks flashed on the red marker. He counted down mentally. Five, four, three, two . . . Bingo! He hit the lever hard. Stephen hit his at the same time. Dynamite skipped across the narrowest point of the valley, blowing the first two trucks into the next world. The second string went off, then the third. Explosions ripped through the earth and burst with fury in the air. The other six trucks were blown off the highway and lay overturned and burning down the embankments. Still the explosions went on and on. Mine

224

after mine blew with deafening roar. Billowing smoke and fire ran in a solid line from mountain to mountain, and the earth lay gouged and gaping below it. A wide chasm had been cut at the mouth of the Salt Lake Valley.

Pausing only long enough to make sure that all lines of explosives were going off, Paulo and Lin Chung jumped to their feet and struck out at a dead run back toward the eastern mountains. If they expected gunfire, they were wrong, but not disappointed. The small convoy lay in pieces, dead or dying, burning, exploding in their own fire. The four men met a mile away and ran on together as long as they could run. Finally, they paused, sides bursting, five miles from the blast and looked back. Smoke and fire obscured a good look, but they could see that the trucks were burning and the devastation was complete. There was no stopping long for rejoicing. Panting, they jogged on, then walked as they began to climb. The arms of the forest welcomed them. It was Halloween night, and they were safe — for the time being.

Three days later, when the Soviet base commander in Las Vegas had not been able to raise communications with his convoy in Utah, another convoy was sent. This one was larger — twelve trucks, one tank equipped with land missiles and two chemical, nerve-gas missiles. About two hundred and fifty Nicaraguan, Chilean, and Panama Communist soldiers rode in that convoy. Most of them were very young, with only scanty actual experience. The second convoy experienced the same unnerving strange observations as the first had. But this time they were on guard, knowing something had apparently happened to their comrades.

They explored the mountain pass at Spanish Fork and Springville. It was blocked by the cavein from dynamite explosions. They turned north and explored Provo and the canyon to Heber. It too was securely blocked — even the river had been stopped in its flow. Still, there had been no fire from the mountains. The Soviet officers suspiciously scanned the mountain fronts, looking for guerilla fighters they sensed were there. They detected absolutely nothing!

After two days of exploration, they continued northward. In the American Fork canyon, more than a thousand men lay concealed. National guard, army reservists, and civilians had all joined together. They had set up the M2HB .50 cal and M-7.62 mm machine guns and had several 81 mm mortars and 106 mm recoilless rifles ready. The resisters had anticipated that the soldiers would explore until reaching the death site of their earlier convoy, then turn toward the canyons for combat. They were right.

The remains of the previous convoy threw the Communists into immediate combat mentality. After examining the great chasm cut across the valley, they turned their sights to the canyon. Here, at this point, American resisters had dared to strike a Soviet armed convoy! Now they would pay. The highway into the canyon was deserted except for Soviet trucks and tanks. As with the others, the pass was sealed off very effectively with thousands of tons of Wasatch rock and earth. The Soviet commander scanned the mountainside with binoculars, passed communication back through each truck, and alerted the tank. Then in one burst, they assaulted the mountain fortress.

The Mormon freedom fighters were ready. The entire face of the mountains erupted in fire. High-powered rifles were the lowest rung; then came the machine-gun layer, as greater height put the rifles out of range, and finally the mortars and recoilless rifles from well-camouflaged positions drove the invaders back. Communist casualties were heavy from the first round of fighting. Their trucks and soldiers lacking any cover were almost sitting ducks for the resistance fighters. The Soviet commander lay dead in the front seat of the lead truck when the battle was over. Regrouping was carried out five miles back down the road. A decision had to be made, fire bombs or nerve gas. Nerve gas it was to be. They knew the debilitating effects of that weapon. It was immediate, and they had no intention of letting the local resisters get the upper hand. The field Howitzer was moved forward. Before they could get it loaded, a 66 mm light anti-tank rocket streaked across the canyon. It hit the lead truck and blew it skyward as the ammunition exploded and damaged the Howitzer. The Soviets pulled back further.

Night was coming on now. Half of their numbers were dead at the mouth of the canyon. Their major was gone. The second in command was dead. Only Nicaraguan squad leaders remained to rally the soldiers. They were somewhat stunned. They had severely underestimated the resistance capability of the Americans. With four trucks lost and long-range communications damaged, they had to get the Howitzer repaired if they were to knock out this camp of resistance. But the South Americans had no expertise with heavy Soviet machinery.

Night settled in with a dark chill. Their camp was just outside range of the fire of the mountain defenders. The soldiers established night watch, while two of their men radioed Las Vegas for instructions, and two more puzzled over the damaged Howitzer. At about one o'clock in the morning, repair attempts were abandoned, and they retired until daylight. It was an uneasy sleep for the Communists, one from which they never awoke. During the night, a chemical artillery round — perhaps faulty in construction — began to slowly leak its poison. The fatal gas spread quietly, imperceptively, overcoming the sleeping soldiers and then the night watch. Now their sleep was no longer restless. It was deep and permanent. The destroying angel had come and gone.

The morning blushed pink and gold through the mountain passes. It lit the cobwebs of fog and seemed to bless the valley with its light. The bands of men, dug into the mountainside, behind boulders, in caves, in the undergrowth, watched the immobile Russian convoy below. Colonel Alder watched with his binoculars. Nothing moved. He had expected another, more vicious attack, even aircraft fire. Chemical weapons were also an expected assault. Soon the morning shadows were gone. The bright light of day gleamed, and still the Russians did not attack. Moving the men with LAW rockets down the mountainside, Colonel Alder called for one strike. With a piercing whine the missile shot high and exploded with a vengeance a few yards from the trucks. Still nothing stirred.

Alder called his core of men.

"I can't figure what's going on. Maybe they've radioed for air support and aren't moving until the bombers show — in which case, we're in for trouble. Maybe they're playing possum, hoping to make a hit when we become unwary. We need to find out where their pawn is."

"I'll be a scout," Paulo volunteered immediately.

"Me too," Stephen put in quickly.

Lieutenant Jackson grinned. "Count me in."

227

"Not this time," Alder refused him. "It's too dangerous. They could be just waiting for us. It just takes one. I don't want to risk any more than that."

Stephen argued. "More than one. It takes two to cover each other's flanks. You never go out alone. I'm with D'Agosta. We already know this road and the cover. We'll be careful. If we disappear, you'll know something's up."

Armed with grenades and an M-60 machine gun, an M-14 rifle, and two belts of ammo, they made their way down the mountain. When they left the cover of trees and oakbrush behind, Stephen and Paulo split up and crawled along the ditch on each side of the road. Both men expected any moment to be sprayed with ammunition, but nothing happened. They grew a little bolder, sprinting to cover and waiting, sprinting again, behind a tree, behind bombed Russian trucks. Still no fire. Twice they stopped and stared across the road at each other. What could it mean? When was the explosion of bullets coming?

As they drew close to the convoy parked in a tight formation, they crawled and wiggled to within two hundred yards. Paulo set up the machine gun behind a clutch of trees and oakbrush, and in a sudden burst, he peppered the inert convoy. Nothing. No return fire at all. Stephen and Paulo paused for five minutes, watching. Finally, Stephen could stand the suspense no longer. He jumped to his feet and ran full tilt toward the trucks. Paulo had the machine gun ready if they fired on Stephen. But nothing moved. Stephen disappeared behind a truck, then a minute later stepped out and signaled Paulo to come.

Still cautious, Paulo walked toward the trucks.

"Look at this!" Stephen said. "Their own nerve gas got them. I saw this stuff in Vietnam. It's a horrible death."

Paulo looked at the contorted faces of the young Latin American soldiers. The day before, these same children would have killed them if they could. He shook his head. "'And the angel of the Lord went out and smote in the camp of the Assyrians an hundred fourscore and five thousand; and when they arose early in the morning, behold they were all dead corpses.'"

Soberly, they stood looking at the dead. Then, Paulo said, "We could always claim we scared them to death. Let's see, that's about fifty for you and fifty for me."

Stephen grimaced. "Right! Think they'd believe us?"

"We can always try. After all, fishermen are allowed some exaggerations. Why not us? Let's go. They'll be anxious."

It was five months before another Russian convoy invaded the desolate Utah valley.

*　*　*

TO BE CONTINUED

(Because of the length of The Millennial Story, the second half will be published in Fire and Glory: The Millennial Story - Part II. It will be available in August, 1989 and will encompass the trek to Jackson County, the building of the New Jerusalem, the return of Adam to Adam ondi-Ahman, the battle of Armageddon, and the second coming of Christ in glory! Don't miss the exciting fulfillment of the great prophecies of the last days. And don't miss the beautiful love story of David and Rachael, the resolution of love between Paulo and Shielah, and the tragedy of Buck, Bridget, and Cherri.)